BY THE SAME AUTHOR

The Frights
Dangerous Pursuits
Falling Apart
Forces of Nature
The Grimace
The Garden of Earthly Delights
Rogue Female

NICHOLAS SALAMAN

A STATE OF SHOCK

HarperCollins*Publishers*

HarperCollins*Publishers*
77–85 Fulham Palace Road,
Hammersmith, London W6 8JB

This paperback edition 1998
1 3 5 7 9 8 6 4 2

First published in Great Britain by
HarperCollins*Publishers* 1996

ISBN 0 00 649030 1

Set in Janson

Printed and bound in Great Britain by
Clays Ltd, St Ives plc

For Heather Meredith-Owen
who would have helped me write it.

Stone walls do not a prison make,
but pleasure is inescapable.

SHOCK: SIGNS AND SYMPTOMS

Weakness
Confusion
Drowsiness
Fainting
Giddiness
Anxiety
Restlessness
Nausea
Vomiting
Extreme thirst
Cold, clammy skin
Sweating and shivering
Rapid shallow breathing
A weak rapid pulse which may also be irregular
Unconsciousness

URGENT MEDICAL ATTENTION IS ALWAYS NEEDED.

One

Too fast. She must be doing eighty. Even the milder bends made the car skip and slither on the greasy roadway, but she dared not slow down.

Any minute now that heavy gunmetal shape would be showing in the mirror.

A truck came towards her, hooting furiously. She pulled the steering wheel and swung the car back onto her side of the road.

With a fresh surge of panic, she wondered whether the keys to the cottage would be in her bag. Hadn't the secretary come in with a question just as she was taking them out of the envelope? . . . How could she be so stupid?

She fumbled across to the passenger seat and tried to undo the clasp. It was always a stiff one. She had meant to have it seen to. Too late now.

Damn the thing. It wouldn't open. Another bend was coming up, with beyond it the bridge over the estuary.

She checked the rear mirror, looked ahead, and saw a van stopped – the idiot – at the roadside just as she rounded the curve. Even that would have been all right but just at that moment the shaking began again, and the bridge started to bend and writhe as though it were a living thing. She slammed on the brakes and the car began to ski in slow christies, first left then right. It clipped the side of the van – she could see the driver's white face inside – and skidded on.

This was it, she thought. The moment so long dreaded. No

way out. Funnily enough, it was almost a relief. Time seemed to go in and out like potter's clay. Up and down went the bridge in serpentine undulations.

Left . . . right . . . a car came towards her . . . she could see quite clearly a woman with children in the back . . . please God, not the children . . .

The cars passed as if they were waltzing together.

She heard herself making noises but it was as though someone else was doing it.

She gripped the steering wheel as if it were life itself but she could do nothing with it. She saw her face white in the mirror. She could feel her heart racing. Where were her careful systems of behaviour, her useful arms? Everything was happening fast now.

The car went up onto the bank, slid down, up onto the other, hit a thorn bush, turned over and started cartwheeling as it dropped from the carriageway down a gentle incline towards a miniature ravine. Trees, grass, and pebbles flew in front of her, and as the car rolled, lines she had learnt at school filled her mind.

> *'No motion has she now nor force,*
> *She neither feels nor sees.*
> *Whirled round in earth's diurnal course*
> *With rocks and stones and trees . . .'*

A flock of little birds fluttered up.

Then with a last shattering of glass and a wail of metal, the car hit the boulders of the stream.

She hung there upside down in the sudden silence, not knowing whether she was alive or dead, whole or injured. There was no pain. She could not move. Sounds now came from above, voices and then faces. They meant nothing to her. She saw his face among the rest. He could do nothing now. Arms reached out to her but she could not feel them . . .

Perhaps that was death after all. To be aware for ever but to be locked in perspex like a paperweight. The thought horrified her but there was nothing she could do. She could not cry. Weep no more, sad fountains.

Someone was shouting.

'Get her out. It could go up any moment.'

'She was going too fast.'

'What's that got to do with it?'

It had all been too fast . . . what was the phrase? . . . the fast lane . . . She wasn't even on the hard shoulder.

'I'm not on the hard shoulder,' she thought. 'And if I were I wouldn't cry on it.'

She wished they wouldn't swing her so. Or if they must, would they do it the right way up, with not too much jerkiness, the way her father did.

There, she was crying now. But why were her tears red?

Two

'You'll like this one,' the lawyer said. 'A particularly unpleasant rape and murder.'

He was a pear-shaped man with a bald head and an invariably emollient tone which had given him his nickname of Soapy. His enemies called him Pontius, though his real name was Patrick Protheroe. He had a way of knowing which side you liked your bread buttered so he was popular with barristers.

'This is a great opportunity for you, Heather,' Sir Peregrine Eardley QC, Head of Chambers, had told her. 'Soapy's very particular. I won't say I'm surprised he asked for you, but he has a reputation for being conservative. He wants you – you in particular – working as my junior on this case. It's unusual because women barristers aren't generally his thing.'

What his thing was became evident to Heather as the solicitor eyed her across the meeting-room table. She smoothed her official skirt down as far as it would go and tried not to imagine the smell of his shiny dome. There had been a maths master called Currie at her school with just such a pate. The combination of name and baldness had inevitably given him the nickname 'Eggs' . . . He too had had a penchant for glancing up one's uniform.

'Are we distracting you, Miss Semple?'

She blushed.

She had to cure herself of this tendency to let her thoughts go free-range. The successful barrister knew when to concentrate and how to concentrate. She collected herself. The nose and all-seeing chilly little eye of Arthur, the senior clerk, appeared round the door in urgent profile, followed by a deferential but conspiratorial finger, beckoning Sir Perry to come and sign something of enormous importance. The great man made his apologies and left the room while Soapy sat with his hands pressed together.

'Well,' he continued as the door closed, 'is that it? Better things to think about?'

'Not at all, Mr Protheroe. I was just thinking . . .'

'Yes, Miss Semple. And please call me Patrick.'

'I was just thinking . . . er . . . Patrick, how pleasant it is to find myself in the company of someone who is . . . well . . . something of a legend.'

'A legend in his lunchtime, eh?'

The portly man smiled as if it were his own joke.

'That's not what I've heard,' she said. 'Just a legend.'

'Well, at any rate, I hope you will join me for lunch.'

Sir Peregrine had informed her that a meal might be on the cards, and advised her, for the good of the chambers and herself, to accept – though it was, of course, entirely at her own discretion. She was both irritated and impressed with the finesse of the solicitor's invitation.

'Thank you. I should like that,' she said.

'I'll fill you in on the case while we eat.'

It was a two-edged asset, being attractive in this business, she reflected.

Half an hour later, the restaurant was softly warm, with pink tablecloths and an air of being patronized by company plastic. The chairs were smooth with the polishing of corporate bottoms.

Heather had lunched there once before with Sir Peregrine when she had first been taken on. He too had looked at her legs. Not that she objected to people looking at her legs. What was the use of having good legs if they were ignored? She might as well have legs like Dorothy, the clerks' secretary, of whom some politically incorrect barrister had remarked, 'The only good thing you can say about her legs is that they reach the ground.'

But there was looking at legs and looking at legs. And then there was looking up legs. Soapy and the head of her chambers were in the third category. Still, there she was in one of the best chambers in town and a job from a legend in and out of his lunchtime. That was where her legs had brought her.

No, she must guard against her tendency to flippancy. That was where a second-class degree in history and a hard-worked-for pass at law school had brought her also.

It irritated her sometimes to think that effortless attributes like long legs could get you further in life than any amount of sitting up late with *Criminal Law Review* after a chaste supper of gelid baked beans and a cup of instant coffee. She hadn't done anything to deserve her legs. They were what she'd been issued with. Dorothy would give her eye-teeth for them – although the exchange, it had to be said, would not have worked out in the exchanger's favour.

It was unfair, really. She sometimes thought there should be a beauty tax, so that pretty girls should be made to wear spots and handsome young bucks have obligatory black teeth. And then of course there would have to be an intelligence tax as well so that self-satisfied barristers should commit mandatory *bêtises* at least twice a week . . .

Barristers were generally argumentative, bolshy, analytical, but most of all smug. She sometimes wondered whether she liked the profession; whether, even, she liked herself for following it.

She forced herself back to concentrate on the matter in hand. Soapy was saying something about some grand person he knew, and her mind wandered again. It wandered into a conjecture as to why she was allowing it to wander. What kind of future was there in a wandering mind when an influential lawyer was giving her lunch? She should be on the qui vive, agog at his every sally. She was good at her job, she knew that. Perhaps a little too introspective, too sensitive – but since when was sensitivity a disadvantage? Sensitivity was what told you that you – and other people – were alive . . . Perhaps she should have read English. She had a good memory and quotes kept pushing their way out of her mind like feathers from a pillow, but it hardly suggested a career.

'Quite so, er, Patrick,' she said suddenly, noting a pause in his discourse and sensing a rhetorical question.

It seemed to do the trick.

The trouble with me, she thought, is I'm bad at making up my mind – not professionally, that's relatively easy – but in my own life. She comforted herself by reflecting that Hamlet had the same problem.

Soapy was moving easily into his restaurant routine now, calling the waiter by his first name, demanding the removal of the restaurateur's own estate Chianti that adorned every table.

'Take away that muck, Piero. We don't want any frooty tooties here.'

'Is very, very good year,' said Piero whose real name was Pedro and who came from Portugal.

'Bollocks,' said Soapy. 'It's been universally vilified.'

'Ah, the signor is such a perfectionist . . .'

'Bring us two glasses of Prosecco and then a bottle of Brunello '83. That suit you, Heather?'

'Fine. I love Brunello.'

She would be drowsy in the afternoon, but it was a price she would have to pay. Better to be drowsy with a job than alert with bugger-all.

The glasses arrived – changed by Soapy to champagne at the last moment – a decision he regretted, rightly in her opinion; it was acid stuff.

'The Italians don't understand champagne,' he said and the small talk went on; where she lived, where she was brought up, gossip about mutual acquaintances. Smoked salmon appeared. She could not recall having ordered it but doubtless Soapy's lunchtime ritual was so established that Piero simply slipped into automatic pilot.

'Can't eat that messed about Italian stuff,' said Soapy. 'That all right for you?'

It was not a question. Heather did not ask him why he came to an Italian restaurant for smoked salmon but he told her all the same.

'Nobody does British food better than the Italians,' he pronounced. 'Sole all right to follow?'

'Fine,' she replied, though querying inwardly the red wine with the fish.

There was evidently more to Soapy than met the eye for he read her thoughts as though they were a tenancy agreement.

'Always have red wine with fish,' he said. 'It's a myth that they don't go together. And white wine gives you breast cancer.'

It was an outrageous remark, designed to be challenged, so she did not challenge it. She wondered whether Soapy was worried about his own fat little bubbies.

'Quite so,' she said again.

The sole, perfectly grilled, and served with Elysian chipped potatoes and a side salad, lived up to Soapy's pronouncement.

She was beginning to endorse his good opinion of the wine and even to a slight pleasurable buzziness – the very table seemed to quiver as if picking up some distant significance – after her second glass of the Brunello when she felt his hand on her knee.

Well versed in evasion (she was after all thirty-five), she contrived to drop her napkin. It necessitated her leaning over elaborately in order to pick it up – a manoeuvre that dislodged the offending paw without causing embarrassment.

Soapy gave absolutely no indication that his hand had been anywhere except his knife or his glass. If anything, he seemed more affable than before. Perhaps it had been some kind of test.

'Now,' he said, 'to business. Let me tell you about the case. I want you to work with Sir Perry to defend a client of mine charged with murder having first, it is alleged, raped his male victim. As you know, he's very hard-pressed at the moment so you are going to be the linch-pin.'

She tried not to show she was flattered.

'A *male* rapist? They didn't tell me that.'

'Rape's rape and murder's murder,' Soapy said briskly. 'Only naturally our man says he didn't do it.'

She now knew why she had been selected. Soapy was a wily old bird. He knew his client stood a better chance of getting off if he had a woman junior working for him – as well as one of the best defence counsels in London.

So she had been chosen not for herself but for her sex. When she had started as a pupil at chambers she had had all sorts of romantic notions about being valued as a person not as a woman, but she had been forced to modify them long ago. A job was a job, whenever, however it came. Even so, there was something so arrantly sexist in the lawyer's attitude that her eyes narrowed a little.

Soapy, as before, anticipated her.

'Come on,' he said. 'Don't tell me you want to be loved for brains alone. Yes, it's sexism. But the boot is on the other foot. It's getting you a job. I'd hate to tell Perry that you were less than enthusiastic.'

She wasn't keen on that either. Her head of chambers had mentioned earlier in the month that work seemed a little slow coming in for her. Of course she could have made an issue of it – certain rather earnest women barristers were hot on this sort of thing – but how much store did she set by the feminist question? Not enough to pass up an opportunity like this. Her father had been a military attaché. 'If you can't take a joke, you shouldn't sign on,' had been one of his maxims. If she wanted to get on, there really was no choice. Besides, maybe the man was innocent . . . maybe she could help the poor bastard and do well by doing good.

'Tell me about it,' she said.

'Good girl. Coffee, I think,' remarked Soapy to the hovering Piero. 'Coffee all right for you?'

'Fine. Cappuccino, please.'

But Piero had already disappeared.

'There's this transvestite rent-boy, see. Locks his door. Ties his hands first, violently buggers himself. Then hangs himself in a cupboard in his room. Impossible, of course. Police have charged a chap . . . my client. He was seen to leave a wine bar with him, some material from his jacket was found in the flat, but he swears he never touched let alone murdered him. It appears that, uh, a condom was used so there's no help there, I'm afraid, and no condoms either . . . at least not on the premises. Our man's already been committed for trial, of course.'

'What do you think?' It wasn't as though she'd asked if he thought the client were guilty. One never did in so many words. Even so, what she had said was too early, too direct. She knew she shouldn't have asked. It was not the sort of thing you said to Soapy. She noticed his hand go white around his wine glass, but otherwise the mask hardly slipped.

'If I thought he was guilty, I would hardly have asked you to defend him, my dear. We don't want any professional embarrassment. We have to believe in our clients' innocence, otherwise where would justice be?'

She knew she had been let off lightly. It had been stupid of her – perhaps the Brunello was stronger than she had realized.

'What sort of man is he?' she asked, choosing to ignore the fact that Piero had brought her espresso.

'I think perhaps I'd better take you to see for yourself.'

'Go to the prison with you?' she asked.

It was rare for a junior to attend an interview with such a big player as Soapy.

'I'll send someone along,' he told her lightly, changing his mind, reminding her of her unimportance. 'The important thing is that you should form an impression . . .'

Three

Alan called at her flat that evening, as they had arranged. They had been planning to go to the cinema.

He was a television presenter and researcher on one of the more responsible (his word) weekly comment shows. The comments covered more or less everything, which suited him well for he had an eclectic sort of mind. There was hardly anything Alan didn't know about, although once or twice she had wondered about the depth of his understanding.

He was a good-looking man in his forties with a mop of boyish brown hair and an engaging laugh, divorced long since, with no children. He had a slight American accent, she never quite knew why: something to do with spending a year at an American school as an exchange student – or was it because it went down well on television? He was good at his job, with a suitably forensic manner; indeed he was currently riding a crest. Success of that kind had done what she had so often noticed, however – it had made its victim coarser, encouraged a certain arrogance, a tendency only to want to meet other successes. He wasn't so interested in ordinary people, just as he didn't really want to take on board any new notion unless it was endorsed by his peers. In this, as in certain other respects, she found him surprisingly immature. Politically, perhaps rather unfashionably, he tended to run with the hare and hunt with the hounds. He called it not taking sides, he was on the side of truth.

For all that, or perhaps in spite of that, he was intelligent and even sensitive, with a good sense of humour so long as it wasn't about himself. He was also a rather good lover.

They had been together for over three years now. They often stayed in each other's flat – more often in hers than his. His was bigger, but he said – rather tritely, she thought – that he needed space. Marriage had been discussed, though very briefly and earlier on. They had both agreed their jobs meant a lot to them. Time enough for marriage later. Did she want children? It was a question she had asked herself. His view was that anybody (almost) could have children. Not everybody could be a successful television presenter – or, he added, a successful woman barrister. Both of their jobs took them away a great deal; his to research, hers to provincial assizes. In the circumstances, they had both agreed (although perhaps he had agreed more strongly), what would marriage provide that their present arrangement could not?

'Hullo, darling,' he greeted her, giving her his infectious, slightly crooked-toothed smile. He had had many letters from admirers offering everything from cakes to copulation on the strength of it.

'Mmmm, you smell nice.'

She had splashed on a little Eau de Ciel by Annick Goutal which she had bought on their last visit to Paris – nowhere in London seemed to have it and she knew it always got a good reception from Alan. Maybe it would encourage him to take her to Paris again; he seemed to have been working particularly hard recently.

She sat down in the living-room and he offered to pour her a drink.

'No thanks,' she said. 'I had lunch.'

'Oh?'

'With a solicitor. He wants me to take on a case.'

'Interesting?'

'A rape and murder. Rather unpleasant. Male rape.'

'That *is* interesting. Male rape and murder, eh? Well done.'

'It wasn't so well done for the poor man who got killed.'

'No, of course. Of course.'

His professional interviewship was often – though not always – good at modulating his reactions.

'Sorry,' she said. 'It's been rather a day. I had masses of paperwork on the case in the afternoon and half a bottle of wine on top of the champagne made me feel . . .'

'I know how you feel after champagne,' he smiled.

He was right. It acted as a mild aphrodisiac.

'Not in the office, I don't. It made me feel like a wasp in a curtain. Do you mind if we don't do the cinema tonight?'

'Of course.'

His smile faded slightly. He had been looking forward to the film.

'I'll cook something,' she said. 'Steak and salad do you?'

She knew there was food in the fridge. Alan scorned the new crop of low-calorie foods, functional foods and – philological obscenity – nutriceuticals, but he still looked after himself with a preference for simplicity in his eating. Her shopping tended to reflect his taste.

'Fine, fine. I'll open something.'

She rather hoped he wasn't going to say champagne, but of course he did.

'There's some Bollinger I brought; got it from a man I interviewed.'

She knew where Bollinger led but she didn't like to let him down. He wanted to make love later. Let him make love later. She had always found her body responsive even if her mood wasn't. It was one of the reasons to feel grateful about being a woman. When Alan didn't feel like it he couldn't and that was an end of it.

'We'll celebrate your new case,' he said. 'Male rape, eh? It's in the news. You're bound to get a good write-up.'

Perhaps love-making would stroke away the image of the man in the cupboard, stained tights round his ankles and a string round his neck. And then again perhaps it wouldn't.

Alan came into the kitchen with a glass while she was preparing the food.

'Thanks,' she said, changing her mind about a drink. The aristocratic bubbles slipped down more obligingly than the bumptious acid of the restaurant. She started to feel better.

They made love, and the dead man did not intrude on the delicious sensations that spread across and through her as Alan caressed her. There was something indefinably different about his love-making today. Almost as though he had been taking a refresher course, or boned up on a few tips from an Ecstasy Aunt. There was no shortage of advice these days in the men's magazines, along with articles on penis enlargement. Not that Alan seemed to need the modification.

Afterwards they lay and talked. She remembered a former boyfriend, a barrister (of course), who had once remarked that carnal activity needs some kind of verbalizing post-coital digestive process. She mentioned it now to Alan. He was not the sort to mind about former lovers – more interested in useable lines.

'Yes,' he agreed, 'a smokescreen after sex. It helps women come to terms with their contentment and men to dissipate their sorrow.'

'Sorrow?'

'*Post coitum tristis* . . .'

She almost felt guilty for feeling happy.

'Bollocks,' she told him.

'Yes,' he said, 'that's the seat of melancholy. The ancients had it wrong. They said it was the bile, the pancreas, but I say it's the balls.'

'Anyway, what have you got to feel melancholy about?'

He gave her his crooked grin.

'Nothing, actually. The series is going ahead. Top priority. Shooting in five weeks . . .'

He had so many projects that she sometimes found it difficult to keep up with them.

'The series?' she asked.

He looked a little peeved.

'You know, I told you, the series on the British Institutions – the Church, the Monarchy, the Treasury, the Bank of England, the Police, the City, yes, and the BBC, and Education, and of course the Law – what's happened to them, why and where have they gone wrong? It's going to happen. We got the go-ahead today . . .'

'Great,' she said, showing proper enthusiasm, 'it could be good. Do you know the answer?'

'The answer?'

'Why they've gone wrong.'

'There are many answers,' he told her. 'But there must be a common thread. We shall be talking to all the top people. This could be the one I've been waiting for . . .'

It had been a fallow year or two, she knew, for the socio-political commentator – at least, that was what Alan had said. Society and politics, taking their cue from the decline of the old millennium, seemed to have become clapped out.

The Conservatives had been thrashed in the 1997 election, and a Labour government under Tony Blair ('never trust a Tony', one of Alan's dictums) had proceeded to mastermind an even quicker collapse of morale than their predecessors. A policy of full employment had meant that the state service sector had become monstrously swollen, and this, with a minimum wage and a degree of City-bashing (as if the City wasn't doing a perfectly good job of bashing itself) together with an increase in income tax and a tax on dividends, had succeeded in putting the country's economic performance into a decline so steep that people talked longingly of the good old days of the 1970s. Meanwhile Brussels piled on more and more onerous, as well as fatuous, contribution demands and Pharaoh-like whips and scorpions. The European Court of Justice continued to give credence – and awards – to preposterous claimants; but like much else that went on under the banner of 'Europe' it had by now achieved the status of farce; to be mocked in principle and ignored in practice.

The celebrations of the new millennium had been prolonged and expensive – employers as well as schools reported pleasure-related absenteeisms of a month or more – and of course it was almost impossible to sack people now. The result was that the country entered the twenty-first century almost completely bankrupt and of course unable to meet any Common European Currency disciplines. The International Monetary Fund once more came up with the cash and a demand for radical reform, and an election was called in 2001.

A new Conservative government had been formed, slightly centre of centre, and this of course had no more success than the last government under John Major. It had now stumbled on for four and a half years. A kind of fatalism had settled over the country. Political and monetary union with Europe seemed as far off as ever. Neither big party seemed to have any profound answer. Foreign investors were picking off what scraps of meat they could find. The rate of illiteracy was rising faster than ever, only matched by the figures for divorce and illegitimacy. The BBC had once again pruned its World Service. Princess Diana had joined a lay healing order and her name had been put forward for the Nobel Prize, though unsuccessfully, for her work among the ever-increasing sleeping-bags of London.

The Queen was still on the throne, while the Prince of Wales's influence had made itself felt in a spate of millennial temples and mosques, and the restoration of two city churches.

As for crime, a whole generation of youth seemed alienated. To the dismay of the retired, violence in the inner cities was now ominously echoed by rural strife. Village gangs proliferated, composed of youths – unemployed and unemployable – super-predators whose forefathers had worked on the land for generations. Now estates that had employed, say, twenty men could do the work with four . . . There was little or nothing for the rest.

Alan's pet hobby-horse was that television itself was now compounding the rot. The old challenging and critical programmes had been cut, and the programme planners exercised themselves ever more basely to compete with the latest and greatest threat to their masters' livelihood – the development of interactive video hardware and software at a price every home could afford . . .

In the face of all this, it was indeed amazing that Alan had nursed his series to production.

But Heather didn't feel elated. Instead, as he spoke, she felt her contentment ebbing away. Suddenly the safe bed, the warm arms about her, the familiar room, the busy sounds of London seemed evanescent, vulnerable, as if poised on some dizzying abyss. She had to say something, anything, that would bring them back from the edge.

'The law,' she said (and what could be safer than that?). 'I could tell you about the law.'

He looked at her for a moment and she saw, just for a micro-second, a hint of condescension in his eye.

'Well, actually,' he told her, 'the Lord Chief Justice has agreed to speak.'

Four

Her mother was slowly dying. There was no emergency.

Indeed, Heather had had no idea that she was ill. Typical of the old girl to say nothing; then one day there had been a call from a hospital in Oxford.

When Heather had arrived on that first day, panicky and upset, she had been asked to wait a few minutes because her mother was being examined by the specialist. He turned out to be a large Scotsman who was still sitting on her mother's bed chatting to her when Heather was ushered in. Apparently they had both been taken to the Summer Isles as children, though Heather couldn't quite understand how the subject had come up. It was one of her mother's attributes that she could extract the most irrelevant information from people and make it seem totally apropos.

'Not at the same time, of course,' said her mother, 'to the Summer Isles, I mean.'

'Not so far behind,' said the doctor, gallantly.

'I'm glad he's a Scot,' her mother confided, smiling. 'He reminds me of my Aunt Florence's husband James. Such good engineers.'

The doctor had smiled, too, but afterwards he had had a word with Heather outside. She could see on his face that this was one old boiler he couldn't repair.

'It's leukaemia, d'ye see, lassie? Slow but sure when they're old. We'll make her as comfortable as we can.'

Heather had thanked him, walked to her car, and sat there,

unable even to turn the starter. For so many years, her mother had been there, solid as a sea-wall. Oh, she had known the wall had been undercut a bit; but suddenly for the cold tide to start coming through . . . it was the most shocking thing she could remember.

Of course, her mother's appearance had been a surprise. Had she looked ill the last time Heather had seen her – six weeks ago? Perhaps she had. The trouble was, mother's years in Africa with her soldier husband had given her a permanently weathered complexion. In the past you often couldn't tell if she was ill, not from her colouring. But you could now. Now she had the colour of an old book.

Heather had sat on in the car park with tears scurrying down her face faster than the rain that dotted the windscreen, and thought about her.

She had had Heather when she was in her mid-forties. That had been a last gasp, her father had said. They had tried to have children for years. It struck Heather now that that might have been one of the causes of tension between them.

'I prayed to St Jude,' her mother often told her.

She came of a High Church family. One of her uncles had been a bishop.

Heather had very nearly been called Judy, an escape for which she had always been grateful. At her first school there had been a Judy and the little boys thought it no end of a game to go up to her and say, 'Are you Judy?'

'Yes,' she would reply.

'Well, here's punch.'

She learned to run away quite soon but it was a painful day or two for Judy. You couldn't do much with Heather except wear it for luck. Why were most little boys such toads, she had wondered as she sat there in the car. And big ones too come to that . . . But thinking of the toadishness of men had cheered her up a little, and at last she had been able to pull herself together and drive back to London.

That had been the first of many visits to the hospital. She

tried to come down every couple of weeks or so. Sometimes the old girl would be awake and comparatively perky, at others she would be drowsy; or drugged and gently rambling away to herself; or asleep. Whatever her condition, Heather always stayed two hours. It seemed the least she could do. Alan never offered to accompany her, nor would she have agreed if he had.

When she arrived this time, the day after the news of Alan's series, her mother seemed half-conscious.

'Mother's just been given her injection,' the nurse said.

Heather kissed the old woman's forehead and sat down by the bedside. A little smile crossed the lined old face. Heather started to talk to her.

'Why do nurses have this sense of economy about the personal pronoun?' she asked. 'I've always noticed – they say Baby, or Doctor or Mother but never the or your. Was it drummed into them at nursing school? Rap knuckles if I catch you wasting your personal pronouns. Do they feel in some way it's like treatment? You can't have them unless they're prescribed. I see Mr Bulstrode is on three personal pronouns a day – up his bottom . . .'

Her mother heaved slightly beside her. It was the nearest she got to laughing when she had had her injection. Heather tried to make her laugh because she'd read somewhere that laughter produced an anti-cancer hormone.

'Silly girl,' whispered her mother. 'How you do go on. I pity those prosecutors.'

Heather squeezed her hand.

'Next time I come to see you,' she said, 'it'll be your birthday. I'll bring a cake.'

'Ha. Don't bother about such things. What good's a birthday to an old crow like me? It'll be my last.'

'Don't say such things. The world will stop if you die. You've got to live to ninety.'

She would be eighty in a fortnight.

'Nmph. The world will not stop for me. The world's been going faster and faster ever since I was born. It's never gone faster – ever. I'll stop for the world. It won't stop for me.'

Heather shook her head.

'It'll stop if you die,' she repeated.

She didn't like to think of the world without her mother.

'Silly girl,' her mother said again.

There was a pause and then her mother added:

'Dying's not difficult. It's living that's a bugger.'

Heather thought suddenly of the dead transvestite and wondered whether he would have agreed with her. Dying had been a bugger for him. She made a conscious effort to dismiss the image. She didn't want such things around the sickbed.

'When I was born,' said her mother, 'King Edward had only been dead a dozen years or so. There were still horses in the streets. I can remember . . . clip clop in the nights . . . and the pools of light made by the street lamps . . . a different sort of light, you know . . . and a bag of bullseyes for a penny . . .'

'You should write it down, Mother. People will forget these things. Write about Boar's Hill.'

Her mother's father had been a don at one of the Oxford colleges and her parents had had a house on Boar's Hill, where the air was supposed to be good, high above the city. There had been a number of eminent academics and artists of various kinds – John Masefield, Sir Arthur Evans, Gilbert Murray among them – who had made it their home. Robert Graves, as a young man, had run a shop there.

'You write them for me, darling. I'm so tired. You write if you like and I'll talk till I fall asleep.'

'All right,' said Heather. 'Of course I will. But don't feel you have to. It was only an idea.'

'And a very good idea. Now, let me see . . .'

Heather fished in her bag for the notebook she always carried; and then she had another idea. There was a small journalist's cassette machine there too which she used for recording notes to herself in the car. She switched it on and sat back.

The old woman lay with her eyes closed, her thin chest rising and falling imperceptibly. Heather began to wonder whether she had fallen asleep. Then suddenly she began to speak in a small clear voice.

'There was a man,' she said. 'I can't remember much about him. Perhaps there wasn't much to remember . . . though now I come to think of it I'm sure there was . . . must have been amusing . . . because he decided to erect a monument to himself. He employed a gardener with a spade and a wheelbarrow to build a mound. It took him ten years but when he finished it was nearly a hundred feet high. It was the highest point of Boar's Hill. Still there now, it always will be there. You can see five counties from it. What about that? Jarn Mound, it's called. The work of slow time. You wouldn't get people doing that now. They'd call up a bulldozer and knock it up in an hour. But it wouldn't be remarkable, would it?'

'Not at all,' said Heather.

She had walked up Jarn Mound with her mother several times.

'Nothing worth while is achieved without effort,' said her mother, one of her favourite maxims. 'Did you get all that, dear?'

Her voice was fainter now.

'Yes, Mother.'

'Well done that man. Now I must tell you . . . Sir Arthur Evans . . . you know, the one who discovered Knossos . . . he had a maze in his front hall . . . and . . . it was rather a scandal, actually . . .'

There was a longer pause than usual.

'What was the scandal, Mother?' Heather asked very gently.

'He was rather too fond of . . . young men . . .'

Five

'The British legal system,' said the head of her chambers when she told him about Alan's series on British institutions, 'the British legal system is falling apart for one very good reason – only I very much doubt if the Lord Chief Justice will tell your boyfriend so.'

'What is that, Perry?' she asked, although she had already heard what he was going to say. It didn't do to point such things out to the head of your chambers and certainly not to Sir Peregrine Eardley QC, for he didn't take kindly to contradiction. Like many barristers, the sound of his own voice was music to his ears. Anything else was, at best, merely the orchestra playing around his solo and, at worst, cacophony.

He was a tall, lean man in his fifties with greying hair crowning a thin, ascetic face lined from long use of that famous contemptuous smile. He had been expensively and exhaustively educated, made a great deal of money, acquired his knighthood and was widely tipped for even greater things.

'The British legal system is falling apart because of the twelve good men and true.'

'Why's that, Perry?'

'Because there aren't any. There aren't even twelve good women and true.'

'You can't write off the whole population.'

'I don't. If I had my way there'd be no juror under fifty. At least the over-fifties have some conception of duty.'

'Not everyone else is bad.'

'I didn't say they were bad. But they're not good and true. They may be good but they're not true. Not true the way Sir Walter Raleigh meant when they asked him which way he'd like to put his head on the block.'

'What was that?'

'"It matters not which way the head lies, so as the heart be true."'

'You mean . . .'

'This new breed of juror confuses do-good with good. They're woolly-gooders if they're good at all. They're so fucking bottomless they'd rather acquit a murderer than convict an innocent man.'

'Nice for the innocent man.'

'But disaster for the law.'

Sir Peregrine had offered to buy her a drink to celebrate their forthcoming collaboration and they were sitting in the Savoy overlooking the river. Prosperous-looking men and women moved to and fro. It was plain someone was making money out of something, even if it wasn't being invested in British industry.

She was keeping her knees especially close together because she knew she had laddered her tights, but apart from that she was feeling rather pleased with herself. It was the first time he had asked her out for so much as a shandy, after her introductory lunch, and now it was champagne again and the Savoy. Outside, the sleeping-bags in the doorways of the Strand proclaimed the failure of politics and commerce, but Sir Perry didn't seem to mind.

'Ah, Lord Beeston,' he greeted a flat-haired man in a dinner-jacket. 'How is the new acquisition?'

'Very smooth, Sir Perry. Very smooth indeed.' He moved on as if on castors.

Heather felt it was time to introduce a little vinegar into the conversation.

'At least God doesn't feel that way,' she said.

Sir Perry's lofty smile modulated to puzzlement.

'Come again,' he said.

'God doesn't mind punishing the innocent and letting the guilty go free – or even rewarding them. He does it all the time.'

Sir Peregrine's eyes narrowed.

'You some kind of born-againer?'

She shook her head.

'Just a comment.'

'You leave all that to your boyfriend's catch-up with the Church. We're talking Law here, woman. What we need's the Scots system. Fifteen jurors and a majority verdict – rather than striving for unanimity as we do. That way we'd get some convictions and the police wouldn't feel so demoralized.'

'Yes, Perry.'

'And next time you come to the Savoy with me, do get yourself a new pair of tights.'

'Bastard.'

The word came out quite unexpectedly. One or two heads turned round. Somewhere a glass fell off a tray.

No one in his chambers had said that to him before. Heather was appalled and rather intrigued. She waited to see how the blow would fall.

He laughed.

'I asked for that,' he said. 'Another glass, d'you think? Who says women don't get a fair crack of the whip in the law? Now, let me tell you what I know of this case – just a *tour d'horizon* – I won't bog you down with details yet. In fact, I'd like you to go along and hear his story for yourself. Soapy's man will give you the picture . . .'

Six

Soapy's man may have been meant to be bringing the case notes with him, but when she arrived at Brixton, she was told that he had called to say he would be late and that she was to go ahead with the conference. She learned afterwards that lateness was the Soapy office synonym for non-appearance. It enabled them to save money and cover ground. She was sorry, however, not to have company because the place was at the best of times daunting, and today, under a light drizzle from a steely sky, it would have made Gormenghast look like a Bargain Break.

The prison had that particular prisony smell that strikes despondency into the hearts of all except old lags and warders; compounded of carbolic, hopelessness, herded male, resentment and captivity, its acrid institutional stench makes even the hardened visitor falter on the inward stride and accelerate, in due course, for the exit. It was not Heather's first visit to the gaol, and her nose went through its customary wrinkle.

'He's in the interview room, miss,' said the prison officer as he escorted her from the lodge, 'talking to the probation officer.'

You had to call warders prison officers, of course, as part of the drive to the sanitizing of occupations. Heather recalled Alan saying he had a soft spot for the term 'gaoler', with its overtones of *Fidelio* and Monopoly, but then he'd never been inside Brixton. There were no shades here of opera-house or living-room.

'He's an evil bastard, if you don't mind my saying so. He'll twist that Probation round his little finger,' said the gaoler.

'I do mind your saying so, officer; as a matter of fact, I'm defending him.'

The warder gave her a look half-weary, half-contemptuous. He was nearing the end of his service and had seen too many evil men and up-and-coming barristers. Even her legs, those limbs of Satan as Alan called them, had failed to impress him, which was about the only point in his favour. She had debated with herself whether to wear trousers for the visit, but had considered the softer look might have its advantages – a decision she was to regret. She followed him as a huge steel door whimpered open, revealing a vast and empty corridor that could have come from Virgil's underworld. The gaoler set off at a spanking pace and she had almost to run to keep up with him. Perhaps it's women he doesn't like, she thought, not just prisoners and barristers.

On and on they went, down tributary passages, with gates clanging like broken promises behind them and new dreary vistas opening up. They passed one or two prisoners under guard who turned and looked at her as though she were a walking orifice.

Finally they stopped in front of a door marked VISITS.

'He's in there,' said the gaoler with a nod. 'He's finished with the Probation. I'll be outside if you need anything.'

He said it as though what he really meant was 'if he attacks you'. It wasn't altogether reassuring, but in spite of having no notes, Heather was determined to show she was on top of things and walked briskly forwards stifling the imp of unease at the thought of being alone in a cell with a man who, if not guilty, was undoubtedly dangerous. This much she had learnt from her briefing.

'Barrister for you, Morbey,' said the warder, shutting the door as he did so.

The prisoner sitting at the table did not get up when she entered. He was a tall man with slicked-back hair, a hawk nose, hard mouth and glittering eyes. Heather's first thought was that his appearance would not be of much help to his case. At least they might be able to do something about his hairstyle.

'I'm not changing my hair,' said the prisoner. 'No way. I could see you was thinking that. I could see you was thinking "evil-looking bastard".'

'Appearances can be deceptive,' said Heather, taken off guard but trying to be businesslike.

'Not in my case,' said Morbey. 'I look like a bastard. I am a bastard.'

'Ah.'

'You know what. I'd like to screw you.'

'That's not very original,' said Heather.

She was on firmer ground here.

'It's not my business to be original. That's your business. You got to get me off. It'll take some originality cos they fitted me up, didn't they?'

'I certainly won't feel drawn to your case if you're going to make sexist remarks.'

'Oh for Gawd's sake. I asked for a pretty barrister cos I thought you'd stand a better chance with the jury. The whole thing's sex, isn't it? Life is sex, isn't it? The charge is sex. That's what I'm supposed to have done, isn't it? Sex.'

'Rape, yes . . . and murder.'

'Ah . . . that . . .' said the prisoner.

'Yes, that,' retorted Heather.

'Not guilty,' said the prisoner. 'I never. Couldn't have done. What was my motive?'

'Sex?'

'I can see you're a Freudian.'

Heather looked at him more carefully. Was he making fun of her? There was more to the man than she had been led to believe.

'You've read Freud?'

'Dipped in,' said the man airily. 'Dipped in and then dipped out again. I prefer Jung myself.'

'You're a rather unusual man, Mr Morbey,' Heather said, opening her briefcase and extracting a notepad.

The act of writing helped to stabilize her impressions. Why had Soapy not warned her of his client's intellectual pretensions? Perhaps indeed they were not pretensions. She wished she'd had the brief or at least some case notes from Soapy. As so often, she was going to have to busk it. Still, it was something to have the chance of meeting the client in good time: often she didn't see them until the day of the trial. But why no brief?

'You're behind the times, Miss Semple, if I may say so.'

He paused and looked steadily at her as though watching the thoughts pass like fish behind her eyes.

'Any self-respecting criminal nowadays gets himself an education,' he continued. 'Three years porridge is enough for a university degree. I have two, as a matter of fact. English Literature and Mathematics. If I go down for rape and murder, I'll have enough time for the whole bloody lot. Two's enough, thank you very much.'

She was impressed by his qualifications, as rare in most clients she came across as in prime ministers and princesses.

'But . . . I thought you said you were a good-for-nothing bastard.'

'I said evil. Evil bastard, that's me. Not good for nothing. Good for a number of things – though perhaps good is not a word I'd use.'

'I don't think improving yourself can be called evil.'

'Depends what ends you put it to, doesn't it? These lads nowadays, they steal a car, they maim an old biddy on a crossing, they kill a baby on a pavement, that's not evil. Anyone can do that. That's just stupid. That's what you get from dropping out of school. Instant kicks – like a ram stuck in a fence.'

Was it her imagination or was his cockney accent modifying as he spoke?

'So what's evil?' she asked.

'Ah. That would be telling. But it isn't raping and murdering and getting caught.'

'So it might be raping and murdering and not getting caught?'

Morbey scratched the side of his nose and looked at her slyly.

'Might be,' he said. 'Might be. But if it was raping, it'd have to be someone prettier than that little rent boy. And then I wouldn't rape a rent boy. It's a contradiction in terms. Murder, now, that's different. I might have killed one or two individuals in the course of business. But I'd never ever rape *and* murder. I'd leave that to the snuff-VR merchants.'

Heather had the impression, just for an instant, that he'd said more than he intended, but she was still far from happy with his attitude. His whole approach seemed pointlessly elusive. What kind of figure did he think he'd cut in court?

She crossed her legs while she searched for another gambit. Why hadn't that junior from Soapy's office turned up, dozy little prat?

'Do you mind not crossing your legs like that,' Morbey said. 'I can hear your pubic hairs rustling.'

Heather stood up. She wasn't shocked. She had heard, in the course of her limited career, almost everything there was to hear on the subject of human anatomy – hers included – in court or out of it. But she was suddenly tired of this man and his intellectual posturing. The interview was going nowhere.

'What you getting up for?' asked Morbey as if he didn't know.

'The interview is over,' said Heather, formally. 'I will take the notes from your solicitors. Perhaps you will feel less like playing stupid games with them.'

'Oh come on now. Keep your hair on.'

She couldn't resist the barrister instinct to score a point.

'I don't think we need any more talk of hair, Mr Morbey,' she said severely. 'You've said quite enough on that subject. What you should be thinking of is your defence.'

The prisoner smiled. Heather suddenly realized he was an extraordinarily attractive man. A filament of desire lit up inside her; absurd, unethical; except, she thought, there are no ethics in desire, only in our pursuit of desire. She watched him, her hand resting on the handle of the door.

'Touché.' He smiled again. 'I apologize. It's the fault of these American films. They make you feel inadequate as a prisoner if you don't say the unmentionable. In the old days, British criminals would never come out with such impoliteness. It would be "bless you, lidy, yer shines like an angel o' mercy". Which I may say you do.'

Heather couldn't help being intrigued by the man. She sat down before she realized what she was doing, half stood up and then sat down again. She opened her briefcase, adjusted her gold pencil and turned over her notebook. The ritual activity steadied her. Now it remained to be seen if the man had a good case.

'Very well, Mr Morbey,' she said. 'I will listen to what you have to say. But I have to tell you that I think you'd be better off talking with your solicitor present. Perhaps you have some kind of block about talking to women?'

She leaned back and nearly crossed her legs again, checking herself at the last moment. Why had she not left when she could so easily have done so? She had other cases to think about. This man was a time-waster; too clever by half. Barristers were a challenge to some prisoners. They had to show they were cleverer.

'I can make you famous,' he said.

'What?'

'We can win a great victory, you and me. It'll be in all the papers.'

It was a not unfamiliar line. Criminals often seemed to have an inflated sense of their importance. Not that the lure of fame didn't have its charms for barristers too.

'I'm glad you're so confident in your case,' she told him, coolly.

'It must be you,' he said. 'Only you can do it.'

They were the words all barristers, however hardened, love to hear. If honeyed phrases didn't work, flattery would be obsolete.

She paused. Outside, in the world of freedom, people toiled away, tied to ridiculous jobs if they were lucky – stencilling harvest scenes on toasters, monitoring the rate of sale of premium goldfish food, devising new quiz shows for sporting personalities. The moon would have risen already, sailing over many-towered Tooting.

Alan would be ferreting about like a starving babushka looking for scraps among the decaying matter of Britain. Babies would be being born, crying that they were come to this great stage of fools. Only here, in this captivity, by these chilly waters, did something important seem to be going on. Who was this man? What had he done?

She turned over another page of her notebook. It really was sickening not having the details of the case – all she had to go on was vague conversations with Soapy and Sir Perry.

'Very well, Mr Morbey,' she said. 'If that's what you want. Now perhaps we should get down to details.'

Seven

As Heather drove back down Trinity Road, exchanging the rum parlours of Brixton for the wine bars of Wandsworth and on through the roundabout land of Wandsworth Bridge, to Fulham, Chelsea and home, she reflected on her meeting with her client.

There was no doubt he was extremely clever and totally amoral. He appeared to believe only half of what he said – a tendency, she felt, that was less dishonest than playful. And yet how could a man be playful when faced with such appalling charges?

She had the lawyer's instinct for liars: but she had never met anyone quite so blithe about his untruths. Normally, people lied out of desperation or from sheer crafty evasiveness or just chronically, out of habit. Morbey seemed to revel in fantasy, almost as though his lies were more real to him than the facts – although equally he was no mere fantasist.

When all was said and done, however, he was still a dangerous man accused of a repulsive crime. She had warned him, of course, about his tendency to fabricate.

'You must be absolutely honest with me. I can't possibly help you otherwise.'

'I see that. 'Course I do. Straight. I'll level with you all the way.'

But there was a glint of mockery in his eye as he slipped into the criminal's patois and turned up the whine of the south London accent.

'You don't deny that you entered his room? What about the material from the jacket?'

She remembered Soapy saying he thought a strand or two had been found, presumably the prisoner's.

'Could've been brought in by anyone. Mine's a Boss. There's hundreds, thousands of jackets like that.'

'Let's hope forensic bears that out. Now, I understand you were seen in that club in the company of the young man shortly before the crime was committed.'

'All right, then. It was like this. I had a drink in this bar and I thought: what's on the menu tonight. Tonight I fancy leg of boy. So I had a drink or two more. And then this boy came up to me and said what about it. Bitter cold it was that night. We was all in our overcoats. So we went off to his place, and when we got there we took our coats off, and there she was dressed like a ballerina. Well, I wouldn't have minded that, but what I hadn't realized was, she was chubby. I can't fancy that somehow. Know what I mean? Chubby? No. Boys should be lissom. Don't you think? Do you like chubby?'

'My taste in the matter is hardly relevant.'

'I suppose not. Anyway, that's the way it takes me. Each to his own. So I fished in my pocket for a fiver to give the pathetic little prat and out I went. Next thing I hear, I'm wanted for murder.'

'What time did you leave?'

'About half-ten.'

The time of death was reliably estimated to be midnight, Soapy had said.

'Did anyone see you?'

'No.'

'Where did you go?'

'Home, of course. It's all in the police interview.'

Soapy's junior was supposed to have provided her with that, of course.

'I want to go through it with you. Was anyone there?'

'I live alone mostly. Less grief.'

'So you have no alibi? That's what the police think.'

'I didn't say that. It's only what they think.'

'Don't mess around, Mr Morbey. There will have to be an alibi notice served in any case.'

'I have an alibi. But I don't know where she is.'

'That's not good.'

'It's not good. But it's not bad. It's in the nature of alibis to go missing. Like the lights in the Finchley Road. They turn against you when you're in trouble.'

'Have you any idea where she might be?'

'I thought I did, but I was wrong, wasn't I?'

There the matter had rested for the moment. She had urged him to rack his brains for a possible location and he had agreed, though without any guarantee of success. The girl was a dodgy little scrubber, he said, and could be anywhere.

'You seem to go in for rather low companions,' she had ventured.

It was out of order. It wasn't for her to comment on the rabid promiscuity and lack of standards of her clients, and she had expected him to say so. Instead he smiled – that slow and charming illumination which had touched her the first time it appeared.

'I like 'em low,' he said. 'That way you don't get disappointed.'

Eight

Alan was already there when she arrived home, and the bottle of Sancerre was down by a third. He was wearing jeans, a white shirt and a light blue cashmere sweater and he looked very young. The contrast between him and the man she had just been seeing was almost shocking; it was good to be on familiar ground again.

'Good day?' he asked, giving her a glass. 'I've been with an influential ex-bishop.'

The wine smelt of gooseberries which made her think of childhood – and of her mother who was always commending them. She gave Alan a kiss, and sat down.

'How stands the Church?'

'Very low.'

She was reminded again of Morbey.

'I was with a new client in Brixton today. He said he likes things low. He doesn't get let down,' she told him.

Alan laughed. His eyes, set off by the jersey, were blue as water mint or, what was that flower Mother used to point out? toadflax. No, perhaps water mint was better.

'Your man wouldn't like the Church. It's crumbling visibly,' he said.

'I always thought it was a mistake to put off the middle classes,' she said. 'In marketing, I'm told, you should never offend existing customers when trying to attract new ones. Getting rid of the old prayer book and Bible was crass. Whatever happened to Matins? They were rather jolly. All you get now is maundering Family Eucharists and kiss your neighbours?'

Alan cocked his head to one side and – a gesture well known to viewers – played with the curly bit of hair over his left ear.

'That was rather the bishop's view,' he said. 'But the trouble's even deeper than that. The Church, like everything else, has gone materialist, he says. The Devil's got into it, not the old red devil but a sort of grey-green variety, according to him. There's no leadership, no will to keep the old truths and spirituality and mystery alive if it goes against the current social knee-jerk. The old boy got quite steamed up. The Church of England, assembled over four and a half centuries, is about to fragment. From giant to pygmy in one generation. Evil, he says, is a seed which regards licence as manure – and that of course is just what we've given it. And when you throw away the Church, you throw away the morality – that's the real baby in the bathwater. Did you know that over sixty-eight per cent of eight- to eighteen-year-olds don't accept the objective definition of right and wrong? I tell you, we're going to have fun with this one.'

'Fun?' she asked.

He was in a mood she knew well: keyed up, buoyant, infectiously enthusiastic; and yet just able, if she said the wrong thing, to be spiky.

'Make a good show. You know . . . Fun? Remember fun?'

She ignored the provocation.

'Any chance it might do some good?' she said.

'We'll have the old boy on the show, of course. He's everyone's idea of an old fogey with a bee in his bonnet, so it'll be good television.'

'That's not what I meant. Won't the series help make . . . don't you want it to help stop the crumble . . . make the Church strong again?'

'Darling . . .' said Alan, rolling his eyes (he really looked rather effeminate when he did that), '. . . darling, whatever gave you that idea? We're journalists, you know. We report. We don't make the news. We're critics, not performers.'

Heather sipped her wine thoughtfully.

'The trouble is,' she said, 'it seems to me, these days all the clever people go into the media. It means the critics are so much brighter than the players. Which is a bit unfair, really. Soon there won't be any players left. Then you'll have to start on each other.'

Something she said reminded her of reading *Troilus and Cressida* at school – the Ulysses speech on order, that was the one. She remembered snatches of it still:

> *'Take but degree away, untune that string,*
> *And hark what discord follows . . .'*

Next there was something about the sea o'ertopping the spongy earth. And then:

> *'Strength should be lord of imbecility*
> *And the rude son should strike the father dead . . .'*

Plenty of rude sons about. She went to the bookshelf and looked up the last bit in the Complete Shakespeare she'd won for the Debating Prize when she was sixteen.

> *'Then everything includes itself in power*
> *Power into will, will into appetite,*
> *And appetite, an universal wolf*
> *So doubly seconded by will and power,*
> *At length becomes a universal prey*
> *And last eats up himself . . .'*

Didn't that sound uncomfortably near home?

She asked Alan if he remembered it, but he failed to see the relevance and told her he'd done *Measure for Measure*, which was all about sex and justice and would have suited her much better. All that deferential twaddle about order might have been all right for the Elizabethans, he said, but had no place in a multi-layered society like ours.

It was a relief, just a little bit, when Alan said he had to get back home that night. He had an early start and had left some notes in the flat.

'What is it tomorrow?' she asked.

'The City,' he said. 'I'm going to talk to an ex-Lord Mayor. God, I'm really going to rub their noses in it. Complacent bastards.'

'I should be careful,' she told him. 'You don't know what you're stirring up.'

'That's the point of investigative journalism,' he told her, kissing her on the cheek. 'If no one gets hurt you're not doing your job.'

She turned out the light and watched him drive off in his old Lancia Integrale, left-hand drive, nearly clipping a cyclist approaching on his blind side. The man shook a fist. Heather could see Alan's white indignant face through the glass. She really felt she loved him at times like this. Pity he was so immature.

Long after the tail lights had disappeared, she stayed by the window looking out on the lighted windows. People living their lives; deceiving their wives; living their lies; sixty-five per cent of them upset (according to Gallup) at what had happened to their country and all thinking that someone else should do something about it; all waiting for the great investigative journalist in the sky to decide how and when they should be hurt.

She knew that when she felt like this she was tired, and sleep was the only cure.

She walked into the bedroom, undressed, stood naked in front of her mirror for an instant, looking at this body that was herself and over which at the same time she had only limited dominion. She had a habit of standing like this – of thinking that the body might not indeed be hers – like a borrowed coat or even a stolen one . . . She was glad she had borrowed this coat. Nicely double-breasted, size 12, and neatly fitting . . . She touched herself with hands that weren't hers . . . making her nipples suddenly start and bloom. She looked down surprised, the reverie broken.

'Take your hands off me,' she said.

She went into the bathroom, took a quick shower to rid herself of the smell of prison, returned and sank deliciously into bed.

In the middle of the night, with shocking suddenness, her alarm clock rang. In the panicky stupor of waking, she pressed the button to turn it off, but it rang on. Bloody thing, she thought in her half-sleep, it's gone wrong. And then it began to speak.

'I'm going to kill you, Heather,' it said – the voice was low and hoarse and indescribably menacing. 'I'm going to kill you but first I'm going to fuck you. I'm going to pull your drawers down and sniff your juicy cunt. And then I'm going to put my cock in it and I'm going to fuck you as you've never been fucked before . . . until you feel you have no body but one enormous cock . . . deeper and deeper, Heather . . . bigger and bigger . . . on and on . . . on and on . . . on on on on on . . . and aaaargh . . .'

She could hear the voice going so thick with lust that it too was spurting and dribbling. She scrabbled for the telephone – she knew now it must be from there – to stop the obscenity but nothing she could do would silence it.

'And then . . . then . . .' said the evil whisper, '. . . I'm going to cut your throat . . .'

She was fully awake now, but it was still nightmarish. Nothing could make a telephone talk when the receiver was down. And then she realized that she must have left the answering machine on, as she occasionally did when she was working, plugged in on the shelf beneath her bedside table.

Finally as the quiet (but not quite quiet enough) new super jumbos whistled through the small hours overhead, as they did all night now, she called Alan, but he must have edged his telephone off the hook as he sometimes did when he put his book down. The line was permanently engaged.

Nine

It is easy to think of barristers, like doctors, as being barristers (or doctors) first, people second. But the reverse is of course the case. You would think of Heather, if you saw her in her gown in court, or simply walking into chambers, as being the epitome of everything a barrister stands for: efficient, beady-eyed, quick-brained, sharp on a question, hard on an answer, and generally more intelligent and combative than the normal run of mankind.

But that air, even more than the wigs and the gowns, is their uniform. Of course, it is important to see Heather in this way. We are what we do – at least in part. But then again, we are what we don't do. We are what we'd like to do. We are what we stop others from doing. And so on.

We are many people, and Heather, when she thought about it, knew she was no exception. It is the dominating characters in the rebellious crew inside us that end up giving us the traits by which others know us. She was indeed a little too Hamlet-like. Her sensitivity sometimes made her good brain see too many sides to a question. She could hear and understand and even be won by another's point of view. This could be – if not necessarily – a weak point in a barrister, but it was certainly a strong one in a friend. She was not stiff in opinion.

Along with that went a certain equivocal quality in her relationships with men which stemmed from her absent father. She needed a male figure in her life and yet she didn't want to need one. It made her put up with Alan because she could see reasons for having him as a lover – and at the same time she could keep her affections ever so slightly at a distance. And yet, if the truth were known, she would have wished to be completely and utterly in love, a most unbarristerly state.

Next day, immediately after the disturbances of the night, it so happened that she was due in court.

Morning had brought a sense of unreality. Of course the thing had happened; it was horrible, disturbing; but the daylight, the woolly clouds, the balmy softness of approaching spring, gave it a distance, an incongruousness. Putting on her court clothes was like stepping onto a barrack square. She was on parade. She didn't call Alan; she was already late . . .

And yet, on the journey to Harrow the tiny threads of anxiety, like the tentacles of dry rot, began to creep back into her mind. A perverted-looking man, rank and white-faced, drooled at her as she walked through an underpass, attempting to block her way. And when she arrived at the court, her pulse was racing. Perhaps she should talk to Arthur, the senior clerk of her chambers, about the threatening call. Not that she wanted to confide in Arthur; he was by no means her favourite person, although you needed to keep on the right side of him if you could stomach it. But it could involve some case she had worked on and maybe he should be told.

Oh, she had had obscene callers before, you could hardly live in London and not have them; but this one was unusual. The man knew her name. It unsettled her. There was quite enough going on in her life at the moment; this sense of unease was an unwelcome extra, eroding concentration.

The man she was defending today was accused of grievous bodily harm: he was said to have attacked his neighbour with a spade. It was unlike her, but her mind kept returning to her answering machine. Normally she had a good command of her attention, sailing the ship of thought purposefully across any currents of emotion, at least in her professional life; but not today.

It did not make for a very good defence. The man with the

spade nearly went down for two years all because of a stupid lapse on her part. It shook her. She was only able to get him off after a prodigious amount of calling back of witnesses and a little eye contact with the foreman of the jury who appeared susceptible to such tactics. The judge, too, seemed indulgent.

'What you trying to do? Give me an 'eart attack?' asked the spade man with never a word of thanks when she spoke to him afterwards.

'I'm sorry, Mr Smallbone. The matter of the common-law wife and her drink problem was crucial to our case and I should have raised it earlier.'

She did not usually say sorry to a client. It was contrary to the unwritten rules of her profession.

'Never apologize,' was Sir Peregrine's maxim. 'God knows we're only human, but it doesn't do to tell our clients so.'

'I wouldn't never have forgiven you if I was sent down when all I did was tap 'im on the 'ead. It was his common law what really clobbered 'im.'

'I know,' she said. 'I think we made that point.'

'Only just, we did. By the skin of our teef. I'm thinking of complaining to the bar code.'

'Council,' she corrected him.

'Yer what?'

'Oh, never mind. By all means complain if you like . . .'

She gathered up her papers. This is what legal aid did to some people. Just because they weren't paying they thought they could treat you like a public park and throw dog shit all over you. Not that everyone was like that. In fact better legal aid, she thought, where the poorest had recourse to law, than the American system which some recommended for England. If everyone had to pay, it produced an under-class alienated from the law, for whom law had no meaning – though that notion too seemed to be finding fertile ground in the housing estates. She pondered the matter in the taxi back to chambers. It took her mind off that telephone call whose sinister tones had kept echoing across her mind.

'I'm going to kill you, but first I'm going to fuck you.'

There; she was listening to him again. Who was the bastard?

'I'll talk to Arthur,' she told herself.

It was not the head clerk's job to sort out such matters, but it could be said that anything that affected the performance of his chambers was Arthur Pollock's business. If Sir Peregrine was the owner, Arthur (in racing terms) was the trainer. A wide boy from the East End, he had started like so many others of his kind, without any legal training, as a gofer running errands. There was another such in the chambers even now, waiting to become another Arthur, with the legal profession at his fingertips and the responsibility of bringing in business – on which he would take a fat commission – all his own. If he were successful, and Arthur was, very, he would be making, like Arthur, hundreds of thousands of pounds a year by the time he was forty. It would be probably more than any barrister was earning. The trouble was, such wealth could breed laziness – and peculation. There had been one or two little signs recently that Arthur might be succumbing to one or other of these temptations. Nothing very tangible, of course. Just a late lunch here and an amused shrug there. You couldn't tell, really. The law could be a very bitchy business.

Arthur was in when she arrived. It was, after all, half past four in the afternoon. She could tell he had had lunch – a faint rosiness around the cheeks, a little too much concentration in the attentive pale blue eyes.

'Could I talk to you for a moment, Arthur?'

'Of course, Miss Semple.'

He led the way into his office. It was the best room in the place apart from Sir Perry's and contrasted peevingly with the shabby den she shared with the other juniors.

'A good day?' he asked. 'I hear there was a momentary hiccup.'

Say what you like about Arthur, she thought; his ear was close to the ground. At least she had some excuse. She comforted herself with the thought that at least she had some excuse for her lapse in court. It would have taken nerves of steel not to have been thrown by such nocturnal unpleasantness.

'We got a result,' she told him – as if he didn't know.

'Good, very good, the solicitors will like that. But I understand . . .'

'Yes. I had something on my mind, I'm afraid.'

'On your mind? Oh dear.'

Arthur never used strong language. It was one of the impressive things about him. 'Oh dear . . . a slight hiccup . . .' such expressions were his stock in trade. They did not disguise, however, the strength of the fellow underneath. What he really meant was: 'My barristers should never let personal problems get between them and the job in hand.'

'Something personal, was it?'

She knew what he was thinking. He had been opposed to letting a woman join the chambers. She had had his words repeated to her.

'It'll be all time of the month and break-ups with boyfriends, I'm afraid,' he had said at the chambers meeting. Strong words for Arthur.

'Personal in a way, yes,' she told him. 'But I think it has a connection with chambers.'

'Tell me about it.'

She proceeded to do so, holding back only a little of the rankness of the message. The description of her vagina seemed hardly to be central to the report, and it was certainly not something she wished to raise in Arthur's office, barrister's training or no barrister's training.

Arthur listened to her story with his best bedside manner, nodding sympathetically, tut-tutting at the sentiments, and taking on the strong language forensically as if it had no shaming or emotive connotations. There it was, part of the evidence, like semen on tights in a court of law – best handled with gloves, but no more or less significant than a thumbprint on a doorknob or a thimble in a brake reservoir.

'Drawers seems a funny word to use,' he said at last, getting up and starting to walk up and down. 'It's a word not much employed nowadays, I understand. Winter drawers on, of course. We like a laugh. But do people go shopping for drawers? In Selfridge's?'

'No,' she said. 'Drawers is definitely out.'

'Or would one say "are out"?' he pondered.

'Is,' she said, shortly. This was no time for grammatical speculation.

'I can understand your concern, of course, Miss Semple. It must have been most distressing. I think you should inform the police and see what they have to say. Perhaps you should have your calls monitored. Can we think of anyone who might have a grudge against you?'

'He didn't say he had a grudge. He just wanted to rape me and kill me.'

Arthur sighed. He fixed her with his pale blue eyes and moved slightly towards her so that she was caught between a table and a tall waste paper bin.

'You are an attractive young lady, Miss Semple. But there are many such in London. There are, however, few attractive lady barristers. I think we can assume he had a grudge.'

'I've won most of my recent cases,' she said. 'So it probably wouldn't be a disgruntled defendant.'

'Someone over whom you've scored in court, then?'

'Not to the extent of cutting my throat.'

She contrived to step over the waste paper basket, but only with an ungainly stride that made her skirt ride up. Arthur watched her discomfiture with asexual satisfaction. She imagined that he had read in an American manual about territorial domination. No doubt he thought you had to read such things if you were to compete with these university dickheads. And in the end, if you read enough and used your wits, you could run rings around them.

'There are some funny people about,' he said. 'Think now. Someone perhaps with an old-fashioned turn of phrase.

Drawers, now. That is surely indicative? What about that fellow you saw yesterday? He's a funny fellow.'

'You know him?'

One thing she was sure of. It hadn't been Morbey's voice. There was something absolutely identifiable in the brittle elastic of that larynx.

'Of old, Miss Semple. Oh yes. A remarkable man in his way. Totally depraved, of course. You're sure it wasn't him?'

'I'm quite sure.'

'You rather took to him, didn't you? It'll be a nice one if you can get him off. Nice for us, I mean. Not so good for others. I happen to know he was in the prison hospital last night.'

It was the kind of information Arthur specialized in.

'Is he ill?'

'They put him in the psychiatric ward. There's a telephone in there, you know.'

'Oh.'

She was positive it hadn't been him. Arthur was advancing again. This time she found herself being edged towards a point between the wall and the door, which meant she would be squeezed when the door opened.

'Why did they put him in psychiatric?' she asked.

'Oh, for observation, you know. They sometimes do with cases like that, in case they're a suicide risk.'

'And is he?'

She managed to sidestep as the secretary came in, but in doing so knocked against a letter-tray which upended a cup, spilling a stream of streaky brown liquid over a filing cabinet covered with papers.

'Oh dear,' Arthur said with satisfaction.

'Sorry about that,' she told him, trying to sound as though she wasn't.

'Accident prone today, Miss Semple? Understandable. Now, where were we? Suicide . . . or do you think we might go for insanity?'

'Insanity?'

'That of course is for you to find out. All I'm saying is, the caller could have been him. He had the means. And he's a bit of a joker. But if you tell me it wasn't him, there's an end of it.'

It was clear that the conversation with Arthur was concluding. He mopped the spilt fluid ostentatiously with his handkerchief, squeezing it into the waste paper bin so it made a hostile excretory sound.

'So what am I going to do about the call?' she asked.

Arthur sighed. She wondered now whether she should have told him about it. After all, she knew he didn't approve of her. It would be logged and used in evidence.

'Women in chambers?' She could hear him saying it to his cronies over lunch. 'All hormones, and lipstick on the teacups, and nasty men on the phone last night.'

'What do you think?' she repeated.

'Personally,' he told her, 'I would forget about it. We all get these cranks from time to time. That's in the line of duty. If you can't take a joke, you shouldn't sign on as Sir Peregrine loves to say.'

Perhaps Sir Peregrine had also had a military father.

'But it wasn't a joke,' she said.

'I hope and believe you're wrong. But there's always the police. And if it happens again, of course, you must let us know. Now, if you'll excuse me, the dead trees are calling.'

It was the way he referred to his paperwork.

'Thank you, Arthur,' she said.

One had to keep on the right side of the man.

'Don't mention it. Glad to help.'

'Anything else for me?'

She meant a job.

'Nothing at the moment,' he said with a hint of relish.

'Right. Good night.'

'Good night, Miss er Semple. And remember: you are not alone.'

'Alone?'

'Goodnight.'

No doubt he meant to indicate that the chambers were behind her, but she could have wished he'd put his token support more happily.

She closed the door, fetched her coat from the office she shared with three other juniors, including her bête noire George Braithwaite (a couple of years her senior, suavely perky, privilege and Floris oozing from every pore, away at Lewes County Court today, thank God), and took a taxi home.

It wasn't that George was unpleasant, she reflected as the taxi lurched and veered over the increasingly dilapidated London tarmac; he was just insufferable. He had a bad case of barrister's overkill. Every conversational point, however trivial, had to be won. Every gathering, however jejune, had to be dominated. Instead of keeping the ball in play, he swatted it. Sometimes it was just about tolerable, but Heather didn't feel like that today.

Ten

When she arrived home she went straight up to the bedroom and turned on the answering machine. She ran the tape back to the beginning, braced herself and pressed PLAY. There were a couple of calls from girlfriends, a man she knew asking her to a dinner party, and a call from the office telling her to call Arthur. These must be yesterday's messages. Arthur had mentioned what it was about when she spoke to him earlier – doubtless he would chide her eventually for not listening to her machine as soon as she got home. She hadn't done so yesterday. She just forgot; sometimes it happened that way. Sorry, Arthur.

She pressed PLAY again. The gentle hiss of virgin tape filled the room as she turned up the volume. What was wrong with it? The bloody thing wasn't working.

She let the tape play until it stopped. There was nothing more on it. She ran it back to the beginning and tried again. She was getting frightened now. What was happening? Who was doing this? Had the whole thing simply been a bad dream? She had had a spate of such things as a child – waking up only to find she was still dreaming.

She made herself stop and think.

She had slept fitfully after the call. She'd got up at four, poured herself a glass of water, and gone to bed again. She must have fallen asleep because it was eight-thirty when she woke up.

That was it. She had turned the alarm off in the night. She wouldn't have done that in a dream. Or would she?

The switched-off alarm had made her desperately late that morning. She had had little more than an hour to get dressed and be on parade in Harrow. She had had no time to play the tape again or try and tell Alan about it (if he hadn't already left home).

It was strange that she found the absence of the voice more frightening than the voice itself. It called into question a number of things. The nature of the evidence, for one thing. Her sense of reality, for another. But of course that was rubbish. She didn't have such dreams any more. The voice had been real enough.

The frightening thing was, then, someone must have erased it. Someone must have come into her flat and done it while she was in court, or talking to Arthur, or sitting in a taxi. Someone – the thought struck her icily down the back of the collar, suddenly, like snow off a porch – someone who might have come in and moved the answering machine to her room in the first place (for though she was notoriously absent-minded when working on a brief, she couldn't positively recall putting the thing in the bedroom) – *someone who might still be here.*

Oh my God.

She was a brave girl. You had to be to get where she was in the legal profession. You had to keep your nerve and stand up to every kind of bully from the successors of Judge Jeffreys downwards. You had to talk calmly to violent men and take abuse from their families. But on the whole you weren't called upon to face physical violence.

Physical violence evoked the most horrible sensations in her. She had a vivid memory, as a very little girl, of a man – it must have been her father – striking her mother. Heather, with the hindsight of grownupness, thought he must have been jealous, probably drunk. He and her mother separated soon afterwards, and shortly after that he had died. He had been in Intelligence, she told Heather, though heaven knew he didn't display much in his business affairs after he left the army.

However it was, the memory of that blow stayed with Heather. She could – and sometimes did – replay the scene at will. The man was very angry about something, and Mother was smiling and trying to explain. And then he just swung at her. The blow knocked her back into a sofa where she lay for a moment, her frock up round her thighs, which was shocking in itself because she was usually so elegant, and then she wiped away the blood that was trickling from the side of her mouth, and she smiled at him once more.

It was the most frightening expression Heather had ever seen, before or since. It said: that's it, finish, don't ever come near us, I never want to see you again. It certainly curled Father up. He implored. He pleaded. But dear, gentle, elegant, sweet, calm Mother was made of stone. So he went away and died. The strange thing was, Heather could remember loving him. She had never raised the subject with her mother, nor she with Heather. Perhaps she thought she was too young to remember; best put behind them. But Heather hadn't forgotten. That was why she was appalled by violence. It wasn't just the act. Throwing a punch was rather like throwing a switch. It was the chain of events which followed which was so frightening.

Or perhaps, she decided, as she wondered what to do next, perhaps I'm after all just an old-fashioned physical coward. I can't imagine the feeling of a knife going through my throat and I don't want to find out now.

She looked at the telephone again, and called the police. She spoke to a duty sergeant who seemed not very interested in her story.

'A threatening message, miss? No longer there? Well, I wouldn't worry if I was you.'

'I think there might be someone here.'

'I doubt he'd come there in person, miss. The telephone's their organ if you'll pardon the expression.'

She put the telephone down rather quickly, picked up a tennis racket – the nearest thing she could find to a weapon – and started to look round her flat.

First, she tried all the cupboards in the bedroom. Then the bathroom: nothing; the spare room: nothing again. She opened the cupboard on the landing and a broom fell out, making her almost choke with fright. Creeping softly downstairs to the kitchen, she put the racket gently on the kitchen table and took a knife from the drawer.

'Put that down or you're dead meat,' said a voice from behind her.

She felt her knees buckle. Was this the moment so often imagined, the terror before the end, unknowable, the secret of the dead tart in the canal, the boy in the cupboard?

She managed to swing round with the knife still held in front of her, and saw a large policeman of the rare avuncular kind, standing there laughing.

'How . . . how did you get in?' she gasped.

'Easy, miss. The door wasn't shut.'

'You nearly gave me a cardiac.'

She must have forgotten to close it in her hurry to get upstairs.

'Sorry. My apologies. My sense of humour again. You looked so comical standing there with your knife.'

She felt anything but comical, but her relief was so great she forgot to be indignant.

'You were quick. I thought you lot weren't interested,' she told him.

'Oh, we like to check things out.'

And check it out he did, but he found nothing either. She gave him a drink and a piece of cake, and lit a soothing aromatic oil that someone had given her for Christmas.

'You need a sense of humour in my game,' he told her. 'Otherwise you think the world's coming to an end. Which, of course, as we all know, it is. Ha ha ha.'

Somehow his large, reassuring presence made her decide after all not to tell Alan about the telephone call, or the wiped tape – not just yet anyway. He had a way of diminishing such incidents, making you feel guilty for having them.

Sometimes she thought that the screen, for him, was more real than reality. If only she could have presented the incident on video tape, it would have immediately elicited his involvement.

Eleven

Alan's parents were a strange couple. His mother was very large, his father very small. The father had been something in tea.

The mother treated her husband as if he were an oily rag but regarded Alan with beaming eyes; he could do no wrong; the sun shone out of his exhaust pipe.

They lived in Richmond, which had the disadvantage of being neither near nor far. His mother wanted to see him too often for Heather's liking. In fact, she had to admit, once a year would have been overdoing it as far as she was concerned.

It was a tiresome drive, even on a Sunday morning. Heather wished there were another brother or sister besides Alan to take the pressure off, but he was an only child like herself. It had been one of the things that had first brought them together (for, whatever they may say, only children are a race apart). The fact that they looked rather alike was another factor.

Indeed, this was about the only thing that could have reconciled Mrs Haddenham to any girlfriend of Alan's. She referred to them as 'my twins'.

'How are my twins today?' she enquired, chasing a peanut round her mouth with a squirt of gin and tonic.

'Oh, Mother, come on now. We're quite different,' Alan said, as he always did.

'Of course, darling. You're prettier.'

This was meant to be a joke, though Heather didn't think it was very funny.

'We all thought Alan was going to be a girl before he was born,' Mrs Haddenham continued.

Heather edged away a little. The woman always tended to stand to close to her.

'How are you, Theo?' she asked the little father who looked more shrivelled and woebegone every time she saw him.

'Theo's got a prostate,' announced Mrs Haddenham in a loud voice.

'Really, m'dear,' said the little man.

'We all have prostates, Mother,' said Alan.

'Ladies don't,' replied Mrs Haddenham.

Heather wished they'd get off the subject. The old boy was looking quite upset.

'Anyway your prostate is A1, Alan, take it from me. It's Theo's that's a bit dicky.'

'Nibble, m'dear,' said the little man, offering a bowl of mixed nuts.

He was rather fond of Heather.

'The prostate is rather like a large nut,' explained Mrs Haddenham, just as Heather was swallowing.

She choked violently and had to be helped to a chair.

'That's better, kitten. Really, Theo, where did you get those things? A simple roasted peanut is all one wants. Get the poor girl another drink.'

Over lunch, they talked about Mrs Haddenham's view of the law. It was a subject she had many opinions on, most of them ill-informed. Her main complaint seemed to be that no one had approached her about becoming a Justice of the Peace. She would be a good JP, she thought. Could Heather help in any way?

'I'm afraid it's quite a different branch of the business, Mrs Haddenham,' she replied. 'Perhaps Alan could help. He's interviewing the Lord Chief Justice soon.'

'Someone very near to the Lord Chief Justice,' corrected Alan.

'I thought . . .' she began.

'Things change,' said Alan. 'It's the Parmenides principle. Everything's in a state of flux.'

'He's way above my head,' said Mrs Haddenham proudly.

'We have a rule, Heather and I, never to ring each other up at work. And do you know why that is?'

'Time's money,' said the old man. 'When I was in tea . . .'

'When you were in tea, I was in cocoa,' said his wife. 'Tell us, Alan.'

'We never ring each other up at work because everything's moving so fast. We'd make an arrangement and ten minutes later it'd be out of date. Waste of time.'

'That's the media for you,' said his mother. 'Always working to deadlines. I'd go mad.'

She was mad, Heather decided. Absolutely bloody raving. She could tell Theo thought so too. Only Alan seemed oblivious.

'I did an interview with Sir Martyn Pike on Friday,' he observed.

His mother made succulent noises at the mention of the City luminary.

'And what are you up to at the moment?' Theo asked Heather.

'Oh,' she said. 'I'm defending a male rapist.'

'You mean,' asked Mrs Haddenham, barging in, 'you mean that some rapists are female these days? Really, this woman's liberation has gone too far.'

'No, Mother,' said Alan, patiently. 'She means that this fellow is supposed to have raped a man.'

'Oh!'

Mrs Haddenham held her napkin delicately up to her lips as she nursed down a forkful of contrefilet.

'Really, Alan. Not over lunch,' she exclaimed at last. 'Just think what they must do.'

'I don't see how they get it in,' observed Theo, who suffered from piles as well as prostate.

'Theo!' shouted his wife. 'I'm so sorry,' she said to Heather. 'Sometimes he thinks he's still back in Mincing Lane.'

'It's all right, Mrs Haddenham.'

'How many times have I told you to call me Daphne?'

'Sorry,' said Heather. 'Next time I will, I promise.'

She just couldn't, somehow.

'And didn't he kill him as well?' asked Alan.

'Horror upon horror,' said Mrs H. 'And you're defending this monster?'

'That's what he stands accused of,' said Heather. 'But as a potential JP, I'm sure you'll understand that in this country a person's presumed innocent until he's proved guilty.'

That took the wind momentarily out of Mrs Haddenham's sails. Alan shot Heather a dirty look and little Theo gave her a grateful one.

'What sort of person is he?' asked Theo, collecting plates and putting them through the hatch to the kitchen.

'Rather interesting, actually,' said Heather. 'He seems to me far more intelligent than some of the people we see in parliament.'

'Perhaps I might interview him then,' said Alan, bringing the conversation back to himself which he liked to do. 'Parliament's one of the things I'm looking at,' he added to his mother.

Theo brought in trifle and crème brûlée.

'You'd never stop if you were to interview all the people who should be in parliament,' said Heather.

'Nonetheless, perhaps I will talk to your man. Get an angle on the law from him, too.'

'Well,' said Heather dutifully. 'I'm not sure it'd be a good idea for him to give interviews.'

Even if it were, somehow she didn't like the idea of Alan poking around in her case.

'It won't come out till after he's tried,' said Alan. 'And anyway, I wouldn't use his face or give attributions.'

'Go on,' said Mrs Haddenham, roguishly sticking her nose in. 'Let Alan have a go. He might find something that would help your case – something you'd overlooked. Brûlée? Brûlée, everyone?'

She had been nettled at Heather's reproof and now she was getting her own back. Heather rose to the bait.

'Alan is not a trained barrister, Mrs Haddenham . . .'

'Daphne . . .'

'Daphne . . .' there, she'd said it. 'He doesn't know exactly what to listen for, what tiny inconsistencies might be thrown up.'

'You mean,' said Alan, pouncing, 'those inconsistencies that might suggest to you he was guilty?'

'That's not what I meant at all.'

'And what would you do then? Hm? Give up the case? Like hell you would. You'd fight the case regardless because that's your business.'

Heather knew it was true. It was an aspect of her profession with which she was sometimes uneasy. But it was unfair of Alan to bring it up over his mother's brûlée.

She smiled pleasantly.

'Alan's critical of the law. I think we all are. There's much that's wrong and there are endless commissions that try to put it right. But one has to say that the law's a pillar of rectitude compared with the polluting smokestacks of the media.'

'Whenever I hear the word pollution I hear the sound of grinding axes,' said Alan. 'But you're changing the subject. Would you or would you not have the courage to resign an important job if you found halfway through your client was guilty – not obviously guilty – only you would know – there'd be every chance he'd get off . . . What d'you say? No weaseling now.'

Alan was in his ace interviewer's mode for the benefit of his mother who joined in the game with a will.

'Would you or would you not? Come on now. Speak up.' Her eyes twinkled with a bullying malice normally reserved for poor Theo.

'Would you or would you not?'

She looked like a judge with her awful curlicues of grey hair and her wobbling malevolent jowls. Heather pushed her seat back. She had had one spoonful too many of crème brûlée, which tasted of Mrs Haddenham's disgusting fridge.

'I think I'll have to go. Not feeling too good. Must've been the shrimps at a party yesterday. No, no. You stay, Alan. I'll get a cab. The fresh air will do me good.'

She left amid a murmur of mock solicitude. She knew that Mrs H. would rather have Alan to herself.

'I'll talk to you later,' she said to him.

'I'll drive you back,' he told her.

'No. Really.'

She walked towards the river. Sunday air smelt different from other days'. It was March, a spring day with that tremulous sunshine that makes the leafless trees fizz with expectation. Whatever was happening to the country, the world, or indeed herself, there was something comforting in the relentless reappearance of the daffodil.

The river was turbid and brown, swollen with the recent rain. Seagulls floated on it in an almost perfect circle like a wreath.

> *'At Richmond I lifted my knees*
> *Supine on the floor of a narrow canoe . . .'*

The nymphs had departed but the salmon were back. Not everything was getting worse, she thought.

She passed a man with a red face dressed in an old brown coat gazing out at the water and looking as though he might throw himself in. She wondered whether she would have the courage to jump in and try and save him. She had just decided she would – she was a strong swimmer – when the man addressed her as she passed, without turning his head.

'Care for a fuck?' he said.

'Not today, thank you,' she said as she walked on.

'Stuck up fucking bitch. I hope you die in pain.'

Twelve

When she got back to the flat she brushed her teeth to get rid of the taste of crème brûlée and lay down for a while on her sofa.

Outside the sunshine played on the daffodils in the window box. A brimstone butterfly, early hatcher, rare in London, suddenly fluttered past, its brilliant yellow upstaging the flowers. She took it as some kind of omen.

As she lay, listening to the Sunday sounds, and the breeze, and the rumble of a bee she would let out presently, she could almost feel the earth trembling, quivering like a mare at the force of the spring. Later she watched an old black and white film with Joan Fontaine and Cary Grant, and dozed and watched and dozed again, exactly as she had done when she was young. It was enough to be alone; a happy afternoon.

Alan was contrite that evening when he called round.

He was always at his worst when his mother was about. Heather knew that, which was why she didn't like going there.

'I know she's a difficult old bag,' he said. 'But I feel I have to go and see them. Blood is thicker than water.'

'But it isn't as thick as that crème brûlée she gave me,' she said. 'It must have been in the fridge two weeks.'

'She wasn't always like that, you know.'

Heather didn't believe it. You could read the truth in the old man's eyes, but she wasn't going to argue.

'What are we going to do tonight?' she asked.

It was a rule of theirs always to spend Sunday evenings together. Other days – not, on the whole, Saturday – but certainly weekdays, they might go out two or three times with cronies. They had agreed they shouldn't live in each other's pockets.

'I know what I'd like to do,' he said.

He cooked her scrambled eggs with smoked salmon and they split a bottle of Hunter Valley Chardonnay. After that, they made love in front of her fire.

He was a good lover, with the most wonderfully sensitive hands. He made her body feel as though it would provide enough electricity to supply a small town.

'You could put me on the National Grid,' she told him. 'Or whatever passes for it these days.'

Her last boyfriend had been quite different, with a much more macho approach; but there was no contest as far as sensuality was concerned.

She sometimes wished he was as good at love as he was good at love-making; but you can't have everything, she reflected, and after making love with him she felt as though she had been given some marvellous high-making drug.

'You're always so cheerful after sex,' Alan pretended to grumble.

'You should put your stuff on the market,' she told him. 'It's jolly jelly. I'm sure it would fetch hundreds of pounds a sample. It's euphoric. Just as well they don't know about it, though, or all the girls would be throwing themselves at you.'

'Who says they don't anyway?' said Alan, filling their glasses and singing 'Deflowers that bloom in the spring tra-la . . .'

He had a pleasant light baritone and had once, long ago, considered training as a singer until his mother put him off it. One of the better things she'd done as far as Heather was concerned, or else she would never have met him. He had been doing a documentary on the Old Bailey, and Heather, as a junior, had been tangentially involved in a case there. They had fallen into conversation, liked the look of each other (because they looked like each other), one thing had led to the next, and here he was trailing the line of moisture that had trickled down her thigh.

'Juicy,' he said.

Heather gave a great start, spilling the refilled glass.

'What on earth . . .' he started, and then looked hard at her. 'Are you all right? What's wrong with you today?'

It was like being hit by an asteroid and spinning wildly out of orbit. One moment the sun was shining, dinosaurs gently munching the gingko leaves and the next . . . tidal waves and winter.

'That word,' she managed to say at last.

'Word?'

She couldn't bring herself to utter it. It was even harder to say than Daphne. By no means her favourite word at the best of times, it was now anathema.

She hadn't told him about the telephone call and the strange wipe-out on the answering machine. Perhaps after all, she thought, it was as the policeman said. A little too much work, a little too much wine, it could happen to anybody . . .

She didn't want to hear Alan say she'd dreamt the whole thing up. He could be rather scathing when he chose, impatient with what he saw as weakness. Astrology and ghosts were two of his favourite victims. Vague fears irritated him.

She told him now, however. Instantly his face grew serious.

'How dreadful, darling. But why didn't you say before?'

'I thought you'd say I was being stupid.'

'My God. What on earth do you think I am? Of course I'm worried. There are a lot of maniacs about. This man could really mean it.'

Though grateful for his solicitude, it wasn't quite what she wanted to hear. She wanted him to say that he was obviously a crank.

'But why wasn't it on the tape when I played it back next day?' she asked him.

'Well, I mean, that's obvious isn't it, darling? In your panic that night you obviously pressed the wrong button and erased it. Quite easy to do. Done it myself.'

'Do you get threatening telephone calls?' she asked.

She thought she glimpsed, just for a moment, hesitation in his eyes.

'All the time, darling,' he said lightly. 'Mainly from blue-rinsed matrons in Eastbourne who want to take my trousers down.'

Neither of them laughed. She got up, went to the bathroom and washed. When she came down, he was dressed again and was obviously intending to leave.

'Won't you stay?' she asked. 'It'd be nice to have some company.'

He shook his head, and finished the glass of wine he was holding.

'Can't do. I have to talk to a general first thing. Mustn't be late on parade.'

'You're doing the forces too?'

'Of course. They're institutions, aren't they?'

'Yes. Yes, of course.'

'They're just about the only things holding this country together. The army in particular. If I were them I'd be considering a military coup.'

Heather was amused. She knew too well, in her father's case, the fallibility of the military.

'You have to be joking,' she said.

'I suppose I am. But twenty years ago you wouldn't have even joked about it, the idea would have been too far-fetched. But now, yes, one could just about imagine a military junta now.'

'People wouldn't stand for it. The whole country would be up in arms,' she told him.

'That's just what a military junta likes. No, the more I think about it, the more possible it becomes. After all, we did have one once. And that was again when politics had failed.'

'I wonder what your general will think about it,' she said.

'He'll probably think you're inviting him to be Cromwell.'

Alan considered.

'I rather fancy myself as a kingmaker,' he agreed. 'Or perhaps as a king unmaker.'

He poured himself another inch of wine and chased it around his mouth as if to freshen the taste of too many words.

'I forgot to ask. How was Sir Martyn, your ex-Lord Mayor?' she said.

He looked serious and started pacing about the room, speaking to her as though she were a camera.

'I talked to him,' he said. 'He gave me the diplomatic answers. Then I did some prodding. The rot in the City started years ago. He thought it was the American influence after the war, but it probably started years before that . . .'

'Maybe with the telephone,' Heather suggested, 'distancing the manufacturer from the money-maker.'

Alan shivered involuntarily as if he had been struck by a bread pellet. Interruption sometimes affected him like this, but it had to be done.

'Anyway, by the fifties, my word is my bond was becoming worthless,' he continued. 'If the lawyers hadn't got it all written down, tied up, sealed and stuck in a vault, my word was no more than my wind. The City had always been full of greed, he said. But it had always given something back. The skill and wisdom of the guilds. Integrity, sound advice. Even enterprise. But these things were being slowly eaten away. By the eighties and nineties, there were unmistakable symptoms of decay like the Lloyd's fiasco. That didn't do the City any good. Even the traditional supporters of the place resented all those insiders making money while the outsiders had to cough up. And then of course there was Barings . . .'

'Surely the last Labour government did something?' Heather asked. 'I seem to recall various measures.'

'More or less cosmetic,' he replied. 'Labour have always been scared of the City. Even up till the millennium, there were still people creating millions with a stroke of a pen or a dab at a keyboard, claiming six-figure bonuses whatever the outcome of their dabbing. An affront to reason, that's what the old man called it. Too many merchant banks with no experience of marketing or of anything but money, making decisions on which manufacturers stood or fell regardless of what they made, or *could* make, or represented to their communities. Too much arrogance, aloofness, self-awarded privilege, short-termism . . .'

'What about invisible earnings?' she asked.

Alan quivered again.

'Doesn't that sum it up, though? Doesn't it make you shiver? Invisible earnings! Where do they come from? Where do they go?'

> *'Never seek to tell thy earnings,*
> *Earnings that never told should be,*
> *For the silent wind doth move*
> *Silently, invisibly . . .'*

misquoted Heather.

This interruption was more successful. Alan laughed.

'Exactly . . . hold on to that one . . . I might use it . . . Anyway, by the eighties, things were going badly wrong. There was an extraordinary explosion of corruption, greed and a sort of desperate hedonism. Everything had a price, nothing had a value . . .'

'Like the last days of Berlin.'

'Very like. The enemy was already at the door. It was our good old friend, technological change. They introduced something called the Big Bang. It was in fact the computerization of the Stock Exchange. It was supposed to be just what the Stock Exchange needed, but it was the stockbrokers who had to bite the bullet . . . It meant fewer jobs . . . and after that it was only a matter of time before it was the money brokers' turn. And they of course have the spectre of Euromoney in front of them, with fewer and fewer currencies to trade. The result is that the City today is a sort of shell. There are only five or six big financial houses left and they're either American,

German or Japanese. The British had nothing left to sell so they sold themselves . . . and another Great British Institution goes into meltdown!'

'Are you going to say all this? Be careful,' she said. 'You're going to make some enemies.'

He smiled his charming toothy smile, and walked towards the door.

'You can't make an omelette without breaking eggs. Goodnight, then, darling. Sure you'll be all right?'

'Sure,' she said.

'If there are any more calls, tell me right away. And the police. Promise?'

'I promise. Goodnight.'

'Goodnight.'

They kissed briefly and he turned to go; then stopped.

'You know,' he said. 'I'd really like to talk to your chap.'

Say what you like about him, he didn't give up, she thought.

'It's not allowed,' she said firmly. 'The lawyers won't have it.'

'I'll get round it somehow.'

'And anyway I don't think it'd be a good thing.'

'It would be a very good thing – for you. If we follow this case, you could end up a star.'

Everyone seemed keen to put her name in lights. Why wasn't she more enthusiastic about it herself? She was too tired to argue. He probably wouldn't get permission anyhow.

'We'll see about it,' she said.

It was her old nanny's way of saying no, but as she held the door for him, Alan took it as an opening.

'It's a possible, then,' he said. 'See you.'

'When?'

'Oh. Tuesday, I should think.'

She didn't tell him she was meant to be going out with a girlfriend on Tuesday, a barrister in a neighbouring chambers whom she saw occasionally and who had chided her recently for seeming self-contained to the point of stand-offishness. Let it wait. Alan would doubtless cancel anyway. He was always erratic when work was in the offing.

He kissed her.

''Night, darling.'

She watched him as he drove off without looking, nearly clipping an approaching Peugeot.

Impossible man, she thought, half irritated, half in affection. And then she thought: was she so self-contained? It was true, being an only child, she didn't feel the need for many friends. But those she had could feel justified in accusing her of neglect in the last few weeks. Why should this be? Perhaps her relationship with Alan, odd though it was in its intimate detachment was now enough for her; or her job was becoming more involving; or was it that she was beginning to feel she was the only person experiencing a slowly accelerating strangeness . . . that it was up to her and her alone to make sense of it all? Of course it wasn't. That way lay paranoia. She was tired, that was it.

Before she went to bed, she double-locked the door, bolted all the windows and unplugged the telephone. In the night, she had a horrible dream in which she was desperately looking for something in a huge overgrown shrubbery and stumbled on Mrs Haddenham, dead, with twigs and leaves growing out of her eyes and mouth.

As Heather looked at her in fear and disgust, the leaves and twigs started to move, and to her utmost horror, Mrs Haddenham began to speak.

'The name is Daphne, dear. It's Greek for laurel, you know. Say it. It's quite simple. Daph-ne. SAY IT.'

The creature, malevolent and implacable was starting to rise now, lifting arms topped with twiggy fingers. The only escape was to say the word, but try as she might, Heather couldn't. She seemed to have lockjaw. She tried with all her might and finally, painfully, mumblingly, noises started to come. Der . . . uh . . . Derr . . . Ah . . . Aff . . . One more try and she would do it. She could feel the twigs now around her neck . . . Quick. Now. Go on, Heather.

'Der Der Deraph . . . ne . . . Deraphne . . . Draph . . . Daphne . . .'

She woke up, still with the words on her mouth. Heart thumping, too terrified to move, she lay there in the darkness. There was something or someone in her room, she knew it.

She must have lain like that for ten minutes before she decided she would rather die than lie there any longer. Apart from anything else, she could feel her gold chain hurting her neck. She'd forgotten to take it off when she went to bed. She lifted herself up and turned on the light. Her familiar bedroom greeted her. Nothing out of place. She checked the alarm clock. It was half-past two. The first thing she did was plug the telephone in again. At least she could call the police now. She'd take it off the hook before she went to sleep again.

Next she locked the bedroom door. She wasn't going to go downstairs, thank you very much. She checked the cupboards again . . . the bathroom. There was no one there. It was just a silly dream, that was all.

Then the telephone rang.

Thirteen

'Miss Semple?'

It was a woman's voice, fractured by a bad line. Heather almost fainted with relief and for a while she could not answer.

'Hullo?' said the voice again. 'Is this Miss Semple?'

There was a note of authority, of spruce efficiency which the bad line could not disguise. There was also something about the voice that rang a distant bell, though at the time she couldn't place it. Heather cleared her throat.

'Yes,' she said at last. 'It's Heather Semple here.'

'Ah, Miss Semple. I don't want to worry you, but it's your mother.'

Heather gasped; she had no doubt it was the news she'd been half expecting. And yet now it was here she couldn't believe it. Mother couldn't be dead. She couldn't imagine the world without her.

Her legs started trembling again and she sat down on the bed. Of course she had known that the old girl would die soon, she told herself. It had been perfectly obvious for weeks; but it didn't make any difference to the shock. I can cope with surprise, she thought. It's the inevitable that breaks one up.

'Miss Semple?' asked the voice again.

'Yes,' Heather said. 'I'm here. Is she . . . ?'

She couldn't bring herself to say the word.

'Oh no,' said the voice, 'not dead. But not very well, I'm afraid. I'm the night sister. Sister Knight . . . with a K, silly isn't it? I always have to explain.'

'My mother . . .' said Heather. 'What happened?'

The relief was almost as shocking as news of her death would have been. 'She's had a slight heart attack. She's stable now, but I thought I should call you. I believe you left instructions, if there was any change.'

'Is she in danger?'

'Not immediately. She's sleeping now, but if you wanted to see her, she'll be awake by, let's see, ten o'clock.'

'I'll come at ten,' said Heather.

That was why she thought she knew the voice. It was someone she'd met at the hospital.

'Make it eleven,' said Sister Knight. 'We'll have her all spruced up by then.'

'Don't spruce her up,' said Heather. 'Just as she is.'

'Only a manner of speaking,' said Sister Knight with a K.

Heather thanked her for her trouble and put the telephone down. She looked at the clock. It was already five. She thought quickly about the day that she had planned; a visit to chambers, ostensibly to pick up some papers but really to see if there was any more work for her; then a journey to Clapham to meet up with one of Soapy's junior partners (if he turned up) and look at the scene of the murder. It could all wait. She would make a call later to the solicitor's office to postpone the meeting.

She decided to get up, drive to Oxford and spend a little time there. It always seemed to do her good. Funny how the place seemed to have that effect on one. Not on everyone, of course. Some people couldn't get away quickly enough. As she drove her Alfa out of the garage and pointed its nose towards Heathrow and the west, she reflected that she had never understood such people. For her and her mother, and all those others who couldn't get Oxford out of whatever part of the brain it is that mixes memory and desire, there was some addictive redolence about the town.

She had sometimes felt in church that all the prayers and good thoughts and sweet sounds had acted like a kind of smoke, embalming the roof. So it was with the University: a multiplication over centuries, of youth, study, wisdom and inclination towards truth, had kippered the place.

As she skirted the Headington roundabout and passed under the mysterious Maxwell footbridge halfway down Headington Hill, she felt the old emotions again, heightened perhaps now by her mother's illness, and her eyes pricked with half-forgotten memories and inexpressible regrets. She wondered if Soapy and Sir Patrick – both Brasenose men – had the same feelings about the place. Probably not, she decided. Success had a way of coarsening people. That was why successful people only tended to mix with successful people – a tendency she had noted in Alan. And in herself? She wondered about that, and thought she probably wasn't successful enough yet. If she won this case, perhaps she might graduate to success and become one of the people who regarded Oxford as something they had left behind like galoshes, relics of their muddy youth.

She crossed Magdalen Bridge, passed Magdalen Tower, remembering vanished May mornings, skirted round Longwall Street and Parks Road and drove up the Broad, parking outside Trinity – her College – where Brian, one of the porters, let her in to park near the chapel. It was impossible to park anywhere else in Oxford these days.

She breakfasted in the covered market, read the *Daily Mail* over coffee and, because it was still only nine o'clock, decided to take the car up to Boar's Hill where her mother had spent so much of her childhood.

Heather felt she knew the place as if she had lived there herself. Crossing the perplexity of ringroads around the city, she took the turning for Hinksey and drove up the hill.

'In the two Hinkseys nothing keeps the same.' Had things changed since Mother's time? The houses perched beside the road still looked comfortably professional-class with their gardens and their fringe of firs. And Bagley Wood, where the Scholar Gypsy had roamed with the charcoal burners, was still brambly and deciduous, with the trees beginning to go blurry with the onset of spring.

She took the first turn after the wood, and drove down the lane, stopping for a few moments opposite the house where her mother's parents had lived. There had been at least two moves in the course of her father's Fellowship: this one had been called Bramcote. It was set back from the lane behind a high beech hedge, its lawn punctuated by silver birch trees. The house itself, with a partly clapboarded front and dormer windows, had a comfortable, slightly hunched appearance. The forest came nuzzling up almost to its back door. Her mother had told her that in the war they had cooked squirrel.

Less gruesomely, Mother had often talked about how she played in the wood and the adventures she invented to amuse her younger sister. What was the song she used to sing at bedtime?

'My mother said that I never should
Play with the Gypsies in the wood . . .'

Heather had always thought, when Mother brought her here when she was little, that this was the very wood referred to by the song; and doubtless the Scholar was one of the Gypsies.

There had been – probably still were – hornets in the wood, and once they had made a nest in that high gabled roof. A Polish major had come and sprayed paraffin on them through a hole in the woodwork to stop them flying, returning later to scoop out the nest with a sickle.

'It was the bravest thing I've ever seen,' her mother had told her.

Heather was suddenly aware of some kind of commotion. A car was tooting its horn behind her. She held up her hand in apology to the very old woman at the wheel, started her car and moved on, turning round in the cul de sac where Gussie Hewitt, her mother's friend, had lived, and where Miss Fish, the mysterious neighbour, had kept the House with no Flowers.

This was Memory Lane all right; plenty of returning room.

She drove on; up the hill past the little dip where Robert Graves used to keep the post office; past the Masefields' house and the other house Mother had lived in when she was a girl;

past the barn where Cecil Sharp rescued the Morris dance; past the Trust Ground with the best of all views of Oxford's spires; past Lord Berkeley's 'castle' on the left where he had retired with a mistress – it was now owned by the Open University; and on to Jarn Mound and Matthew Arnold's field. Here she parked and walked through the rocky garden to the concrete steps which slipped unevenly down the clayey side of the man-made hillock; pausing to read the inscription on the rock. 'Arthur John Evans, 1851–1941, who loved antiquity, nature, freedom and youth, created this viewpoint and wild garden for all to enjoy.'

Climbing the steps, even now, seemed an adventure. There was a notice which said DANGER. As a small child, it had made her feel nervous and she had clung on to her mother's hand, almost pulling her over so that they both tripped.

'Careful, Feather,' her mother had said.

Feather was her pet name for her because she had been so light as a baby.

'Careful, Feather, you'll have us over.'

'I'll float down,' she had said.

'All very well for you. Mummy would come down plump.'

Heather was so deep in thought that she tripped again on the Difficult Step which was almost twice as high as the others. And then she was at the top. It was always a moment of drama.

How many counties? Heather thought it was five. Oxfordshire, Berkshire, Buckinghamshire, Gloucestershire. And Northamptonshire? Or was it Warwickshire?

She was just studying the brass plate engraved with topographical information on the central plinth, when she became aware of someone else coming up the steps.

It had happened before on her return visits, and she had always been irritated. Here was where she wanted to be alone, on top of the world, mediating between air and earth. She always climbed down again as soon as anyone came up. It was usually children with an exhausted mother, or worse, an instructive father; or it could be lovers.

This time, however, it was a man. She knew she wouldn't like the look of him before she even took him in. There was something about the approach, stealthy yet truculent; and now she saw him properly, she realized she was right.

He was about forty, red in the face, probably a boozer. But he was a big fellow. He wore a sneery kind of expression on top of a blue anorak.

He came right up to the top step and stayed there, rocking slightly, and looking at her the way men look at women from football coaches.

Oh fuck, she thought. It would be today. No mothers, no lovers, just me. DANGER, said the steps, and here it was.

She continued to stare at the topographical brass until she had taken in every angle, every minute of its message. She turned and looked at the distant Cotswolds, surveyed the Chilterns, turned back to the brass for pretended elucidation, and still the man stayed there. Although he had said nothing, he was incontrovertibly menacing.

She looked over the edge of the flat concrete top. All around were brambles and impenetrable thickets covering an almost forty-degree slope. Escape was impossible that way. She had to think of something else.

'Excuse me,' she said. 'Do you have the time? My watch has stopped.'

'I've got the time,' the man replied thickly. 'I've got the time to lick your juicy cunt.'

That stupid word again. Was it he who had been ringing her? Somehow the voice didn't fit, even though you had to admit he looked the part. Suddenly she was terribly angry. How dare this lout come up here, desecrating the holy places, disturbing the quiet garden? It was not to be endured.

'Do you see what I see?' she said, pointing west.

'I see, you see, joosee,' he said, disgustingly, but he turned all the same, and she gave him a tremendous push so that he fell clean off the concrete with a 'Way-ay!' straight into a clump of brambles in which he became embedded, every movement bringing on a swarm of thorns. Even so he was up too soon. He was quick for his size.

'Fucking cunt! I'll fucking kill you,' he shouted.

But he didn't know the steps as well as she did. She leapt down like a stag – twisting her ankle on the way, adrenalin lending her painkillers as well as wings – and ran for the car. Thank God she had just brought the key with her, insecurely leaving her bag inside the Alfa.

Then, with huge relief, she saw that the instructive father hadn't failed her. There he was, typical of his kind, coming towards her from the lane, shepherding a small boy through the gate.

'Quick,' she panted, grabbing at her saviour. 'There's a man after me. Help me.'

'What? Where?'

He was a bespectacled, bearded, thin-looking specimen, clearly better at teaching his youngster the position of the Great Bear than at sorting out this kind of hurly-burly.

She pointed wildly behind her.

'There.'

'I see no one,' said the man, disentangling himself from her grasp.

She looked round. There was no sign of the red-faced fellow. No movement disturbed the stillness of the undergrowth. All around, the garden lay at peace as Sir Arthur would have liked it, quietly fizzing with early spring.

'He was there, I tell you,' she said desperately.

His disappearance was even more alarming than his loutish presence.

The bespectacled father edged away.

'Come along, Tarquin,' he told his boy. 'The six counties are waiting.'

Six? There were only five, surely.

'Only five,' she said to the man.

'What?'

He looked at her coldly.

'Five counties,' she told him.

'I think you'll find there are six.'

He started to walk away.

'Won't you help me look for him?'

The man stopped wearily.

'Come on, Dad,' said his son. 'I want to see the trigonometric point.'

'Can't you see you're disturbing him?' the man told her. 'Please keep your fantasies to yourself. You need help.'

'Yes,' she said. 'And I'm not getting it from you.'

She turned and walked to her car. What was the use? There had been a man there. She had pushed him. He had run after her. He had hidden when he saw the instructive father. She hadn't invented it. Had she?

She started the car and drove off, glancing in her rear mirror. Just as she turned the corner, she saw a flicker of blue – could it have been anorak? – emerging from the shelter of the man who loved nature's laurels. This was beyond a joke. She would have to talk to someone when she got back. But who? Alan wouldn't believe her and Arthur would put it down to 'women's problems'. Who?

When she reached the hospital it was quarter past eleven and her mother was dead.

'She can't be dead,' she said when the ward sister broke the news. 'Sister Knight told me there was no immediate danger.'

'The night sister had nothing to do with it.'

'What?'

'Your mother was taken very ill last night. We rang the new number you gave us and left a message as soon as it happened.'

'I gave no new number. I got no message.'

'I'm so sorry – but those were the instructions we received.'

The sister was genuinely apologetic. But nothing she was saying seemed to make much sense to Heather. What was all this talk of messages and new numbers? It was like a game of Chinese whispers. Her mother was dead; that was surely what mattered. She couldn't make sense of the rest.

'I was told she had a slight heart attack last night,' Heather said, her eyes beginning to prick.

'Who told you that?'

'Sister Knight. Knight with a K. She made a point of telling me.'

'We have no Sister Knight. The night sister last night was Sister Meredew.'

Heather felt a tear start to slide down beside her nose. Another tear followed, and suddenly she broke down. Someone fetched a chair, and she sat there sobbing inconsolably. She cried for her mother and for the past – the gentle, kind, orderly, scholarly past her mother had known – full of English Hymnals and sherry before Sunday lunch and the *Dictionary of National Biography* and home-made jam and sloe gin and rock-cakes and brains trusts and beekeeping – all gone now, or going – as surely as Mother was going to slide off into the furnace and those terrible doors shut on her for ever. She cried for herself, too. The loss of the one come-what-may friend was a fearful blow. The world, at a stroke, was colder, more critical, less constant than she had ever known it. She had needed Mother today – not that she would have told her about the man at Jarn Mound, or the telephone calls, it would have worried her – but her implicit support would have given strength. Her mother would have known that she wasn't imagining things. Two is sanity, Heather thought as she sobbed; one alone can look like paranoia. It was Mother who had said perhaps she shouldn't go in for the law. It was Mother who was usually right.

At last she stopped crying, blew her nose and stood up.

'Sorry,' she said. 'I'm a barrister actually. Barristers don't cry except for effect.'

'That's their problem,' said the sister, kindly.

'I'd like to see her, please.'

'Certainly,' said the sister. 'Come with me.'

Heather followed her, still limping slightly, down the familiar corridor.

'Here we are,' said the sister. 'She looks very peaceful.'

She opened the door and followed her into the little room. A nurse was tidying a cupboard near the wall.

'I've put her clothes and things in a suitcase, Miss Semple,' she said. 'I'm so sorry about your mother. She was such a nice old lady. It was like a window on another world when she talked.'

Heather could feel her eyes pricking again.

'Thank you, nurse,' said the sister. 'That'll be all for now.'

'Thank you,' said Heather.

The girl gave her a shy smile as she left.

Heather went up to the bed and kissed the familiar face. It was already shockingly cold.

'Goodbye, Feather,' it said. 'I loved you with all my warm heart.'

'I'm sorry too,' said the sister, 'not that that does any good. We were all very fond of her here. She talked about you a lot.'

'What will I do now?' said Heather, bursting into tears again.

The sister cradled her head on her starchy bosom.

'Soldier on, that's what she would say. You wouldn't believe some of the heartaches I've seen here. She was lucky in a way. A long life . . . daughter she was proud of . . . good memories . . .'

'I know, I know. I should be grateful,' said Heather, drying her tears again.

'Life's a bugger and that's a fact,' said the sister. 'We don't feel grateful for a slap in the face, but at least it keeps us awake.'

'Or not, as the case may be,' said Heather, looking at her mother.

'Or not,' agreed the sister. '"Fear no more the heat o' the sun" as the Bard says. No more slaps for her. Perhaps we should be grateful for that.'

Heather appreciated her robust approach and began to feel a little better.

'Who d'you think rang me up last night?' she asked. 'And who gave you a new number?'

'It's a mystery,' said the sister. 'But I'll certainly try to find out. As for the number, I'll look it up for you later myself.'

'Don't spend too much time on it,' Heather told her. 'I have a feeling we won't catch whoever it is.'

'I hate hoax calls,' said the sister. 'It's the lowest of the low, like stealing. But of course these days they probably teach it in the schools.'

Fourteen

Although they had arranged not to meet until Tuesday (if then), when she got back around six o'clock there was a message from Alan on the answering machine inviting himself round early for a drink. But as it happened – as it often happened – not that she usually cared, for she was not the fussing nor the jealous type – he was late. She hadn't been able to get him on his mobile phone. Besides 'we never call each other at work'.

'Trust you, Alan,' she thought at eight o'clock, pouring herself another glass of wine. 'Fuck you, Alan.'

She didn't normally drink on her own but today there were mitigating circumstances. Tonight she would take a sleeping tablet and if all the weirdos in the world rang up, she wouldn't hear them. She felt exhausted, hollowed out, unstringed.

The clock moved on. Half past eight, and then nine. She was beginning to feel rather drunk, which was good.

'I suppose I'd better eat something,' she said.

She had a habit of talking to herself after a drink or two. Alan said it was one of the signs of madness. She was just cutting herself a slice of bread when she heard the front door open.

'Alan?'

There was no reply.

She had thought she could feel no more emotion today, but fear had a wonderful way of asserting itself.

'Alan? Who's there?'

She put the knife down and walked towards the kitchen door, returned, picked up the knife and went out into the hall. There was no one to be seen.

'Alan?'

It was stupid of her to keep shouting his name. She wasn't going to go upstairs to the bedroom, though, not this time. She would go and knock at a neighbour's flat thank you very much, and ask them to call the police. Quietly opening the front door, she ran out into the hall.

The naval commander who was a spy and lived opposite was rarely in, and was not in now, so she hurried downstairs to Flat 3 where a recent arrival, a commercial attaché from South America, had taken up residence. She could tell he was there by the insistent thud of some Latin American rhythm.

'Where are you off to, darling?'

She looked up. Alan stood there. Outside her door, staring down at her.

'You?' she said, stupidly.

'Me. Seen a ghost?'

'Why didn't you answer me?'

'I was going to surprise you.'

'*Si*?' said the Latin American attaché, suddenly appearing.

He was a very tall youngish man, around thirty-five she guessed, with long bony hands, sallow-complexioned, with an air of the Aztec about him. There was probably some Indian blood there. He cracked his knuckles, not nervously but disconcertingly. As if in deference to his host country, he wore a blazer with brass buttons, cream trousers and a Garrick Club tie. He smiled continually.

'I don't want any bloody surprises,' she said.

'You no want prices? What you no want prices for?'

Heather retreated upstairs, apologizing.

'So sorry,' she said. 'Mistake. So sorry.'

'I give you prices you ask for. What you want – kitchenware? Cocaine?'

'No prices,' she shouted at him. 'Nothing.'

'Crazy woman,' he muttered, returning to his sweet-smoky diplomatic flat.

'What are you so wound up about?' said Alan. 'I said I was going to be late.'

He hadn't but it didn't matter.

'Mother's dead,' she said.

'Oh God. I'm sorry.'

He looked it too. He ushered her back into the flat, sat her down in the living-room and put a glass of wine into her hands.

'I'd better not,' she told him. 'I've had three quarters of a bottle already.'

'It'll do you good,' he said. 'When did it happen?'

'She had a heart attack this morning.'

'I'm so sorry,' he said again.

'The odd thing was, I had a call in the night. Someone who said she was the night sister. She told me Mother had had a slight attack but was in no immediate danger. I said I'd come at eleven. But when I got to the hospital they said she'd had a coronary in the night and died after breakfast. They said they did ring up and left a message at a new number – I didn't give them a new number. They had no record of the name of the person who spoke to me. What's happening, Alan? Do you know what's going on? It's not your series, is it? Maybe someone doesn't like it.'

'I don't know,' he said. 'But I'll damn well find out. I was going to do the National Health soon anyway. In fact, I've fixed to see someone at the ministry tomorrow. There's no mafia like the medical mafia. They'll know how to get some answers from the hospital.'

'I couldn't even see her before she died.'

'Would you have reached her in time if they *had* got hold of you?'

Heather looked at him. She thought it was rather an odd question.

'As a matter of fact, no. Why do you ask?'

'So you don't dwell on it too much, darling. Don't you see? If you couldn't have been there anyway, it makes someone's stupid mistake less hurtful.'

She knew he said it from the best of motives but somehow his reasonableness was not what she wanted to hear.

'Anyway,' he continued, 'I'll get my ministry contact to kick some ass, if that would help.'

She had a feeling that the ministry would know nothing about night nurses and old women dying in Oxford. That was not what ministries were for. Ministries were about their own index-linked pensions and White Papers. But she said nothing. Let Alan find out what was wrong with the ministry.

'The funeral's on Saturday,' she said. 'Want to come?'

Alan was pained.

'Of course I want to come. I'm your . . . friend, aren't I?'

'Yes,' she said. 'You're my friend.'

Our earthly friends may fail us, was what the hymn said.

'Have you chosen the hymns?' he asked.

With interviewer's instinct, he was sometimes uncannily good at reading her mind.

'I haven't decided on the service yet,' she said. 'I've got to do that tomorrow. I think she'd like the Old Service. She wanted to be cremated . . .'

The vision of those crematorium doors closing assailed her again. She was too tired to cry. He suggested he make her some supper, but she shook her head.

'Do you mind?' she said. 'I'm awfully tired. I think I'd like to be alone tonight. Do you mind?'

She was pretty sure he did mind. In fact, she thought, he'd come over wanting food and sex, but even he couldn't coax her into either this evening. With his reservoir of self-confidence, he tended to draw the line lower than other people, but even for him there was a limit.

He smiled at her, line drawn.

'Of course I don't mind. But are you sure you'll be all right?'

'I'll be fine.'

'You know,' he said, candidly. 'I really believe these things have been happening to you.'

'What things?'

She hadn't told him about the man at Jarn Mound.

'These telephone calls and things.'

'Why d'you say that?'

'Well . . . just to reassure you. Just in case you thought it was all going on inside your head. I'll tell the telephone people to monitor your line.'

'Thank you, Alan.'

She meant it. Kindness was all she wanted at this moment.

'I mean . . . I know you're probably feeling as low as you *can* feel. I just wanted you to know that I'm behind you.'

'You're very sweet,' she said. 'Goodnight, darling.'

It was funny how her mother's death had made her see things more clearly. She needed Alan, but did she want him? That was a decision she could leave to another day. She sat for a while, thinking of nothing, feeling the wine whizz round inside her.

There was a ring at the door.

It was the Latin American diplomat; bony, gangling, sporting a preposterous club tie.

'Hey,' he said. 'Boyfriend go? You wanna rumba?'

Fifteen

The next morning she spent on the phone, talking to the undertakers in Oxford and sorting out her ideas about the service. One of the advantages of being an only child was that you had no one else to consult. It was also, of course, a drawback.

The crematorium did not take kindly to the idea of using the Old Service. She asked to speak to a priest and was put through to the Reverend Mr Blisworth.

'We find the modern version very popular,' he said smoothly.

'It's not for popular consumption,' she told him. 'It's for my mother.'

'But she's dead. How can she mind?'

She nearly exploded.

'Don't you believe in the after life?'

'Well,' he told her, 'nowadays we feel that that was simply a term used in the context of a simpler age. A metaphor, a parable if you like.'

'I don't like,' she told him. 'I believe in the after life. At least, when my mother dies I do.'

'Really? Ah well. These things die hard. Have you thought about the hymns?'

'I want "Lead Kindly Light" and "Immortal Love Forever Full" to the tunes in the *English Hymnal*.'

'Dear me. I'm afraid we don't use that any more. May I suggest "Lord of the Dance" or "The bells of heaven are jingle-jangling"?'

'My mother didn't know them.'

The Reverend Mr Blisworth seemed to be about to remind her again that her mother was dead but veered off at the last moment. There was a sort of macabre humour in the exchange, adding to her sense of suppressed hysteria. Why didn't he just shut up and do what he was told?

He must have sensed her outrage at last because he appeared, rather grudgingly, to modify his approach.

'We'll see what we can do,' he said. 'It's always more difficult when people want to go private.'

When she had finished with him, the articled clerk from Soapy's firm rang up. Did she want to go down to Clapham with him next day? Why not? she thought. It would perhaps take her mind off the funeral on Saturday.

Alan stayed away that evening, though he telephoned to see how she was. Telephoning cost virtually nothing these days because so many other services came down the cable. It was hard to get used to the cheapness of it and somehow it seemed to devalue conversation. Sometimes she thought, especially living with a media man, that there should be a tax on words. Sometimes she thought she could feel the cable throbbing like a vein.

'I'm fine,' she said. 'I'm going to Clapham tomorrow to look round the scene of the crime.'

'Oh?'

She thought there was a quickening of interest in his voice.

'I shall take my magnifying glass and curly pipe, of course,' she said. 'To say nothing of the deerstalker.'

It wasn't a very good joke but she should put on a show of cheer. He ignored it altogether.

'I should really like to interview that defendant of yours,' he said.

'I told you. There's no way you'd be able to,' she said. 'After the trial, perhaps. I don't want anything to prejudice the case. It means a lot to me, you know.'

Of course he knew. Her success meant more to him than it did to her.

'Take your point,' he said, 'take your point.'

'Why do you want him anyway?' she asked. 'He's nothing to do with an institution in decline.'

'He's innocent, isn't he?'

'Well. He says he's innocent,' she told him.

'Hasn't a survey like mine got to take the innocent into account? And the guilty, for that matter?'

'Maybe it has,' she said. 'But not my innocent.'

'You just don't want to help,' he said.

'It's not that. It's . . .'

'I know. You don't want to mix your personal life with your public one.'

'It's sort of that.'

'I understand. Of course I understand. Shall I see you tomorrow?'

She hesitated. For some reason, she didn't want sex with him until her mother was buried, and sex would be the inevitable or only with difficulty evitable consequence if he did come round. Better if he stayed away, really; then he wouldn't be offended.

'Collect me Saturday morning,' she told him. 'I'm not very good company at the moment. Nice and early. The service is at half past eleven.'

'What if you get lonely?'

'I'll have a girlfriend round. Honestly . . . I'm all right.'

She heard a faint noise behind him, almost like papers falling, a sort of slapping, flapping sound.

'What was that?' she asked.

'That?' he asked.

'That noise. Did you knock something over?'

'Oh . . . yes . . . Just the telephone directory flopping over.'

'Well,' she said, 'I'm going to flop over pretty soon. I've never been so tired. There was something else, though. Did you see your contact at the ministry?'

'I did but . . .'

'You didn't mention the hospital.'

'Not the right moment. Timing's everything with these things. I haven't forgotten, though. They're coming back to me.'

'I shouldn't bother now. She's dead. I wouldn't have got there in time.'

'I'm glad you see it like that.' Alan was in his mature, judicious vein. 'No point really in stirring it up.'

She knew he wasn't going to jeopardize his interviews. Sometimes she knew him too well.

'I meant to ask about your talk with the general,' she said. 'The army was Mother's life for a while, you know. How's the army these days?'

'Don't you worry about the army. Like I said, it's about the only thing holding this country together. That's why the politicians want to cut its balls off. The army's soldiering on. Meanwhile I'm into the National Health, and doctor says go to bed and sleep.'

Down below the Latin American diplomat had switched to tango. Der-der-DER der-der-DER der-der-DER der. Perhaps he had found a partner with a little black moustache to der-der with.

Her ormolu clock – early nineteenth century with two little dancing figures on the front – ticked away, prancing down the evening.

The present is simply a machine for turning the future into the past, she thought. Her mother used to have an old Ford Prefect and you could see right down the handbrake hole to the tarmac below. How the road sped along! You couldn't take it in, looking at it like that. It was a whizz. That was what the present was like.

The telephone rang again. A voice spoke, filling her with an extraordinary mixture of disturbance and elation.

'I was sorry to hear about your mum. It really filled me with grief, that did.'

It was Morbey, the prisoner.

She took a deep breath, finding to her surprise that her heart was beating faster. She automatically reproached herself. The heart might have its reasons, but there could be no reason strong enough for her to become involved with a client. And if that were not sufficient, her life was quite involved enough, thank you.

'Are you there?' he said.

'Yes. Yes, I'm here. I just . . . wasn't expecting you, that's all. It's very kind of you to think of me, Mr Morbey.'

'It's nothing at all,' he said. 'The least I can do. My mum died three years back and I thought the world had stopped.'

'Are you sure you can talk to me?' she asked.

'Of course I can. I don't know why they think we need a phone in psychiatric when the sane ones can't have one, but there you are. That's the Home Office for you. It just gives nutters the chance to ring up and make nuisances of themselves. But I'm not complaining.'

'You're not a nutter, are you, Mr Morbey?'

'For God's sake call me Chris. No, I'm not a nutter. But they always give murderers the once-over in case they can plead insanity. They've been giving me Rorschach blots.'

'You're not a murderer either.'

'That's for you to prove.'

'With some help from you.'

'But I didn't call up to talk about me. I wanted to know if you're all right.'

'How on earth did you hear about my mother?'

'Oh, we hear everything inside. You hear more of what's going on in the world than if you're walking round the West End. Funny thing, parents. I always say they're like the front line. They take the knocks. They shoulder the sky. And all the time you're somewhere behind, doing mock-attacks, exercises; going through the motions, if you like, but it's not genuine; it's a rehearsal. Then suddenly the message comes through. The battalion's gone, blown up, Mother's dead. Advance. That's when the shooting starts. That's when it starts to be real.'

Heather was silent for a moment. This was a strange mixture of a man: sensitive, reflective, as well as (she must not forget) dangerous.

'What d'you think?' he asked. 'I hope I haven't depressed you. It's bad enough to lose your mother without being told you're going up the trenches.'

'I hadn't thought of it like that,' she said, 'and it doesn't depress me. I suppose you could think of it like shark's teeth.'

'How come?'

'They keep growing from the back. They get to the front, tear and snap a bit, and then they fall out. Then it's the next row's turn.'

He laughed.

'It's certainly a more positive way of looking at it,' he said.

She thought of something.

'Have you called me before?' she asked.

'Called you? From here? Never. Mind you, I've thought about it.'

'I was told you were in psychiatric ten days or so ago.'

'To be honest, I didn't want to pester you. Some of these nutters, they're snivelling on the phone to their shrinks and their lawyers non-stop. All they want's a wet nurse. No, I reckoned I'd see you again soon enough, renew our dialogue so to speak. As a matter of fact, I'm getting bail, I heard today.'

'Bail? But that's most unusual for a . . .'

'Murderer? Say it.'

'For someone accused of murder.'

'Old Soapy got it for me. D'you mean to say he didn't tell you?'

'He . . . might have left a message. I've been having trouble with my answering machine.'

It was a lame reply. Arthur should have damned well told her.

'Right. Well. You want to talk to Soapy. I know you've a lot on your plate, but when I'm out . . .'

'When's that?'

'A day or two. I have to wait for a recognizance of surety. Then we have to meet. Oh sure, we'll meet at Soapy's but I'd like to see you alone. Iron out a few things.'

'We can't do that,' she said. 'It's not allowed.'

'Not allowed? But I'm the client, aren't I?'

'It doesn't matter. It's simply not done.'

'Ah. Not done, mm? I didn't think you were like that.'

'It's not a matter of what I'm like. I'd be up before the Bar Council. I'd be . . .'

Actually, it wasn't an absolute rule – just inadvisable – but she felt she needed the excuse. It gave her time to think.

'When are we going to see each other, then?'

'It's not that I wouldn't like to,' she told him, softening, 'I find you . . .'

'Yes?'

'Interesting,' she concluded, 'as a case.'

'Oh, I'm interesting all right,' he said. 'What about attractive? Do you think I'm attractive?'

'I'm not allowed to find my clients attractive. It doesn't enter into the deal. And even if it did, I certainly wouldn't tell you.'

'Ah, so you *do* find me attractive.'

She had to laugh in spite of herself.

'I don't know how you work that out,' she said. 'The next time we meet it'll either be at my chambers or at Soapy's – and he'll be present as well. Do you find that idea attractive?'

'I'd like to buy you lunch,' he said. 'I have to go now. There's a nutter here with a knife who wants the telephone.'

She couldn't tell if he was joking or not.

'Can't be done,' she told him. 'Sorry. But . . . where would you go if we could?'

She enjoyed a good restaurant and she was interested in his choice even though there could be no question of joining him.

'Langan's Brasserie,' he said. 'It's an oldie but it still has something. I could murder for that spinach and anchovy soufflé. 'Bye.'

It was an unfortunate turn of phrase under the circumstances, she reflected, but undoubtedly, like everything else, he'd thought about it. There could be no question of knowing him in a social context at all.

When she put the telephone down, she found that she was crying again, suddenly touched that he should have rung her in the midst of his troubles, to say nothing of a nutter with a knife; suddenly and desperately missing her mother.

Sixteen

Soapy's articled clerk was very much a Soapy in the making. This time he actually managed to put in an appearance, arriving to pick her up in a 1949 convertible Buick of which he was very proud. Food also seemed to be on his mind. Much of the way he talked about where they might eat, though he did preface his remarks by offering his condolences.

'Thank you, Joscelyn,' she said – that was his name. 'She had been ill for some time, actually.'

It always made people feel better when you said that, though God knew it made the victim feel worse. She hoped he wouldn't say 'a merciful release' but he did. What would have been merciful for her mother would have been no illness in the first place.

'Did you bring the papers?' she asked him.

'I only take the *Telegraph*,' he said.

'No, stupid. The notes. I need the brief. I haven't had it yet.'

'Oh,' he said, vaguely. 'I think Soapy's making some changes.'

It was a fine day, and Joscelyn had the hood down.

She ought to have the brief. No doubt it would come in time, but it wasn't good enough.

'I thought we might try Herbert's for lunch,' he said. 'You know Herbert's.'

She did know Herbert's. It was extremely expensive. Set in the heart of Wandsworth, it was a mecca for foodies from far and near.

'The thing is,' she said. 'I'm not feeling terribly hungry. Even for Herbert's. Sorry.'

She said it reprovingly as though he should know that people whose mothers have just died don't want to take every opportunity of filling their faces with a gourmet menu.

'Ah,' he said. 'Quite.'

She could tell he wasn't pleased, but stuff him. He was quiet for a while and then began a litany of wine bars he rated.

Finally they drew up in a sort of tributary road that dribbled into a High Street. There were one or two shops, a launderette, a run-down video store, an off-licence and a wine bar.

'Our Souls Wine Bar, that's original I must say,' said Joscelyn. 'Original and prophetic when you think what happened to the victim.'

'Not in your food guide, I suppose?' asked Heather drily, not wanting to think about the wretched youth's fate.

Whoever had done it was still walking around, because whoever it was certainly wasn't Chris Morbey. Or was it? Her professional duty to believe in his innocence apart, what did her mind say, what did her instincts think?

'I suppose we'd better go in,' Joscelyn said.

Although it was past midday there were no customers, just a sullen-looking girl smoking a cigarette and reading the *Sunday Sport* behind the bar: PRINCESS DI IS AN EXTRATERRESTRIAL SAYS SEX-CHANGE VICAR.

'Yeah?'

'We're from Protheroe, Osbourne and Gedge,' said Joscelyn. 'The owner . . . Miss, er, Strange . . . is expecting us. We've come to look at the locus.'

'Who is it, Val?' came a deep voice from backstage.

'Lady and gentleman from Proctor, Austin and Gish. Come to look at the locust.'

'I'll be right out. Offer them something, dear.'

'Tell her not to come out. We're not allowed to talk to her,' said Joscelyn.

'They're not allowed to talk to you.'

'Why not?'

'Tell her she's a prosecution witness.'

'You're a prosecution witness.'

'Bollocks!'

'You want something to drink?' the girl asked.

Joscelyn took a brief look at the shelves and shuddered.

'You could have a Sprite if you like. There's a special offer.'

'Sprite I don't like,' said Joscelyn.

'Please yourself,' said the barmaid.

Or was she a man, thought Heather? This was after all a transvestite bar. Appearances were bound to be deceptive. Reality was tenuous in such places. Maybe the evidence would be too. What evidence? Where was the brief? For no reason to do with the case, more curiosity really, she asked what the house wine was.

'You want a glass?'

She was definitely a girl, Heather decided, if not a maid.

'No. Just the name of it.'

'It's Vin Coquille.'

'I don't know that one,' Heather said. 'May I buy a bottle?'

'You must be out of your mind,' said Joscelyn. 'It's probably Congolese claret.'

The barmaid gazed at him from under sultry lids. Joscelyn was a good-looking lad.

'It's very popular, actually,' she pouted. 'Red or white?'

'Red, please. I've got a chum who writes a wine column,' Heather explained to Joscelyn. 'I sometimes bring her discoveries.'

'That's a nice way of describing Vin Coquille. I don't think your chum will thank you for it.'

Heather paid for the wine and looked at the label: *Vin Coquille Rouge 11% 75cl Produce of France Imported and bottled by Eurovin Ltd for Our Souls Winebars London England.*

There was something about wine going on at the back of her mind. Something she had seen before. However, she had learnt long ago that the harder you try to remember such things, the more elusive they are, like soap in a bath. Better to wait and let them come to you.

'Here we are then.'

It was the owner of the deep voice, a big cheery-looking woman who didn't look quite so cheery on closer inspection. The sex here was much more questionable. Little eyes too close together glittered instead of twinkling. Still, today she was pushing the boat out.

'Val, champagne.'

'No, really, er, Miss Strange . . .' Heather started.

'It's all right. It's Veuve Cliquot, and call me Mandy.'

'Tell her we're not allowed to talk to her,' Heather said to Val. 'Tell her not to waste her money.'

'I usually have some around now, anyway.'

'The widow, eh?' said Joscelyn. 'That's a bit of a quantum leap from Vin Coquille.'

A tray appeared, and the champagne gambolled into the glasses.

'It takes all sorts,' said Mandy. 'Some of the people who come here are grateful for Vin Coquille, a very decent drop of plonk from the Pays d'Oc. Good quaffing wine.'

'If you say so,' said Joscelyn. 'I'll settle for the widow.'

Mandy took a long sip before she put the bottle down.

'Who says you're not allowed to talk to me?' she asked.

'She may be a prosecution witness,' Heather told Val. 'I can't address her.'

'Who says so? Who says I'm a prosecution witness?'

'You should've brought the bloody papers,' Heather gritted to Joscelyn.

'I didn't know. I thought your clerk would've shown you the draft . . .'

Heather didn't feel like explaining all the background at this point.

'Ask her if she's a prosecution witness,' she said to Val.

'Of course I'm not. They got one of our regulars, Charlene,

who saw the whole thing. And besides, I was off that night. Wasn't I, Val?'

'If you say so,' said Val.

'She thinks I'm off all the time, don't you, Val?'

'Right off.'

There was a strange kind of bad-tempered camaraderie between the two of them.

'My God,' said Heather, 'then I suppose Val is the witness.'

'No, they got the other manager, didn't they? The one who was standing in, my alter ego as you might say.'

'Who was that?' asked Joscelyn.

'Walter. That's the one. My Walter Ego as I call him. He was here.'

Heather felt a great sense of relief. Now at least she could ask some questions.

'You must have heard all about it,' she said to Mandy. 'What exactly happened?'

Mandy took another mouthful.

'Let's see now ... Thursday night it was ... the twenty-third ...'

'Pissing with rain,' said Val.

'... Pissing with rain, so we didn't have as many in early on. Thursday nights are very popular. We have a show and quite a party. You'd be surprised where they come from – miles and miles. Isn't that so, Val?'

'They come from Watford,' said Val. 'Pissing with rain.'

'Is that right?' said Joscelyn.

Heather had started to wonder about Joscelyn. Next thing he'd be lisping.

'Are they all transvestites, your customers?' she asked.

Mandy drew deeply on her cigarette, held the smoke, looked at her outstretched nails, exhaled gently across the back of her hand so that her fingers looked like pillars of rock in a sea of mist, rubbed her chin thoughtfully making a sandy sort of sound.

'A lot of 'em are. Transvestites and cross-dressers, not that they're the same thing. Some of 'em are as hetero as you are, I should think. Others are into their own kind. Not that we allow anyone getting up to anything on the premises. They can do what they like outside. Some have a gender crisis, some are raging queens, some just like to dress up. We get ladies here too, you know. Oh, it's all go at Our Souls.'

'Are you the owner?' asked Joscelyn.

'The manager, dear. One of the managers.'

She seemed slightly guarded on the subject, so Heather pressed her.

'Who is the owner?'

'It's a consortium, dear. Businessmen. Nothing significant. All above board.'

'You're sure of that?' asked Heather.

'You're very forensic today,' Joscelyn said to her.

'That's right, dear. She's a barrister not the fucking police, if you'll pardon my French.'

'I'm only asking,' said Heather. 'If you don't ask, you don't get. Tell me more about the night in question? What did your colleague say?'

'There was a crowd that night. Someone's birthday, Nicky someone, don't ask me to remember names, Stevie, that's the deceased, he was here. We always notice him because it's unusual for him not to come in, but he was a bit pissed that night so Walter told him to go home. And then he started talking to this feller, evil-looking bastard he was, slicked-back hair and a face like an 'awk.'

'Why did Walter notice him? He must've been busy with all those people? Why him in particular?'

'He was worried about Stevie, like. He's one of the regulars. Walter wanted to see him go home all right. Lovely dress he had on, he said. Almost like a designer number it was. Next thing he knew, they'd gone. This evil bastard must have gone home with him and topped him.'

'Well, that remains to be seen. Did, er, Val see him too?'

'Nah, I didn't see nothing,' said Val.

There was something about the way she said it that Heather found almost too glib. She looked searchingly at the girl and Val looked away.

'Keep polishing them glasses, Val,' Mandy told her. 'They were looking like they been used for a smear test last night.'

Heather decided she'd heard enough for the moment. She could always come back when she'd extracted the brief from those limpets at Soapy's.

'Well, thank you very much,' she said. 'Maybe it's time we made a move.'

She held out her hand and Mandy took it in a robust grasp.

'Not at all, dear. Come again sometime. Thursdays, Fridays and Saturdays are good. Very lively we are then. Au reservoir.'

Seventeen

Cloud had gathered from the west and hung almost motionless overhead, the colour of pavement.

They walked up the road away from the High Street through a little network of two-up two-down cottages connected by narrow lanes. Beyond these they came to a row of huge, dreary-looking red-brick tenements, some already boarded up. Heather felt the ground shake for an instant: perhaps there was subsidence round here, but it could have been a passing tube train. It didn't seem to register with Joscelyn.

'I understand the block is scheduled for redevelopment,' he said. He led the way towards one of the entrances, Number 40, and produced a key. The door swung open, and they entered a narrow hall which smelt of cabbage, urine and dry-rot. A bicycle without its front wheel stood against the wall.

'No buttock's sat on that seat for many a moon,' said Joscelyn cheerfully. 'Man's, woman's or transexual's.'

They climbed cracked stairs illuminated by a grey light filtered through dust and cobwebs. On the second floor he produced another key and, fumbling in the semi-darkness that seeped across the landing, he finally turned it in the lock of Flat 5.

To enter a place where a murder has been committed is always something of a psychic ordeal, at least to the sensitive – and Heather was sensitive. Her mother's death had made her doubly so. She stood for a moment in the doorway, unwilling to go in. The smell in here was worse, a chilly, clammy smell redolent of nameless practices and long-cold bachelor cooking. The place was in almost total gloom apart from one or two pale rods of light admitted through the knot-holes. No doubt to shut out prurient sightseers, or others who might wish to pry, the police had boarded up the windows.

Joscelyn groped for the light switch, found it and clicked. Nothing happened.

'Fuck,' he said. 'They've turned the bloody electricity off. I think they said there were some candles somewhere.'

He'd brought a torch along, but it was only a small, pocket-size thing. The scene revealed by its beam did nothing to lift the spirits. They were in a living-room about fourteen foot square. There was a table by the window with two meagre chairs drawn up to it. A spindly sofa faced a boarded-up fireplace. An armchair of the same make confronted a black and white television set. A plastic bowl of obnoxious design sat like a toad on a coffee table.

Joscelyn found the candles inside it, and lit two, handing her one and pocketing his torch which showed signs of going on the blink.

'I'd kill myself if I lived here,' he said.

Heather shuddered. She had seen some pretty depressing places in the course of her career, but nothing beat this for sheer hopelessness. It wasn't so much that the room breathed poverty or squalor. It was just utterly miserable.

The furniture was derelict, the carpet was of an indecipherable colour under a moonscape of stains, even the mantelpiece above the boarded-in fireplace was encrusted with ash; biscuit crumbs, old packets of cigarettes, half a pair of bicycling tights and what looked like spilt Horlicks but could have been anything really, added to the general squalor. The candlelight threw eerie shadows. Even Joscelyn seemed to be jumpy.

'I suppose we'd better look at the bedroom,' she said.

The bedroom was where the body had been discovered.

'You go first,' she urged Joscelyn.

He opened the door and she followed him inside. Here too

the windows had been boarded up. The candles revealed a small room dominated by a double bed large by even courtesans' standards. It almost filled the place. There was just space on either side of it to sidle round and reach the substantial built-in cupboard at its foot.

'Generous hanging-space,' said Joscelyn, sliding open the doors.

'That's not funny,' said Heather, although it was. She started laughing, tried to stop, then laughed till she cried.

'I say, are you all right?' asked Joscelyn.

'I'm fine,' she told him, drying her tears, and sitting on the bed to blow her nose.

Joscelyn sat beside her.

'I lost my mother when I was seven in a car accident,' he said.

She was glad he'd told her that. Strange how sensitive young men can be sometimes, she thought. It was just exactly the right thing to say. It made her glad for all the years she'd known her mother, and it took her mind off herself.

'How dreadful,' she said. 'I'm so sorry. Just the worst age for that to happen.'

'I suppose it'd be worse if I'd been four,' he replied. 'That's what my father used to say.'

'I'm so sorry,' she said.

'I was cut up about it at the time. She was a rather nice person as it happened. Oh well. *C'est la vie*, and a bloody awful vie it is too, sometimes. Look at this poor little bastard. All the trouble of being born, of someone making sure he didn't get whooping cough or measles or diphtheria or smallpox, making sure he didn't swallow a pin or run across the road or take sweets from strangers, teaching him to walk and talk and do his poos in a pot and his two times table, and how does he end up? Hanging in a clothes cupboard in a pair of dirty tights.'

'Joscelyn, I'm surprised,' she told him.

'Just because we're solicitors, it doesn't mean to say we don't pause and reflect sometimes. Sometimes we even have visions.'

'Ah,' she said. 'Now that can be dangerous.'

She turned reluctantly to the cupboard again.

'Let's confine ourselves to the facts. What was the poor lad hanging from?'

He showed her a stout hook screwed into the solid wall at the back of the cupboard, more than six feet from the ground.

'Odd to have a hook there at all,' she said.

'I am told there is a certain satisfaction some people derive from near-asphyxia,' he said. 'It apparently shoots out of you like a howitzer. Sometimes elderly colonels are found in this way, dressed in black tights, having forgotten to unhook themselves in time.'

'Thank you, Joscelyn.'

'I only mention it because you asked,' he said. 'Is there anything else you want to see?'

'We might as well look at the rest of the place. There's just one thing, though.'

'What's that?'

'They said the front door was locked from the inside. How did the murderer get out?'

'There was a window open, a large drainpipe and then a balcony. Easy for anyone reasonably fit. We'll have a look again when we're outside . . .'

'All right. Let's finish in here first.'

The kitchen was tiny, more like a ship's galley, and provided nothing in the way of inspiration for the defence. The bathroom seemed equally unhelpful, apart from offering a basic resource.

'Do you mind if I have a pee?' she said. 'Won't be a minute.'

It was while she was sitting there, thinking of the dead boy and how he was the last person to sit like this – one touch of nature makes the whole world kin, and so forth – that she noticed something on the ground, far back, touched by the candlelight, between the base of the pedestal and the wall, such as might have fallen out of someone's pocket as he sat with his trousers down.

She leant down and picked it up. It was a small piece of silver metal, square, almost the size of a postage stamp, with no name, no information on it, no clue as to what it might be or what it could be used for. Perhaps it was something to do with the police, she thought, part of their forensic equipment. And yet, if it were, they would surely have come back for it? Or perhaps it was not significant in any way. She sat there, thinking about it. It had a vaguely electronic look about it as if it might be a small part of a radio or television, or it might simply be a fragment of an electrician's current counter or a plumber's mate. She almost left it where it was, but something prompted her to pocket it, as one pockets a pebble on a beach.

'Are you all right in there?' Joscelyn shouted.

'Fine, thanks. Just reading a back number of *Gender Bender*.'

There was something about the awfulness of the place which encouraged jokes like that. She was sorry about it as soon as she said it.

'Don't get hooked on it.'

'Now, now, Joscelyn, that was a jest too far.'

Not that he meant harm, but one has to observe the dignity of death – especially, she thought with a sinking of the heart, especially when it's your mother's funeral on Saturday and you don't know how you're going to manage without her.

'Feeling better?' asked Joscelyn when she emerged.

'Much better thanks,' she said.

'Nothing in there, I suppose? Evidence? Clues? The meaning of life?'

'Nothing,' she said.

After all, the thing was probably no more than that, an irrelevance at best, part of the wretched boy's dismal life, or of the equipment of those who had come to rootle around the scene of his last humiliation. It was a no thing.

Better, certainly, to check it out before exposing it to the wits at chambers. She could hear Arthur reviewing it already. 'And I found this teensy little thingy in the lav . . .'

'Nothing shall come of nothing,' said Joscelyn.

'Not so in quantum physics,' she told him. 'In quantum

physics, nothing can fluctuate. It is thought the universe may have come out of such a fluctuation. We are made of nothing.'

'I don't know about you, but I'm beginning to feel that way,' said Joscelyn. 'What do you say to going for a beer and a sandwich at a little place I know in Chelsea?'

Eighteen

It was a small party that gathered in the sunshine outside the crematorium chapel.

Sir Perry had asked her if she would like him to come but she knew it was only politeness. He hadn't known her mother, who would probably have found him insufferable. She never cared for people who were too fond of themselves. Indeed she had never much cared – though she never said it – for Alan.

Heather was just congratulating herself on having only the small group who had been friends of her mother: Daisy Singleton from her schooldays; the village's retired admiral; her elderly solicitor; a fellow ornithologist; a representative from BBONT (Berks, Bucks and Oxfordshire Naturalists' Trust); a retired Fellow of her father's college who reminded her that the body of C. S. Lewis's tragic wife had also passed this way . . . when she saw Alan's parents coming in.

'You didn't tell me they were coming,' she hissed at Alan.

He shrugged hopelessly as though he were dealing with a force of nature.

'You know Mother,' he said.

'Hullo, Mrs Haddenham.'

She looked at the woman with dismay, remembering her dream. There had been something prophetic about it. Death had got the women mixed up, that was all, and taken the wrong one.

'Call me Daphne, dear. We had to come. After all, we're virtually family.'

Little Mr Haddenham approached and shook her hand.

'So sorry, m'dear. So very sorry.'

'D'you know if there's a loo in the vestry?' his wife asked in a loud voice. 'He's very weepy these days.'

'Really, m'dear.'

She punished him for his protest.

'Still, he has what I call his intercontinentals on . . .'

Alan had moved away and was talking to the retired Fellow – he had an instinct for the most distinguished member of any gathering.

Heather felt she should mingle with her mother's friends and walked over to Daisy Singleton, an elderly upright woman dressed in a dark tweed suit. She looked poor as a crematorium mouse, but you could see she managed. She had that air about her. Her mother had always said Daisy was a good sort, no nonsense about Daisy.

'I remember you, Heather, when you were a baby. Such a sweet little girl.'

'Not so sweet now,' Heather smiled.

'Oh. I wouldn't say that. There's a fellow over there looking at you as if you were *very* sweet.'

Heather turned, almost stumbling with surprise. It was her client, Christopher Morbey. How on earth had he got here? He held up his hand in a gesture as if to say: don't speak to me now, talk later. She turned back to Daisy.

'Not that one wants to introduce such a note on an occasion like this,' said the old woman. 'But life must go on. Your dear mother was the first to take funerals with a pinch of salt. I remember when her own father died, she . . .'

Heather put her responses onto automatic pilot while her mother's friend reminisced; not that she wished to be rude to the old thing. She had often thought how galling it must be to be old and for people to listen as unattentively to you as you listened imperfectly to them. The young and the old don't share quite the same world, that was the problem. For the old, the past is the thing and memories are more real than what passes for reality.

For Heather, though, the present was a matter for urgent consideration. What on earth was Morbey doing there? She was impressed and pleased that he had managed to come. At the same time, she didn't want him to speak to Alan. For some reason, every time Alan raised the possibility of such a meeting, she became more and more resistant to the idea. Besides, it would give the wrong kind of complexion to the funeral; they were there to cremate a parent not to make a television programme; or indeed to pass the time of day with her client. The man from BBONT approached.

'A fine day,' he said. 'I see the celandines are out already. There'll be primroses in Bagley Wood. If you have to go, I do think spring's the time to go in. In Nature, life and death are inseparable, aren't they? Shakespeare full of that sort of thing. The red blood reigns in the winter's pale, and so forth.'

Her eyes filled with tears.

'I'm sorry,' he said. 'Tactless of me, but she was a great one for her flowers.'

'It was a very nice thing to say,' she said. 'Don't worry about me. I'd probably cry if you said "cheese sandwiches".'

'I'll try to avoid mention of those,' he said. 'Though it's funny how hungry a funeral makes you.'

She gave him a smile and moved on towards the retired admiral, but Mrs Haddenham overtook her.

'There's an extraordinary black-haired man over there,' she said. 'Did we invite him?'

She gestured to where Morbey stood looking out over the cemetery. There was a man in a dark blue overcoat beside him whom she hadn't seen before.

'I think he's . . . something to do with the undertakers,' Heather said.

'Extraordinary man. I gave him a straight look and he smiled most evilly. Shall I send Alan to have a word with him?'

'No!' Heather exclaimed. 'I mean, no. He's fine. Everything's fine. Please don't interfere.'

'Well!'

Mrs Haddenham drew herself up. She wasn't used to being spoken to like that. Alan came wandering over.

'Everything all right?'

'I was only trying to help but Heather says I mustn't interfere.'

Alan gave Heather a look, half sympathetic, half admonitory. Before he could enquire further, the Reverend Mr Blisworth arrived.

'We're ready now. Would you all like to come in? Mother's going to have a lovely send-off.'

And indeed the chapel was full of spring flowers, though happily, as the man from BBONT remarked, they were not wild ones.

The service went mostly according to plan, though the organist played the wrong tune for 'Lead Kindly Light' which meant no one sang it.

Heather had another little weep over the lines:

> *'And in the morn those angel faces smile,*
> *Which we have loved long since and lost awhile . . .'*

Mr Haddenham lent her one of his enuretic tissues.

The Reverend Mr Blisworth, being deprived of his modern service, read every archaism, every thee and thy and hath and doth, as though they were part of an impenetrable foreign language.

The old Fellow made rather a hash of Ecclesiastes: 'Consider now thy Creator in the days of thy youth when the evil days come not, nor the years draw nigh when thou shalt say, I have no pleasure in them . . .' But Alan redeemed the situation with a splendid rendition of Pilgrim's final progress across the river to the City of God, and when he read 'And all the trumpets sounded on the other side' there was not a dry eye in the house.

'He's a lovely reader,' sniffed Mrs Haddenham.

He was a lovely reader. A little too lovely, perhaps.

The coffin containing the body in which she had been conceived and from which she had been born, flesh of her flesh, now started trundling away while the organist played 'Ave Verum Corpus'. The doors, the terrible doors, opened, the sound of a discreet furnace filled the chapel, and the coffin slid towards eternity.

The moment she had so much dreaded being over, Heather felt a little better. She turned to see how Morbey was getting on at the back of the chapel, but he had gone. The man in the dark blue overcoat also seemed to have disappeared.

The little party emerged again into the garden of rest. They were all that was left of her mother's life, and soon most of them would be gone too. Heather shivered in the sunlight as Alan took charge, directing them towards the pub in Beckley where a room had been booked.

The wake was short but well-received. Mrs Haddenham, fulsome with sherry, distinguished herself by buttonholing the retired Fellow, whom Alan had told her was a distinguished medical theorist and prizewinner, and asking him in-depth questions on the lining of her womb.

'Should one have it out? Should one keep it in? That's the burning issue,' she kept saying.

The old man was quite overcome. Happily Alan was able to revive him with an account of his latest researches on the National Health Service.

'It is, after all, one of the country's institutions even if it is less than sixty years old,' he said. 'And it seems that it's falling apart. Not because it's under-funded, but because it's overloaded. The middle-class, the managers, keep climbing on top of it and paying themselves handsomely for the privilege. The thing is, of course, it was designed as a life-raft but they've turned it into a cruise-liner for their own benefit. And then there's medicine itself. Technology's way ahead of a system designed for yesterday . . .'

The old man thought about it.

'You say you're doing a series on the British Institutions?'

'That's right.'

'On why they're all breaking down?'

'Absolutely.'

'It seems to me – there's a parallel here – everything's gone too fast for them. They've been built up over hundreds of years – even the NHS has been going for more than half a century. It's the rate of technological change, d'you see, shaking it all down. Things can be obsolete in ten years these days. It's like Greek columns in an earthquake.'

The old man sipped his sherry.

'Go on, Professor,' said Alan intently.

'Of course, as animals, we're adaptable creatures. We can quickly adjust to change. But our institutions can't. Now what happens when things go too fast for humans? In a car crash for instance? We go rigid. We can't believe what's happening. Our pulse rate goes up. Our eyes dilate. Adrenalin rushes through the body. We're in a state of shock. And that's what's happening here.'

'Brilliant,' said Alan. 'Thank you, Professor. You've given me the title for the series.'

Nineteen

She met him at chambers in the Temple at the appointed hour, or rather five minutes after the appointed hour which was chambers practice – in fact five minutes past anything was called Perrytime – it indicated a plethora of cases and proper barristerly to-do. It was five past five, which was the time conferences were held at the end of a court day.

He was out of sight, waiting in the library when she arrived. Sir Perry wouldn't have anything as vulgar as comfortable chairs or sofas in reception.

'No, no,' he had said to Arthur, when the issue was raised, 'we wouldn't keep guests sitting in the hall at home, would we?'

Well, actually Arthur would but he did not say so. He would keep them sitting on broken glass with a bramble up their bottom, but he did not say so.

'No, Sir Perry,' he said.

'We would show them into a room where they could sit down, look around, read a book, turn a globe. We have a globe?'

'No, Sir Perry.'

'Acquire a globe.'

'Yes, Sir Perry.'

And Arthur did, as he did everything, making a nice little bit of profit on the deal.

Anyway, already in the library, quite possibly twiddling the globe, sat or stood Mr Christopher Morbey when she arrived punctually in Perrytime.

Arthur buttonholed her before she went in to greet him.

'Mr Protheroe's office called, Miss Semple. Mr Protheroe's been detained, and Mr Joscelyn's been called away to some family crisis. I expect a deer has escaped from the park or something.'

Was this a joke or was he serious? You could never quite tell with Arthur, and if you asked you were wrong.

'Mr Protheroe wants you to proceed with the interview,' Arthur added. 'The meeting-room is being redecorated so you'd better talk in there. You won't be disturbed. Miss Jerrold will be joining you presently, but she called to say she'd be late. Sir Peregrine sent her off to the Law Courts.'

Lucy Jerrold was her pupil, a sickly girl not often in evidence, and now *in absentia* yet again.

Heather was glad that she would be alone with her client. She had gone to some lengths to look agreeable; new suit, hair washed, Fogal tights at fifteen pounds a pair. She knew she looked good because a couple of admen from the local agency, weighed down by their presentation bags, stigmata of their trade, had turned their heads as she walked down Fleet Street. She thought he deserved it for coming to the funeral, that was all. One had to keep a sense of the niceties as well as of professional decorum.

However, decorous or not, she noticed her heart quickening again as Arthur opened the door for her and she saw the man – no doubt just barristerly interest. Arthur waited a little longer than was necessary or polite.

'Thank you, Arthur,' she said.

Arthur looked cryptic but closed the door, and Morbey moved towards her to shake her hand. She wondered absurdly whether he was going to kiss it, but it was just as well he didn't because Arthur opened the door again very quickly.

'Anything you want?' he asked. 'Tea? Coffee? Soft drink?'

'A bottle of Meursault, please, and two glasses.'

Arthur looked daggers and slowly turned on his heel, shutting the door with quite a thump.

'Why Meursault?' she asked.

'I thought of nothing else when I was in prison. Well, not quite nothing else.'

He gave her a quick smile, and she frowned a professional frown, but she couldn't help warming to the man. It hardly seemed possible that it was the same person she had interviewed in Brixton. Even the slicked-back hair had become fluffier.

'I think you've upset him,' Heather said.

'Good,' he said. 'Now to business. I didn't kiss you on greeting, not because that clerk was lurking but because everyone kisses everyone nowadays to show how continental and sophisticated they are. But what they've done is debase the coinage – like just about every other kind of coinage around these days. Our grandparents never used to throw kisses around like that. A kiss, in my book, means the sealing of love.'

'It would have been quite inappropriate,' she said, but she smiled to take the edge off the words.

'You're probably right,' he told her. 'However, I must say, Miss Semple, that you look good enough to eat. Talking of which, I don't suppose I could persuade you to come and have dinner with me after this?'

'Sorry,' she said. 'It's not allowed. I told you.'

'Not allowed? Who says it's not allowed?'

'It's etiquette. We went through all that.'

He seemed absolutely deflated.

'Oh my good Lord. I thought you were just . . . you know . . .'

She tried to cheer him up.

'Never mind,' she said. 'We can talk here.'

'It's like a banquet you're not allowed to touch.'

'You'll get over it,' she laughed, patting his arm in mock consolation, a silly thing to do.

He grasped her hand and suddenly put it to his mouth and kissed it. A shiver passed through her, as if a breeze had stirred things untouched for too long. There was a silence between them.

'Thank you for coming to the funeral,' she said. 'It was the last thing I was expecting. I was completely . . .'

'Flabbergasted? Timber-shivered?' he teased.

'Not to put too fine a point on it.'

'You seemed to have a mixed bunch there.'

'How on earth did you manage it? Mrs Haddenham thought you looked extremely sinister.'

'The old bat with the little husband? Poor little chap. She'll swallow him one of these days.'

She opened her briefcase and extracted a notepad.

'I don't like talking to paper,' he said.

'I have to get things down. You've been in luck so far. We usually have interviews in the meeting-room where Sir Perry's experimenting with one of the new high-security voice processors.'

'Ah. So nobody else will hear this?'

'Not this. I'll make notes later and send them to Soapy. Talking of Soapy, tell me, how on earth *did* you get bail? It's most unusual in a murder case. Unheard of these days.'

In fact, she had been livid that she hadn't been informed. She would be making a scene about it. Everybody seemed to know everything except her. However, she had at last been able to extract the brief from Soapy's lot, noting with relief that it was indeed a Walter Muscott who was the prosecution witness from the wine bar.

'Soapy's a wily old bird,' said Morbey. 'I had to get a mate to put a load of money up. Couple of hundred grand.'

She was impressed.

'Still, you're out, that's the main thing,' she said.

'May not be for long. And I can't leave London.'

'But you came to Oxford.'

'That was compassionate. I had to have a screw along with me. You probably saw?'

'I did. Why didn't you stay?'

'I didn't want to be an embarrassment, did I?'

She smiled at him and impulsively reached out and took his hand, her turn.

'You're a good egg,' she said.

'I'm a rather strange egg,' he said suddenly formal. 'I'm a cuckoo's egg, Miss Semple.'

'I don't understand. And please call me Heather.'

'One day I'll tell you about it.'

'Is there something I should know?'

'There's lots you should know.'

'Then you should tell me about it now. I must know everything.'

'It's not as simple as that,' he said. 'Heather.'

He said it as though he had been repeating it to himself a great deal but never said it out loud before.

'Who are you?' she asked him. 'There's something strange about all this.'

'Christopher Morbey, born February 4th 1960, sign of the Rat.'

'A rat? Not a cuckoo?' she said. 'Are rats good eggs?'

'Rats are clever and social,' he said. 'We've been given a bad name by the Black Death. We are attentive and loving. We do not like to be caged.'

'Quite so,' she said. 'That's why we have to get you off.'

'If only it was as simple as that.'

'It is simple. You didn't do it, did you?'

'Of course I didn't. I was only joshing you along first time I saw you. The only time I ever went with a man was in Singapore and then I thought he was a girl. It was one of those Boogie Street creatures. My twin brother put him up to it. I nearly had a cardiac when she took her clothes off.'

'I imagine you won't want me to make notes on this,' she said.

'He had a sort of pouch. A bit like an inverted pop-sock. Not like the good thing at all.'

'Enough. No more,' she said, stopping her ears.

It was time to change the conversation.

'I didn't know you had a brother,' she said. 'I don't even know if you're married. I should have had this down on file.'

'I was married,' he corrected her. 'Divorced long since. Started too early, romantic nature.'

She noted in herself a little surge of irrational interest at the news that he was single.

'And what does your brother do?'

His face clouded over.

'Now,' he said, 'now he's no good. No good, period. A bad seed. Evil.'

His face was closed, almost again as if he felt he'd said too much. Well, she could do that too; she had been quietly saving up for this.

'Why did you play games with me?' she asked.

'Games?'

'What you call joshing. You've changed your story since I spoke to you in Brixton. What you told me wasn't what you told the police or your solicitor.'

'To be honest, I was making it up to shock you.'

'Why on earth would you do that?'

'Because I fancied you. And because I thought you were just another little tight-arsed barrister girl, making your way by sleeping with the seniors.'

'You were wrong, weren't you? And you were wrong to try and confuse the issue. My fault perhaps for coming to see you before I had your documents but . . .'

'Yes?'

'Soapy's clerk *was* supposed to be coming too.'

'I'm sorry,' he said. 'Sometimes reality's a bit of a greasy pole. Especially when you're sitting in Brixton.'

'I think we should get the story right now, though, don't you? Perrytime marches on.'

He chuckled.

'You're a strange person, do you know that? Most women would have taxed me with lying long ago. You just kept it to yourself.'

'I knew you were playing some kind of game,' she said, 'but if that was what you wanted, it was all part of the picture. My job was to get to know you first, work out a strategy for your defence later. That's why we're here now. The facts, as I have them at the moment, are that you went up to the High Street to buy electronic equipment you needed for your work as an engineer. Is that right?'

'Yes,' he said. 'It's funny that High Street. They've got some of the most specialized electronic shops in London, in Europe, and they're all cheek by jowl in this funny little street. Open till all hours, some of them are.'

'Right, and I understand you made a purchase in S&J Electronics of a particular part that you wanted for some new machine . . . Will you take it from there?'

'I bought it at around quarter to seven, and then I mooched around to one or two of the other shops to see what they had in. After a while, I got a bit of a thirst on, and I remembered a chum who said you must look in at Our Souls Wine Bar. It's a hoot, he said, just round the corner from the shops. So I went up there, and a hoot it was too, though I didn't know I'd be laughing on the other side of my face. I stayed there and had a couple of pints, and then I caught a bus back at around ten o'clock to Prince of Wales Terrace. End of story.'

'But the prosecution will say that you were seen leaving with the boy at around ten o'clock.'

'Whoever says that, they're lying. Or it was just coincidence. I never met him. He went one way, I went another. Simple as that.'

'The trouble is, nobody saw you. You don't have an alibi.'

'I know. That's the bugger.'

'You've said it,' she told him.

He did not seem particularly worried.

'We have to find an alibi for you, Mr Morbey.'

'Christopher.'

'We have to do that, Christopher. Someone who will say that you were elsewhere at the time. A bus conductor, a taxi driver, a traffic warden, anything . . . the caretaker of your flat. Your girlfriend . . .'

'I don't have,' he said. 'I told you.'

'No,' she said. 'You told me you *did* have but she was unreliable.'

'Just joshing,' he said.

'No, no girlfriend. But someone. You see, it's the weak part of your case. Oh, the witness who says he saw you leaving may not stand up to cross-examination. There are no fingerprints of yours at the scene of the crime, but there are no fingerprints of anyone's apart from the victim's. There are strands of material, but whose? There are a lot of questions to be answered but . . . we try to leave nothing to chance . . .'

'Oh . . . right . . .'

He seemed almost bored with such details.

'You don't seem to be very . . . involved . . . in your case, Christopher.'

'That's because I'm involved in something much more interesting,' he said.

'Oh. What is that?'

'You.'

'Ohhh. Come on,' she said exasperatedly.

She supposed she had been expecting something of the sort. Instinctively she closed her notepad for a moment. Why wouldn't he let her just get on with his case?

'Have I said too much? I can't really think of much more than you – especially when you're there,' he told her.

'I have a boyfriend, you know,' she said. 'Quite apart from the impossibility of my having an affair with you.'

'I know.'

'How do you know?'

'I made it my business. Do you love him?'

She paused. The conversation was getting out of control, but something made her reply. Why fool around? The truth shall be thy warrant.

'I'm not in love with him, but I love him in a way.'

'That's all I need to know,' he told her.

She pulled herself together. It was a cardinal rule of all successful barristers that they never get emotionally involved with their clients. It was more than a rule. It was common sense.

'We really shouldn't be having this conversation,' she said. 'If I'm to defend you properly, I mustn't be emotionally involved. It's very important to me, this case.'

'Me too, lady.'

'Of course. I didn't mean . . .'

He put his hand on hers for a moment, emotionally involving.

'I know. Don't worry about it.'

The door opened. It was her pupil, Lucy Jerrold, with Arthur standing behind her. Christopher did not take his hand away.

They all stared at each other for a while. Heather thought, trust Lucy, who was never there, to turn up at the wrong moment. Anyway, it was inexcusable to interrupt a conference.

'Close the door, Lucy,' she said. 'I'll speak to you later.'

Arthur spoke up. It was obviously he who had put Lucy up to do it. He himself would never be seen to interrupt.

'The thing is,' he said, 'we've got a bit of a bottle-neck here, due to the decorating in the meeting-room. Any chance you might, ah, finish the matter in hand in the next half hour or so?'

'Fine,' she said. 'We've finished now.'

Arthur looked surprised, even mortified. He had wanted to be awkward. Still, there it was, Mr George could have the library now. He turned and went back to his office while Lucy, who looked as if she had an even heavier than usual period, slunk away to the pupils' room. They were alone again.

'What d'you mean, we're finished?' said Morbey, agitatedly. 'We've only just begun.'

'Then we'll have to have another meeting, won't we?'

'You mean . . .'

'I'll walk down the street with you,' she said.

She just wanted to be perfectly sure there was no one listening, no record anywhere of what she wanted to say. She waited while he put on his coat against the chill daffodil-shaker that had blown up from the east, and walked with him a little way towards Holborn. From his window, Arthur had watched them go with a quizzical expression half-frown, half sardonic.

'I always think this is one of the vilest streets in London – big, noisy, charmless, dirty . . .' she said.

'But today it's feeling better.'

She laughed.

'Where shall I see you tomorrow?'

She reflected. The library would be booked, George would be in the office, a conference room could be had at an office suite but Arthur always made such a fuss of the expense, and she had already told him they were finished . . . Really there was only one place to go.

It was strictly against all the rules for dealing with clients, especially one accused of such crimes. Soapy would be livid and have her guts for his sock-suspenders, but if one didn't trust one's instincts, what could one trust? One would be better off working for a multi-national conglomerate. Her experience both as an individual and as a professional told her she could handle the situation.

A fire engine hurtled past – an acoustic asteroid. Buses throbbed and burbled. An old man at a stall proclaimed the headline of the day, indecipherably, in a voice like a cracked bugle. But above the urgent clamour of the street, above the motorbikes and the baleful chunter of the taxis, above even the other voices in her head that told her that what she was doing was madness, Heather knew she could hear the sound of a die being cast.

'I think you had better come to my flat,' she said.

Twenty

It was already six o'clock. She said goodbye to Christopher and walked through to Covent Garden where she had a cup of coffee and watched the buskers in the piazza. When she reached the Temple again it was nearly a quarter past, but Sir Peregrine was not yet back from court and nor was Arthur to be seen. George, however, was in. It was he who was meant to have been using the library.

Her old Etonian stable-mate had been having a successful time of late. He had won two cases of burglary with assault, and had managed to get a bullion robber who was patently guilty acquitted; so he was pleased with himself, which meant he was more insufferable than usual.

'Ah, Heather,' he said as she came in. 'What brings you in today?'

'I work here,' she told him. 'Remember?'

'Well, it is rather hard to remember, actually. We see so little of you.'

'My mother died,' she said.

She hated to bring her mother into it, but she knew it would put a spoke in his wheels.

'Ah yes,' he said. 'Awfully bad luck. Too bad. Sorry to hear about that.'

'Thank you,' she said.

'Did you hear about my bullion robber? Bloody marvellous. I must say, Arthur was chuffed. Bought me a magnum of Bolly '82.'

'That was nice of him. Why weren't you using the library just now?'

'Oh, I had a conference arranged with a manslaughter but he bottled out at the last minute.'

'Thank you, George. I just about got turfed out for you.'

'Sorry and all that.'

A pretty girl she had not seen before came in.

'Sir Peregrine's back, Miss Sepal. He'll see you now.'

'Semple.'

'Pardon?'

'Semple, not Sepal.'

'She's not a flower, you know,' said George. 'Not the way you are, petal.'

The temp batted her long lashes at him. He was odiously good-looking. They smirked in sexual semaphore. Really, thought Heather, they might as well wave their genitals at each other and have done with it.

'"The wren goes to it and the small gilded fly does lecher in my sight",' she said.

'Pardon?'

'Oh, never mind. Tell him I'll be with him in a moment.'

The girl went out.

'I must say, Heather, you don't have to be so condescending to the poor girl. We don't all have your education, you know.'

'That's rich, coming from an Etonian.'

He opened his mouth with a rejoinder but she forestalled him.

'Sorry. Mustn't keep Sir Perry waiting. Save it for later.'

The great man was standing in front of a blazing smokeless fire when she entered.

'Ah, Heather. Good to see you. Take a seat.'

How the room embodied the Establishment. The bookcases lined with leather-bound tomes, the genuine Georgian windows looking out onto the tree-fringed lawn, the deep armchairs, the stiff invitations in the Chippendale mirror, the scent of hyacinths standing pink and blue in their huge Harrods bowl . . . This was changeless England.

'How are you getting on then, Heather?'

'The Morbey case, Sir Perry? Pretty well, I think.'

'We want you to do very well, Heather. We set great store by this one. It must look good.'

A strange choice of words, she thought. She waited for what he had to say next. The fire spluttered with a little outpouring of gas. The Tompion grandfather clock tut-tutted away the seconds as if regretting, ever so discreetly, the irreparable flight of time. A pane rattled, very very quietly, as if caught in a tickle of light.

'Soapy and I pulled a lot of strings and . . . you know.'

'I heard. I think I should've been told.'

'We tried to get in touch but your answering machine's playing up, and you were out, I think that's what Arthur said.'

'I've been seeing the client today, as a matter of fact.'

'Seeing?'

'Conference here at chambers.'

'Well. That's good. Getting my schedule together, are we?'

'I only got the brief a couple of days ago. It seems Soapy's lot have been re-drafting it.'

The schedule was the junior's priority: a presentation of all the relevant facts to the silk.

'Soon as you like, soon as you like,' Sir Perry told her.

'It's unusual for him to get bail,' she said.

'It is,' he agreed. 'But good if you can get it. We got it. One up to us.'

You mean one up to you, she thought.

'I shall want my schedule in due course, very particular about my schedule. Times and dates, places and faces . . . you know the form. Oh, and sorry about your mother. You got the wreath?'

'I did. And thank you.'

'It's not easy, is it? Sometimes I think it's almost too difficult to endure.'

'We must have patience,' she said.

'I often think of those last ten, or was it sixteen, silent years of Shakespeare's life. What on earth was going through his mind? Ah well, must get on. There's plenty to occupy *our* heads with things the way they are. How did this country get into such a state – and so fast? Our children will blame us, you know, just as I used to blame my parents for Hitler.'

The door opened and Arthur popped his head in, bright blue eyes a-twinkle and just a little flushed around the jowls.

'Ah, Arthur. Wanted to see you. Miss Semple's just going.'

'I'll be right with you in a moment, Sir Peregrine.'

Outside, Arthur collared her.

'I was rather surprised to hear your client ask for wine. And Meursault no less!' he said. 'I trust you won't be putting in for expenses.'

'We didn't get it, Arthur, remember?'

'Of course not. You know Sir Perry doesn't like drinking in conference. Besides, we don't have Meursault.'

'Actually he offered to pay for it himself,' she lied.

'Good heavens!'

It was the strongest expletive she had ever heard Arthur use. She didn't suppose he had ever personally paid for a drink in his life. The notion prompted a sudden quirk of memory. That was where she had seen the name Eurovin. On a case of Club Claret being delivered to the chambers bar. They must be more respectable than she had imagined. Arthur seemed to pick up on her thought.

'You went to the scene of the crime, I hear,' he said.

'That's right.'

'Did you . . . find anything?'

She wondered if she was right in thinking there was an extra emphasis on the word 'find'.

'It was just routine, really,' she told him. 'I like to get a feel for the case.'

'Nothing special then?'

What was he driving at? Did he know that something had

been lost? It seemed hardly likely. No doubt he was just being Arthur, ever inquisitive; what did the Australians call it? Sticky-beak. It was Arthur sticky-beaking. Why should she indulge Arthur?

'Nothing special,' she said, 'at this stage. But you never know what may be important.'

He looked at her, twinkling coldly; Mercury on a frosty night.

'No,' he said, 'you never do. Sorry to hear about your mother.'

'Thank you, Arthur,' she said.

'I think we may have a motoring offence for you down in Stratford East,' he went on smoothly.

'In Stratford?' she asked. 'Couldn't George do it? He lives in Docklands.'

It was clearly a case at the very lowest end of the Richter scale of earthshakingness. Arthur laughed without humour.

'Oh no, Miss Semple. I'm afraid that's out of the question. You see, he's very much in demand these days. And you're next on the list. Sorry.'

There was just the very slightest bit of emphasis on the 'he', which was Arthur's way of putting her down. And sod you too, Arthur, she thought.

And then she thought, I'm not going to take much more of this.

Twenty-one

When she got back to her flat there was a tall, bald policeman on the landing talking to the South American diplomat. She could hear their conversation as she came up the stairs.

'I see nothing, I hear nothing. Then I come out and I see the open door. I call to Mees Semple to come and dance. Then I think she leave door open by meestake. I look in and I see all thees mess. Then I see you walk past, bobby in blue, how you do?'

'Did you hear any noise, sir?'

'I play rumba very loud. It is the dance of my country.'

'What's happened?' asked Heather, breathlessly.

She had run up the last flight, hoping uncharitably that the diplomat might have been burgled, not she; but the evidence was all too plain. Her front door stood ajar.

'Miss Semple?' asked the policeman.

'Yes.'

'This is your flat, I believe.'

'It was my flat. Have they done much damage?'

'I've only just arrived. We'd better have a look. Not you, sir,' said the policeman to the diplomat who showed signs of wanting to come in.

'You like to dance after, you tell me,' the diplomat said to Heather.

'Thank you, sir. That'll be all.'

The whole place had been expertly rifled.

'Whoever it was, knows what he's looking for,' said the constable.

'Or she, I suppose. Mustn't discriminate,' she observed, wryly.

The impact of the thing had not properly sunk in. Thank God, she thought, I haven't moved Mother's things in yet. I couldn't have borne the idea of all her stuff being hawked on a stall in Bermondsey Market tomorrow morning.

'I buried my mother on Saturday,' she said. 'Cremated, I should say.'

'I'm sorry to hear that.'

'It's all right. In a funny way, it makes this easier.'

'Any idea what they might have been looking for, miss?'

'Oh, the usual, I suppose. Clocks, jewellery, small things like candlesticks, silver . . .'

'But they haven't taken your clock.'

She looked at the chimneypiece, and there it was. One of her grandmother's wedding presents – an Edwardian carriage clock – it ticked away crotchetily, as if almost affronted not to have been purloined. The ormolu clock was in its place as well.

'I'd better look at my jewellery.'

'Try not to touch anything, miss. The fingerprint man will be along presently.'

'I can't very well look if I can't touch . . .'

'As little as possible, please.'

They went into the bedroom. It was awash, embarrassingly so, with her clothes. Stockings, tights, skirts, knickers, bras, rings, dresses, shoes, belts, shirts lay scattered around as if the place had been blown up by a soft howitzer. The policeman stood on a particularly sexy nightdress with his big boots while she opened her jewellery box. Everything was there.

They progressed to the spare bedroom which was the scene of lesser mayhem. The suitcases which she kept there were scattered about the floor. Every drawer of her desk – she used the room as an office sometimes – had been taken out and its contents upended on the carpet. But this was mild compared with the mayhem downstairs.

'Nothing missing?' asked the policeman.

'Not that I can see.'

The kitchen and bathroom had also been subjected to the same attention.

'Weird,' said the policeman. 'A rum do. You didn't bring anything into the flat that might have been valuable to someone? Any object of beauty or . . . interest?'

She could think of absolutely nothing.

'Perhaps they made a mistake,' she said. 'They mistook my flat for someone else's. I had a couple of weird calls. Maybe it was that.'

'Maybe, miss. Well, I'd better be off now. You'll no doubt contact your insurance people.'

He gave her a Crime Number to quote and told her that counselling was available.

'I'd rather have an arrest,' she said.

'Not very likely, I'm afraid. Though the fingerprint man may come up with something. Burglaries are two a penny these days, and if we catch 'em they're usually back on the streets within a month. Law and order? This government couldn't get a grip on a bunch of goose-grass . . .'

The bald policeman said goodbye and left Heather alone in the wreckage of her flat. She couldn't even begin to clear up until the print man came. Her fortitude under the circumstances surprised her, but when the worst happens it's sometimes better than the *fear* of the worst. Those telephone calls were perhaps just a burglar checking her out. Or, as she'd said to the policeman, perhaps it was all a mistake.

Damn it, she thought. At least I'll have a drink, prints or no prints.

It was while she was sitting and sipping a glass of Cloudy Bay that she thought of the bit of metal she'd found at the flat in Clapham. For heaven's sake, no one knew she had found it. It had been so low on her list of priorities that she hadn't even thought whom to ask about it, whether it was even worth asking.

It was, insecurely, in her handbag even now. Perhaps those who wanted it back couldn't believe she would treat it so lightly.

She hadn't even bothered to hide it. If it were so important in some way, she really had to find someone now to talk to, someone whom she trusted. But who? She certainly didn't want to tell anyone at chambers – or, come to think of it, at Soapy's office. In either case, she would be censured for not having mentioned it earlier or laughed at for thinking, even for a moment, that something so obviously trivial could be important.

'The womb was formerly said to be the seat of hysteria, and it is not difficult to understand such a notion.' She could hear Arthur now, twinkling away, showing off his reading to his cronies. 'Let a woman loose on evidence and they go wild. Any little thing is grist to their mill. You'll never guess what she's come up with now. Clever me! A plumber's tubelet governor. Useful, of course, if you're plumbing, but as I keep saying to Sir Perry, this is the law . . .'

She hated being mocked by these people. No, she would think of someone else. Alan perhaps? He was certainly a possibility, but he again would be whimsical if it were unimportant. And if it were not, wasn't he a little too elusive, a little too insecure? Media people are by their nature communicative. Only Alan as a last resort, she decided.

She took the thing out, moving to the window, and looked at it again. Perhaps it was, after all, something electronic; a chip maybe, though a little larger than any chip she'd seen.

Oxford, that would be the place. There must be someone at Trinity who would know. She would call up her old tutor tomorrow. Meanwhile it was getting late. She telephoned the police station and asked them when the fingerprint man was coming.

'Which fingerprint man, miss?'

'The one that was coming to check out my burglary.'

She gave her address.

'Nothing's been reported, miss.'

'But there was a constable here. Number 3759. A bald man.'

'We don't have an officer of that number, miss, bald or

otherwise. I'm afraid you've been the victim of a masquerade. I'll send someone round. It's a serious offence.'

'Burglary, a serious offence?'

'Masquerading as a police officer, miss.'

'No, burglary's a serious offence.'

'Quite, miss. Like I said, we'll send someone round.'

'How will I know he's genuine?'

Reality seemed to be misting up around here. Perhaps the physicists were right. There were parallel universes in which anything that could happen, did happen. Certainly it seemed her own life appeared to be plagued with such mergings and dissolvings of possibility. She did not know what was true any more – not of course an insurmountable condition for a barrister – but, in her own life, worrying.

In due course, a policeman arrived. This time at least she knew him. He was the one who had surprised her prowling about with a knife in her hand. She told him her story and he looked sympathetic.

'You *are* having a rough time and no mistake, miss. Would you like some protection? We could put a man outside for a while.'

'For a night or two, perhaps. I think it may all be a mistake.'

He spoke on his portable radio.

'We don't seem to have a spare man at the moment, miss. Sorry about that. The good news is, the fingerprint man will be along any minute now. In fact, I thought he might be here before me.'

He looked round briefly, took a statement from her, gave her another Crime Number and asked particulars of the masquerader.

'From what you say, miss, it seems he might have been in the force, might even still be in it. He certainly knew the form. We do have some rogues in our midst, I'm sorry to say.'

There was a ring at the door.

'Ah, here's our man now. I'll leave you to his tender mercies, if I may. Don't hesitate to get in touch. And I'd get Banhams or someone to do you a new lock in the morning. Goodnight, miss. I trust it can only get better.'

The fingerprint man was a little chap with an irrepressible sense of humour.

'I don't suppose you'll find anything,' she told him.

'Possibly not, possibly not, but nil desperandum. You know why Snow White is the patron saint of our trade?'

'I have no idea.'

She was beginning to suffer a reaction now.

'Some day our prints will come. Ha ha . . .'

She had the feeling it was not the first time he had made the joke, but she made an attempt at smiling. It must be a depressing job blowing chalk among other people's misery.

While he was still doing the spare bedroom, Alan came in. She had made a start of clearing up downstairs but had just decided to quit and wait till morning. The bottle of Cloudy Bay was now half-empty.

'I had a burglary.'

'It's all happening to you, isn't it, you poor thing.'

'I think there must be some mistake,' she said, vaguely, as if to ward off the imputation of external malevolence.

'Mistake or not, they've certainly done you over.'

'The policeman said that, one of the policemen, the false policeman . . .' she started.

'Hold on. A false policeman?'

'He must've been. He seemed all right at the time. A bald man. I came back and found him talking to Mr Hernandez. But the police didn't know anything about him when I called. By that time he had gone . . .'

It sounded confusing to her, God knew what it sounded like to Alan.

'I think I'd better have a glass of that Cloudy Bay,' he said.

An idea struck her.

'You don't think . . .'

'What?'

He turned as he poured so that the wine missed the side and

slopped onto the carpet. He swore and dabbed at it with his handkerchief.

'Don't bother,' she said. 'There's enough mess round here already. Chaos is the norm. Order stands out like a sore thumb.'

He laughed.

'I'm glad you're taking it so well. You were saying, before I so obtusely interrupted?'

'I was going to say, you don't think all this could be connected with you . . . your series, I mean? You know I talked about your making enemies . . .'

Alan thought about it, his head cocked on one side, pulling at his ear, the interviewer's endearing idiosyncrasy, and started talking about how a journalist has to take risks.

Heather put her mind into neutral; blanking, her mother used to call it.

Somewhere nearby a police car, ambulance or fire engine – you could never tell which was which these days, they all combined their sounds in a unison of crisis, especially at night, whether it was a cannabis pedlar, a road accident, a broken-down lift or a cat stuck up a tree, it was all part of some policy (it could not be coincidence) to make the public's adrenalin race – whichever it was, something was shrieking its way up from Kensington High Street now. Blue shift as it approached . . . red shift as it went . . . doppler of anxiety, involving all citizens in the crisis of one. Therefore seek not to know for whom the siren wails, it wails for thee.

Her mind free-wheeled away until Alan came back to the burglary again.

'It could be me, I suppose,' said Alan. 'I've never had any trouble of that sort before. But why wouldn't they do *my* flat over? If they were looking for material, that'd be the place to go for.'

'Perhaps they think I'm your soft underbelly,' she said.

'You are,' he told her. 'Nice and soft.'

'Perhaps they think you're here more often than you are.'

'It's not for want of trying,' he said.

It was, as a matter of fact. He was just as keen to preserve an independent part of his life as she was, perhaps even keener. She sometimes wondered whether he was having a little something on the side. She hoped not. You couldn't be too careful these days even though the AIDS lobby, still adding its shrill wheeeeEEEEeeeee to the heterosexuals' adrenal burden, was perhaps protesting a little too much. No, no. He wouldn't be unfaithful, not good old spooky-tooth.

'I don't think it's me,' he told her, 'but I'll check around. We're certainly stirring it up. I'll ask Den.'

Dennis was the producer of *A State of Shock*. Heather knew that he would play it down because he wouldn't want the series upset. Den would be totally negative.

'Otherwise,' Alan went on, 'it's something you've got into. This whole thing started, if I remember right, around about the time you had this murder job.'

'Yes, but . . . It's not that sort of case. No drugs involved, no political sensitivities, no Mafia. Just a rather grubby little killing in Clapham.'

'That's as far as you know.'

This was her opportunity to ask him about the bit of metal she had found, but her instinct still favoured the dons.

'Oh come on, Alan. You reporters always want to make things more dramatic than they are,' she said.

He hated to be called a reporter, but tonight he made an effort not to be riled.

'Whatever you say, darling. I know you're tired. Look, I'll go and see if the man's finished now. The best thing for you would be food and bed.'

He went upstairs and stayed there an unconscionable time. It was nearly ten o'clock. She was meant to go to a solicitor in Stratford in the morning to talk about that driving offence, and then she had to get back here to meet Christopher later. She wanted time to look at the brief again – she had at least made sure it was still intact up there among the snowstorm in her office.

At last Alan and the print man came down.

'What on earth were you doing up there?' she asked.

'He had to do the cupboards in your bedroom. We had a very interesting talk. I might do a programme on a day in the life of a fingerprinter.'

'You could do worse, you could do worse,' the little man said. 'If you asked me to think of a better idea, I wouldn't be able to put a finger on it.'

She thought Alan laughed immoderately at the joke.

It made her cross to think of them stumbling around amid the depths of her cupboards – intimate things like an old cap she'd once tried and hated, Tampax, panti-liners, condoms, NSU pills, they were all there scattered around, advertising her type of period, her sexual activity, her occasional itch.

'I'd like to go to bed now,' she said crossly. 'I'm sorry. I've had enough.'

'Sorry to keep you,' said the print man. 'I do sympathize. Everyone hates the print man. Everyone laughs at the print man. But he sees the individual in all of us. He sees the hand of God, as you might say.'

'I didn't mean to be rude.'

'That's quite all right. I'm used to it. See myself out. Might be hearing from you about the programme,' he said to Alan. 'Here's my card in case you're interested. That's about it then. Whorls well that ends well. 'Night all.'

When he'd gone, Alan said it was maybe time for him to go too.

'I didn't know fingerprinters had cards. Is nothing non-commercial?' he added as an afterthought.

'Stay with me tonight,' she asked. 'I'll have new locks fitted tomorrow, but I don't feel very safe.'

He looked a little doubtful.

'I have to interview the Industry Secretary at crack of dawn, and then tour factories in Bedfordshire. After that it's Education, if you can call it education in this country . . .'

'Alan,' she said urgently.

'Of course I will,' he told her, 'dear old soft underbelly.'

'And none of that either,' she said. 'I'm shattered.'

She didn't tell him about her meeting with her client. It seemed hardly germane.

She slept once her head hit the pillow, almost dreamlessly, though at one stage she dreamt that Alan had got up and was rummaging about among her underwear, seeking just what it was that had undermined the works of time and sapped the pillars of the state.

Twenty-two

For some time now she had been aware of a very faint and intermittent tremble, like the one she had noticed in her flat after that Sunday lunch, nothing really when she had first been aware of it – in fact she had thought it was pins and needles, or the onset of some dreadful disease when it happened several times, but she was sure finally that it was outside her. She had seen her biscuit tin lid rattle in the kitchen, the mugs swing on their hooks, and the water waiting in the bath before she got in, on various occasions had become confused.

In the end she had asked Alan whether there might not be some seismic activity, but he pooh-poohed the idea of earth tremors in London.

'London's not built on a fault,' he told her. 'We *are* the fault.'

Still, she had persisted with her research, finally running to earth, in a basement office smelling of damp paper, a man recommended by *New Scientist*. Like many another whose job seems to influence his appearance, Desmond Festing, though small and otherwise unremarkable, had extraordinarily exuberant and sensitive eyebrows.

They had quivered when Heather first appeared, and went on quivering throughout the duration of her visit. It seemed, in truth, that he too was in tune with the tremors that she felt. He told her that London had had a few quakes in its time. There was a minor fault running across England from London through the Midlands; but there had been nothing larger than 3 on the Richter scale.

She had asked him if there was any record of seismic activity at the moment and he obligingly called the relevant laboratory, but there was nothing. Not so much as a quirk of a needle, he told her.

'Extraordinary,' she said. 'I'm sure I've been feeling something.'

She was not the sort to imagine such a thing – sensitive perhaps as barristers go, she had at the same time a good analytical mind. She had always liked to find the reason for things, to see how they worked; as a small child she remembered taking apart a perfectly good and rather valuable musical box. It had not been so easy to put together again.

She looked at the little man and his eyebrows.

'You,' she told him, 'you feel it, don't you?'

'It's a fellow feeling,' he said.

They did not get many pretty women in the basement office near Paddington.

She had returned to her flat, gently declining his offer of lunch, vindicated and baffled. London *could* have earthquakes, but it wasn't having any at the moment.

And yet she could feel it now, today, as she woke up, there, as if the whole building had its hair standing on end, tense as a terrier.

She wondered whether Alan would notice it too, but he was having re-entry problems with consciousness; it always took him at least ten minutes to make the transition between sleep and wake. She decided to say nothing, leave him to introduce the subject; he couldn't help but feel it; but when he finally got up, he had other things on his mind.

'The trouble with this country,' he told her, pulling on a shirt and hoisting his Y-fronts, 'one of the troubles with this country, one of the almost infinite number of troubles with this country, is that all the clever people go into the media.'

'Present company excepted of course,' she said.

She could afford to stay in bed for a little longer. It was nice watching someone get up first, even if he didn't notice the tremor. It wasn't the central heating – she'd had it checked.

'Indeed. What's left over, a few dribs and drabs, more drabs than dribs, go into the City and make vast quantities of money. And only the duffers go into industry. So no one *makes* anything very well any more. Or not many people anyway. With the result that we're a nation of brilliant critics and hopeless performers.'

He was repeating almost word for word what she had told him; flattering in a way, and typical Alan.

'Are you going to say that to the Industry Secretary?'

'Not in so many words. I don't want him to rise into the air squawking. But as he's never had any first hand experience of industry anyway, how should he know?'

Alan went off to his flat to have a bath and change. It was only five minutes' drive away. There had been a time when he kept clothes at her place, but it was like having a weekend cottage, he said. The to-ing and fro-ing got too much for him. It was then that she wondered whether he was having an affair, but he made such a fuss when she mentioned it that she was totally persuaded of his constancy.

She got up, showered and dressed. The locksmith came, and while he plied his trade, she set herself to cleaning the flat. The bedroom was relatively easy as were the kitchen and bathroom, but the living-room – which was where she intended to interview Christopher – took longer than she had thought. All the books had been taken out and thrown on the floor. There was a whole wallful of shelves. Some of the books had been damaged. It was going to take longer than she could allow.

Hell, she thought, he might as well see it like this. If it's anything to do with his case, he might have some views on the matter.

The locksmith departed. He had seemed authentic – she had checked with Banhams – but melancholy. Perhaps it was hearing Love laughing at him all the time.

She was just about to leave for Stratford when she remembered she had meant to call Oxford. She dialled the familiar number and talked to the porter's lodge.

'Morning, Brian,' she said.

The porter prided himself on never forgetting a voice, and she had been a particular favourite of his.

'Morning, Miss Semple.'

'How are you doing?'

'Oh, not so bad. It's non-stop these days. As soon as term's over, we get a course in. Advertising Role Reversal Seminar. My word, they put away a lot. They make the Claret Club look like schoolboys. Well, of course, they are schoolboys now. I always say it's never been the same since they stopped National Service.'

Brian had first come to the college as a lad of seventeen, escaping National Service because of flat feet.

'Good for college funds, though, all that drink.'

'Oh yes, they're not so bad, the advertising gentlemen.'

One always had to go through a certain ritual with Brian, however pressed one was. The mention of the seminar reminded her it was vacation.

'Dr James in?'

'Well, I think you're in luck. I believe I saw him come in five minutes ago. I'll try him now.'

She heard the line go dead, then ring again.

'Hullo, James speaking.'

'It's Heather Semple here.'

'Hullo, Heather. What can I do for you?'

The very sound of his voice made her feel she was back in the big leather armchair in Kettel Hall reading him her essay on Lord Chief Justice Coke while he poured sherry.

'Do you have anyone in college who's an electronics man? I have what I think might be a chip that I'd like someone to look at.'

'Let me see . . . Yes, I think we do have someone. Our physics man, Dr Bawtree, has a graduate from Hong Kong working with him. I think she might be the person for you. She's called Mei Noon. I know. It sounds like a Morris dance, but she's very bright. She's in Oxford, I know, but I don't have her number. Shall I get her to call you?'

'Yes, please. I have to go out now, but if she could call around four, I'll definitely be in.'

'Very well. I'll tell her.'

'Thank you so much. I'll probably bring it down myself, that is, if she can help. Perhaps we can have lunch?'

'That would be very pleasant.'

She replaced the receiver well satisfied, and was just about to leave when a thought struck her. If there really was someone after the chip (if it was a chip), she'd be crazy to go on carrying it about. The best place for it now would be the flat. She put it carefully in the butter-dish under a (wrapped) Lurpak, and pushed it to the back of the fridge – a place that had been scrupulously examined by the intruder on the previous evening. After that she left for happy Stratford.

Her morning there was a mixed success. For one thing she was late, which she always hated. The tube train decided to blow a fuse and sat in the tunnel for half an hour. And the man she was supposed to be defending had changed his mind at the last moment and decided to plead guilty.

'Sorry,' said Mr Grillsman, of Grillsman and Lutosovski. 'To say the boy is not a little indecisive is a grotesque litotes. But I did tell your head clerk yesterday evening.'

Right, she said to herself, that settles it. One way or another I'm going to fix that bastard Arthur. He could perfectly well have made sure she got the message. However, revenge being a dish best eaten cold, or at any rate tepid, she decided to bide her time and dish it out when it suited her. Meanwhile, the good news was that she could have the rest of the day off on full pay.

We like a guilty plea, she thought; though it would be nice not to have to go all the way to Stratford to hear it.

At least she had ample time now to do some more clearing up, wash the smell of the Underground out of her hair, maybe even have lunch with one of the few girlfriends she wanted to see these days, Chloe – a part-time model who did 'young mumsy' work and had a useful cottage in Suffolk. After that, maybe more clearing up and general preparation for the appointment with her client at six-thirty.

It was pleasant to find, when she arrived home, that the front door was intact and Mr Hernandez was nowhere in evidence. The first thing she did was to call chambers.

'Arthur there?'

'Yes, Miss Semple. Just got back.'

'Hullo. Miss Semple?' asked Arthur. 'I was trying to get hold of you yesterday evening to tell you about the guilty plea, but your telephone was off the hook.'

The wind was taken right out of her sails. Was Arthur, after all, all right? Was her dislike of him mere paranoia?

'I had a burglary,' she said.

'Oh dear, Miss Semple. We *are* accident-prone.'

At least Chloe was in. They had a pleasant lunch at Riccardo's, inexpensive and very cheerful, in the Fulham Road. Chloe specialized in soap powder commercials. She was thirty-five, good-humoured, pretty and clean-looking; she was also exceedingly naughty. She used her cottage in Suffolk for week-ends with boyfriends while her husband sailed rich Germans and Japanese round the Hebrides in a luxury steam yacht that had once belonged to King Farouk.

'You can have the cottage any time, Heather. Just say the word. Take Alan up there. Or anyone.'

'Anyone?'

'Oh. You like to be faithful, don't you?'

'Do I?'

Chloe laughed.

Heather didn't know Chloe that well, but she liked her feckless approach to life. She told her so and Chloe laughed.

'I suppose you can afford to be irresponsible if you're a model,' Heather said, ruefully. 'Barristers are supposed to be so bloody full of rectitude.'

'You should kick over the traces now and then. Take the cottage any time. Just say when.'

Heather thought for a moment. The murder trial was billed for April.

'Maybe we could take it, Alan and I, for the May Bank Holiday? My trial might be over by then. Anyway, I'll be glad of a break.'

'Sure. We won't be there. Guess where I'll be? The new season starts and I'm going up for the first cruise. Skye and the Butt of Lewis. Good naming there by someone . . .'

Twenty-three

After lunch with Chloe, Heather went back to the flat and made some desultory attempts to restore further order; but after a while a kind of cloudiness spread across her thoughts. She made a cup of tea, and sat and listened to one of Handel's great Concerti Grossi Opus 6, finding the strangely moving Musette with its low mysterious tones and dotted crotchets, deeper than tears.

For some time she sat, pondering the course she had set herself, knowing that it was still not too late to turn back. As a young barrister, junior to a famous QC, it was more or less career suicide to ask a client to one's private address, especially a client who was out on bail, charged with such a murder.

But that was not all, was it? A visit she might be able to get away with; but there was more. The man Morbey had a strange and troubling presence that she found attractive, no doubt about it; there was a mystery to him which she found attractive also; and there was, behind it, a sense of tension, almost of helplessness, nothing to do with the trial, as though there were things of which he could not speak and knowledge which could never be exposed, like the subterranean stirrings of Handel's Musette. It was perhaps this which, most of all, appealed to her. It made him, even with his strengths, surprisingly vulnerable.

For a few months now she had been questioning herself about her career. She knew she had it in her to be a good barrister, but at the same time she did not like herself for doing what she did. It seemed to her to be a game, dangerous, difficult, adrenalin-pumping, which she was no longer certain that she wanted to play. Her mother's death had perhaps heightened this feeling, making her question her own directions and her values. She knew of others in the profession who had experienced similar self-questionings, especially on the death of a parent, spouse or (lately) in one case a child. Some of them had left and become people again.

At this point her thoughts took a more cautious cast. Having no mother meant a greater sense of isolation, brought home to her her own insecurity. Having no job would bring its own problems. Did she really mean to bring such anxieties and dangers on herself? It was one thing to talk to Chloe about kicking over the traces, quite another to shoot oneself in the foot, if not the heart. Yesterday she could have persuaded herself that this was some kind of game, a dare such as one used to play at school, but now . . . ? She could not answer. And then there was Alan. He represented security of a kind; and yet, at the same time, was security enough?

When finally the doorbell rang, though, its hard little prrrring had a no-nonsense quality; and she got up and walked to the hall with a mixture of relief and misgiving. This could be the end of life as she knew it – but did she know it? – and did it matter if she didn't? For God's sake, all she was doing was interviewing a client.

She opened the door. It was one of those moments, she realized, when in the most mundane of circumstances – her own flat, a mild spring day slightly overcast, Telecom engineers just down the road, builders opposite – momentous and world-changing events occur. War may be declared. Or peace, she thought, as she looked at him, standing on the landing and holding a bunch of flame-coloured roses.

Now was the time to tell him that she had changed her mind and they must meet at chambers.

'For you,' he said, extending the flowers towards her. 'I always think red's overdone.'

She took a deep breath.

'Come in,' she told him.

There. She had done it. She almost hurried him inside. Stupid, really. No one could be watching. Of course he noticed.

'What's the hurry? Ah, I see. Not the done thing, I suppose?'

'Not the done thing,' she said, smiling. 'But the right thing.'

She knew, now that he was here, that it was. There was something about this man, about the way things were at the moment, about the whole case, that made it necessary to break the rules.

'Come and sit down,' she said. 'I want to take some notes. Sorry about the room. I've been clearing up. I had a break-in.'

'Bastards. Did they take anything?'

'Nothing I could see.'

'Police no good?'

'No good.'

'Par for the course. Soon they'll have so much body-armour they'll be like medieval knights – unable to move.'

'Would you like a coffee? Tea?'

'Nothing,' he said. 'I don't want to waste any time.'

'Are you in a hurry?'

She was disappointed.

'I mean,' he smiled, 'that I would rather just look at you than drink tea. It is refreshment enough.'

She blushed, stupidly pleased, then pulled herself together. There was still a case to be made.

'To business, then,' she said. 'But first I must ask you to say nothing of this meeting to Soapy . . .'

He laughed easily.

'Soapy? Why should I talk to him?'

'He is your solicitor. He'd fire me if he knew.'

'Mum's the word,' he told her.

'This meeting, here, is strictly against procedure. I'm being totally unprofessional.'

'Will I get you into trouble?' he asked, suddenly anxious. 'I'll go, of course. Strike today off the record.'

'Don't go,' she said quickly. She had made the decision now. 'It's just that . . . I'm putting myself in your hands . . .'

It was perhaps stupid to tell him that he had such power, but it was after all in his interests that she was risking her professional name.

'All right,' he said. 'But this meeting has not happened. Right? We're in each other's hands, it seems to me.'

'I just wanted to get some things about the case straight in my mind,' she went on, giving words to feelings that she hadn't yet properly expressed to anyone. 'There are things that puzzle me, things happening that I can't explain. It seems that somebody wants to frighten me. Or I've got something somebody wants. I'm confused, to tell you the truth. Is it to do with you or is it to do with me? That's why I wanted to see you here. I can ask you things that maybe you wouldn't want to say in front of your solicitor. I don't mean bad things. What I mean is . . .'

'What I mean is,' he said, 'is that I want to make love to you. I've thought about nothing else since I first saw you.'

'I thought you said it was Meursault you dreamt of in prison?' she said, falling back on argument, the barrister's stock in trade.

'Just you. Though Meursault did come into it – and still does.'

He opened his briefcase and showed her the bottle. She found a corkscrew and they poured the wine, drinking without speaking, looking at each other. Then she found herself doing something that she knew to be madness, and yet seemed absolutely inevitable.

She led him to the bedroom and he undressed her, kissing her through and under her clothes, kissing her clothes off, with a passionate tenderness that was surprising in a man. When she was naked, he licked at her neck and breasts as though they were delectable canapés before a feast and then, sliding his head down her stomach, he tasted her as though she were some rare ambrosial banquet.

This is not happening to me, she thought, this is happening to a changeling body because mine never felt like this. My body, the legal body, was taken off with the clothes.

He entered her neither boldly nor diffidently but with the possessive assurance of a hero at a homecoming, and she came with such force that all the breath was knocked out of her and she lay there gasping like a guppy.

The shocking, the irresistible strength of reality, gave her a momentary conviction. That's it, then, she thought, finish with the law when this case is over, hand back the wig and gown, end the charade, *finita la commedia.*

Later they lay in bed and drank Meursault which they agreed was better when not too cold. But the wine and the sex, normally so good at bolstering fortitude either jointly or severally, today seemed to have the reverse effect. She looked around at her familiar room, at her life which had seemed so ordered, at her things – her hair brushes with the initials in silver on them, the little Goanese ivory statue of Jesus treading on a serpent that she had bought at an antique shop for her mother when she was twelve – all these seemed to say, you're mad, what the hell are you doing, life is hard out there. She felt the obligations, the habits of her existence pressing in upon her. She looked at this man in bed with her. She thought of Alan.

'Oh my God,' she said. 'What have I done?'

'You've done well,' Morbey said. 'The girl done well.'

'I've done ill. I've deceived him.'

'You never pretended to him that you hadn't slept with me.'

'Of course not.'

'Then you mean you *will* deceive him.'

'I must get up,' she said. 'I must be mad.'

She started to put on her clothes. Suddenly she was angry.

'Who are you?' she asked. 'What do you want? What is it you want of me? I was more or less engaged to Alan. God, what a shit I am.'

'When a woman puts on her clothes it's like wiping out a drawing with a Magnadoodle,' he said. 'Bed's forgotten, on with the show.'

'Same for a man, isn't it?' she said crossly, hating herself.

'Strangely enough, it isn't. We tend to be more transparent. Anyone can see we've been to bed.'

'Well for God's sake get them on anyway,' she said. 'We'll go downstairs, go through your story, I'll take some notes, and then . . .'

'Then?' he asked, buttoning his shirt.

'Then we'll say no more about it,' she said, nannyishly.

Tears before bedtime were one thing; tears after bed were another.

He followed her to the living-room and sat down in an armchair opposite her. Strange, to be sitting there like strangers while he smelt of her, she thought, and while he still trickled inside her. She crossed her legs and reached for her notebook.

'Now,' she said, 'I want the whole story.'

'It was a wet evening,' he began.

In spite of her anger with herself, she was impressed by the way he did not try to apologize or excuse his behaviour. His strategy was more like the mariner's – wait, and it will blow itself out – though she doubted in this case whether the blowing-out might not come too late for him and whether she might not get blown out herself – right out of her job, out of her life.

'Before all that,' she said, 'what are you? I know when you were born, but where? What sort of life have you had? What kind of electronic engineering do you do? What were you drinking in the wine bar? Tell me.'

It was mostly written down on the brief but she wanted to hear him explain himself, to establish her authority once more, put on her professional clothes.

He looked at her as though he understood exactly what she was doing, but answered her evenly, without irritation.

'I was born in the east,' he began.

'China? Singapore?'

He laughed. Rather nice of him, she thought, under the circumstances.

'The East End,' he said. 'My mother was Jewish – her parents never forgave her – my father was a Geordie. I was a bastard, of course. I have a bastard brother. I went to the local school where I turned out to be good at mathematics, so they sent me to Leyton Grammar on a grant. Then I went to London University, and I never went out of this country, hardly out of London, till I was eighteen. I graduated with a First in Maths, and got a job with a company in Leicester called "Virtuality" where I worked on games. I married and got divorced.'

'Games?'

'You know. Interactive games, first for kids, then for adults too.'

It was an area she knew little about, except that every family now seemed to own one of these machines with their new lightweight headsets. She was told they even allowed you to taste and smell, if that was your game . . .

'Artificial intelligence, that's what I was into,' he continued.

'Interesting things going on,' she said. 'So I hear.'

'Bloody amazing. You can even have an interview with someone you've never met. The manpower services are all over it.'

She crossed her legs again. She was going to have to go upstairs to the bathroom. The whole situation seemed absurd, unreal, like a childhood embarrassment when you just wanted to laugh.

'That's why I was up there in Clapham High Street that night. The night I was supposed to have done it. I was up in the High Street.'

'For manpower services?' she asked stupidly.

'No, no. For a chip.'

She had enough of her wits about her to ask the important question: 'Did you get a receipt for the chip?'

'I'm sure I would've done.'

'Excuse me one moment,' she said.

She thought about the chip while she washed and changed her pants. She was half-inclined to ask him about the thing she'd found in the Clapham flat. She could show it to him now. But something prompted her to keep her counsel. If he was holding something back, if the thing really were a chip, if he had anything at all to do with it, it might help her to surprise him with the information when she knew for certain what it was. What if he had in fact dropped it when he was in the flat, before he killed the boy . . . ? No, no. She was sure beyond any doubt that he had not done that. She put it from her mind and shut the door as her grandmother used to do with the cat she hadn't wanted to trip up on.

When Heather came down he was reading her notes. He did not put them aside guiltily, but laid them on his lap as he looked up at her. Again, it was a point in his favour. Even so, the chip, so insignificant-looking, so powerful, seemed to have come between them.

'Feeling better now?' he asked.

'Those are my notes,' she said. 'Not for reading.'

'They're about me, aren't they?'

He handed them back to her with a smile.

'So you're into artificial intelligence,' she said. 'A clever man.'

'Just a mathematician,' he corrected her. 'If I were clever, I wouldn't be in trouble, would I?'

'A lot of clever people have got into trouble,' she told him. 'Look at Oscar Wilde.'

'I'm not sure I find that comforting,' he said.

'Oddly enough,' she told him, 'I think I'm in trouble too. I have the feeling something's going on, and yet every time I get close to it, it changes shape. Do you know that feeling?'

He gave her the most extraordinary look, compounded of affection, sorrow, concern and apology. It worried her.

'I should like to know the truth,' she told him. 'I can't help you if you tell me lies.'

'The truth is,' he said at last, 'I can't tell you.'

She shut her notebook with a terminal snap.

'In that case, I shall waste no more time,' she said. 'I do have other briefs, you know.'

'You have to,' he said.

'Have to?' She was incredulous.

'You have to,' he repeated.

There was no alternative.

'I don't understand.'

'There's something going on,' he said, as though he'd told her too much.

'And you're involved in it?'

'I'm just a small part of it,' he said, 'a creature. Someone else pulls strings. No one knows who.'

'I don't believe that. You're so . . . yourself . . .'

'No man is an island,' he said. 'Not in these islands anyway. I have to do what I'm told. Also, I believe in it, funnily enough.'

'It?'

She had a growing sense of being caught in some dark matter. And now, she thought, we're coming to the heart of it. Surely there had to be some reason for the things that had been plaguing her – beyond simple paranoia which had been her first explanation (it would be Alan's). Comforting if there were; at least dark matter can be shared; of course it depended how dark . . .

Her mother used to warn her about diving into Bobs Wood's pool on Boar's Hill. There was weed at the bottom of the pool, or the arms of doomed spirits – she had been at an impressionable age – which it was said had drowned a boy. Now she too was out of her depth, and struggling.

Still, the great rule with barristers is: never to be seen to struggle. If she must drown, she must drown quietly.

'It?' she repeated.

'Ah, that is the question. Can't answer, I'm afraid. Don't even know.'

She sighed with frustration.

'I'm going to have to give your case up,' she said.

Not, of course, that she could – or would – short of leaving the law.

'Look,' he said. 'I can't tell you more. It'd be dangerous for you if I did. It's dangerous enough already. I shouldn't be here – not just because of you but because of me. If they thought I was passing on information, you'd be for it. Not just phone calls but . . .'

'Do you know who's been calling me, then?'

'Calls?' He looked at her strangely, almost – she thought – apologetically again.

She told him about the obscenities in the night.

'Bastards,' he said.

'Do you know?'

He shook his head.

'We don't know what goes on. The whole thing's closed.'

'Closed? You mean you have cells? Like communists or terrorists? That's what terrorists have – cells. And communists . . . cells.'

'We're not terrorists, or communists for that matter,' he said.

'What are you then?'

'Look, you have to help me.'

It wasn't an instruction, it was a plea.

She opened her book and looked at the notes again.

'So the account you gave the police, and the one you repeated yesterday in chambers is true?' she asked.

He paused. She knew his story was false, and he knew she knew it, but he himself was like the ram stuck in a fence he'd talked about when she first interviewed him. The more he struggled, the deeper he was in.

'"What is truth?" said jesting Pilate,' he said at length.

She snapped.

'For God's sake,' she shouted. 'True or false?'

'True enough,' he said.

He looked as though the stuffing had been knocked out of him, and her pity almost overwhelmed her better feelings, but there was no more to be learnt from him now. If he wasn't going to be straight with her, she certainly wasn't going to tell him about the chip even if he was an electronics man.

'I suppose you feel pleased with yourself?' she said, getting up.

'Pleased?'

'You got me into bed and you've told me nothing.'

'I . . .'

But she almost pushed him out into the hall. His acipitrine looks, dark and proud, seemed to have undergone a sea-change. He looked young again, as he must have done at school when he was in trouble, more like a bedraggled blackbird than a hawk.

'You will still act for me?' he asked. 'I'm counting on you, not Sir Wotsisname.'

'When we meet from now on, it'll be at chambers,' she told him.

'Thank you, Heather.'

'Don't thank me, thank Sir Perry. He's your counsel, so you'd better learn his name. Here . . . your coat . . .'

He was almost leaving without it.

'Thanks,' he said. 'And Heather . . .'

'Yes?'

'You didn't find anything up there – in Clapham, I mean.'

'Find?'

'Anything?'

'Of course not.'

There, the lie was told. Her first lie to him. One lie deserved another. She had a question for him in her turn.

'Do you have a head for heights?'

'Heights?'

She saw his knuckles clench.

'Yes; like, er, did you as a boy climb trees? Or go mountaineering?'

'Trees? Where's all this leading?'

'Did you?'

'No. As a matter of fact, it's a weakness. I have vertigo. Is that all?'

His admission of weakness made him angry, and her relieved. He would never have locked a door from the inside and gone shinning down a drainpipe – unless he were a very good liar. Would he? Was he?

As he walked down the stairs, Mr Hernandez came out. He must be permanently stationed at his spy-hole.

'Hey!'

'Yes?'

'That not your boyfriend.'

'No.'

'You like other men? Me maybe?'

'Listen, Mr Hernandez. Do you know what fuck off means?'

'Fuck off?'

The diplomat pondered, furrowing his brow, and produced a grubby pocket South American phrase book.

'Ah,' he said at last after much fingering, 'I understand. You have the women issue. Tomorrow I call again and maybe it will be fuck on.'

Twenty-four

That night she had another dream, knowing at once, as one sometimes does, that what was about to happen was both inexplicable and alarming.

She saw a man who was half familiar, and whose thoughts in some strange way she could read. It was almost as though she were part of him. He was huddled in the liquid darkness against the wall of an old walkway above a crumbling sewer. Below him, mingling with the syncopated drip-DRIP-dripdrip from the roof, came the sound of flowing water.

She knew where he was. This was the old Tyburn stream, one of the rivers of London, turned by the Victorians into a cloaca maxima. The smell was sour and rancid, street rubbish and dog shit, but the man was past caring, almost beyond sensation. Every now and then he gave a retching sound that seemed to tear at his guts, but he had almost lost the pain of that too, for it was cold down here, tomb-cold, cold beyond hope of midsummer morning or St Paul's Epistle to the Corinthians. Even the fires of hell would sputter down here.

Clammy, fungoid, slime-coated, the crumbling tunnels ran in all directions. Sometimes there would come the sound of falling brickwork. They had never been made for so many people, so many new kinds of filth. It was a wonder they had held up for so long.

The man waited at this foul crossroads, hunched in his misery, seemingly in the last throes of exhaustion.

Suddenly he sat bolt upright as though something had

alerted him. A faint scraping sound coming from far away down the network of tunnels to his left, as though someone or something was feeling the wall in stealthy pursuit. The buggers weren't going to let him get away, no, not they. But he'd give them a run for their money.

Coughing quietly as he ran, he set off again, splashing through the stinking glistening darkness towards he didn't know where, his goal he didn't know what. He had no other thought than escape . . .

Twenty-five

The dream was so vivid that when she woke up, gasping, she instinctively looked around for the glistening walls, but finding none, she at length recovered herself and lay wondering what kind of cold and terrifying vision she had experienced. Who was this half-familiar man? What was this sinister pursuit?

It was almost morning. She dozed a little and then, unable to sleep, got up and worked on some case notes. Every now and then her mind returned to the inexplicable (and yet decipherable, if she only knew how) images of the night.

The remainder of her week passed routinely enough. She had a couple of minor cases, a dangerous driving for which she secured an acquittal, and a plea of guilty for which she was again duly grateful. After that, as Arthur had warned her, there seemed to be something of a lull; so Friday saw her at home again, and on Friday morning the telephone rang. It was Mei Noon from Trinity saying she was in London for the day. She understood Heather wanted something looked at. She might be a Noon from Hong Kong but she sounded as English as Stanford in the Vale or Hinton in the Hedges, with an attractive, quiet rather breathless voice.

'Fine,' Heather told her, 'come round as soon as you like.'

She spent the next half-hour clearing up more books and thinking of Christopher and his case once more as she did so. How did she feel about him now? No, better to leave that. What had he been doing in Clapham? Had he really been buying a chip? He seemed vague about it, about the receipt. It was a weak link in his story. He agreed that he had been in the wine bar, but he had left as soon as he saw what sort of place it was, so he said. It was an unlikely tale, knowing him. He would have known what sort of place it was a mile away. The prosecution would have a field day with it, making out that he was looking for trouble, a habitué of such establishments, he had been seen chatting to the murder victim, drinking with him, simply waiting for the moment to gratify his dark impulses . . .

She knew that he wasn't like that, could never have been; that under his sardonic exterior nested an odd blackbird; but how could she prove it if he wasn't willing to trust her with the truth? She would have to speak to Perry about it. Perhaps he could persuade the odd bird to sing . . .

The doorbell rang, delicately this time. Strange, she thought, I hadn't considered it an expressive instrument; but when she opened the door there was a Chinese girl of extraordinary grace and beauty standing there who had somehow coaxed a quiet note from the thing. She could hear already the scrambling noise of the chain on the diplomat's door (did he never go to work?), so she quickly ushered the girl inside.

'Come in. Mei Noon, isn't it? It's so good of you to take the trouble.'

The girl smiled. It was as if she had some secret gift of happiness that was immediately captivating.

'It's no trouble,' she said. 'Dr James is a wonderful man. Anything I can do for a friend of his . . . He helped me come over here, you know.'

'I didn't know that. Oh, please sit down.'

Heather indicated the sofa and the girl perched elegantly on its edge. She was wearing a simple blouse and skirt but they might have been a gold-encrusted silken cheong-sam for the finesse with which they were worn.

'Yes,' she said. 'My family were very poor. Dr James met me when I was at university over there and took an interest . . .'

I bet he did, thought Heather, and I don't blame him. But there was such a simplicity and innocence about the girl that you couldn't resent her beauty. Her very name expressed warmth and freshness. She was pearl-like; her secret places, you would think, must be like the heart of a rose, distilling only the quintessence of a dew.

'I believe you're an expert on computers,' she said.

'More artificial intelligence,' the girl replied. 'I am a mathematician.'

You too, thought Heather.

'And you're taking a doctorate in electronic engineering?'

'That's right. Sorry to be so boring. Arts subjects are always more fun, I think.'

The girl got up and walked to the window, gazing down the hill past the big wedding-cake houses towards Kensington High Street. The builders opposite whistled and blew kisses.

'Anything has to be better than the law,' Heather smiled. 'Thank God I read history when I was up. Where did you learn to speak such brilliant English. I mean, your accent is . . . pure Oxford.'

The girl laughed.

'Where else but the BBC World Service,' she said. 'One thing I am good at is imitation. I used to imitate my brothers when I was little. Then I learnt to imitate the newsreaders. It made me very popular at school. They used to fall about. But here nobody falls about. They think I am Home Counties.'

Heather felt she could trust this girl totally.

'I've got something I'd like . . . looked at,' she said.

'What is it?'

'A chip. At least I think it is.'

'May I see?'

Heather went to the fridge and took it out of the butter dish.

'Ever seen anything like that?' she asked.

Mei Noon turned it over several times, looking faintly puzzled.

'It is very unusual,' she said slowly. 'It's obviously not a commercial chip. If you ask me, this is something very new. I believe that there are one or two small firms producing this kind of thing to carry the latest games. To be honest with you, I don't think I'm going to be able to help. Rather like historians, we all have our particular areas of study and frankly this isn't mine. I know Dr James always thinks I can solve everything. It's only because he understands nothing . . . in terms of computers only, I hasten to add.'

She rose to go.

'I wish I could be of more help,' she said. 'But it's very nice to meet you.'

'I'm sorry I've wasted your time,' Heather told her.

Mei Noon still seemed fascinated by the chip, examining it for a last time by the window and shaking her head.

'Anyway, it's been extremely pleasant to meet you,' she said. 'That was no waste.'

Her eye fell on one of the books Heather had been about to put back on the shelf.

'Oh look,' she exclaimed. 'That life of Babbage, the Victorian computer man. You've read it, I suppose.'

'Well, no, I haven't actually. I was given it by the publisher years ago.'

'I've been meaning to read it. It's meant to be brilliant.'

'Here,' said Heather, 'you have it.'

'I couldn't possibly.'

'I mean it. It'll mean more to you than it does to me.'

'That's really kind of you. I'll bring it back.'

'Come and see me again – but keep the book. Okay?'

The Chinese girl put the book in her bag and, rather unexpectedly, kissed her. Heather felt a quite extraordinary flutter of love for her. How could anything so beautiful survive?

Just at the door, Mei Noon stopped and struck her palm against her head in mock horror.

'I've put your chip in my bag along with the book,' she said. 'You must think I'm quite mad. Crazy electronics brain.'

Heather watched as she rifled through the hold-all.

'Here it is. I'm so sorry. You didn't realize you were harbouring a kleptomaniac.'

'Nice kleptomaniac,' said Heather. 'Come and see me again.'

This time it was she that gave the kiss. The touch of her skin was impossibly soft and smooth. Somehow she seemed to Heather incredibly vulnerable in her beauty as though entropy would work overtime to break her in pieces.

Heather watched her leave the block and walk down the street. She was tall for a Chinese girl, with exquisite legs. But then she would have, wouldn't she? As if sensing the beam of her thought Mei Noon looked up and waved. Heather waved back. Across the street, a curtain twitched, builders yodelled.

The strange vibration started up again, fuzzing the glasses in the cupboard, dancing the dust the Hoover hadn't reached at the skirting board's edge. Too many tunnels, Heather thought, as she turned from the window. There were bound to be complaints. Whether it was the Millennium Line – five years late, of course – or still more fibre-optic cables for the new VR sets that were flooding the market or cracks widening in City confidence, it was hard to say and even if one could, and did, would one ever really know what was going on?

Twenty-six

She had the strange subterranean dream again that night, though it seemed to start at another place, another time.

She was still in the sewers, but she now knew more about the man who was being followed. He had been a bouncer in a South London night-club which was a front for a drug racket. He had beaten up people who owed money, poofters and junkies – it was sometimes all three rolled into one – until one day he had gone too far.

Then it was like a dream of its own, shot through with pain, anger and the frustration and deprivation of imprisonment; but what he did remember, clearly, were the dark pleasures that came after, when the man showed him the machine.

It wasn't his fault that the thing had broken down. She knew that. It just stopped. All he knew was that, when it did, he suddenly realized he wanted to get away. Anything – pain, hunger, filth or terror, or all of them together – was better than being hooked on to it. He had almost lost who he was. So he had hit the white-coated man who came with the pabulum – that's what he called it, a food with everything you needed, tasting of whatever you wanted it to taste of.

He had hit him hard, over the head, put on his jacket, stolen the token from the machine – he might want to look at it again some day – but he lost it somewhere, didn't he?

Taking advantage of some confusion at the main gate, where the guards were in process of changing (the only guards in the place, just about), he was out before they checked the pass against his face.

They realized soon enough, though. He hadn't expected them to be so quick. The thing was, he found it difficult at first to tell real life from the one they had given him inside, where they had provided all the things he liked, only better. Torturing and killing drag queens and poofters was one of them. And he had been unlucky enough – or was it more than bad luck, had he known the place before? – to find himself in that place of all places where he had started the game once more – just like the other game – the pretend flirt and the sudden shock, the imploring and the screaming, the kicking and the twitching – only messier afterwards . . .

That game had been a mistake because it was big news. He might as well have left his calling card for them. And now they were after him in earnest, because the Commissioner of Police and the Home Secretary and God Almighty wanted this one cleared up – there had been too much violent crime in London – the public mood was turning ugly . . .

Even so, he might have got away with it if only he could have had a wash and grown a decent beard and had a nose job or a hair dye. And then that bloke had spotted him on the Embankment.

After that it had been like this, dodging and weaving – underpasses, warehouses, foreshores, crowded tube stations, cardboard cities and finally sewers – you couldn't get lower. Lucky the white-coat had had a small torch in his pocket with one of the new hi-life batteries. He used it as little as possible but he'd be done for without it, although there was sometimes light of sorts coming from gratings far above . . .

He stopped and listened, and Heather listened with him as if she were part of him and yet still herself.

There was no sound save for the variations of drip-drip from the roof. He sat on the rusted ring of an iron ladder and rested his head in his hands, oblivious of the water that fell onto his jet-dark hair.

Then the sound behind him started again . . .

Heather woke to an opalescent early dawn, her ears still tuned to the noises of pursuit, but all she could hear was the chirping of birds in the garden; and slowly all the intricate sharpness of the nightmare's detail – like gossamer in the wind – began to fall apart.

She had more pressing things to worry about.

Twenty-seven

On Monday, Arthur's eyes were twinkling like a hole she had once seen in a Norwegian glacier, ice blue and bitter cold.

'Ah, Heather,' he said. 'Come in for a tea and a biscuit?'

'You know as well as I do why I've come, Arthur.'

The man was not in the least discomfited. How sleek he was, how condescending! Rumour had it that he had an expensive habit. Surely those red veins around his cheeks were getting redder? Was the nose a little too runny?

'Ah yes, to be sure. Our schedule for Sir Perry. Got it all tied up?'

'Pretty well.'

She wasn't going to admit that there were aspects of the case that troubled her, not to Arthur; to Sir Perry perhaps, bloody well certainly in fact. After all, he was the silk, he was going to have to carry the can.

'Sir Perry will see you now.'

His secretary, Miss Rodber, was a stern woman of whom even Arthur was wary. Rumour had it that she had been a school matron, but had been sacked for being too rigorous. For Sir Perry, of course, she could not do enough nor for George either, come to that. Those were her favourites. Heather was not on the list.

'Miss Simple to see you, Sir Peregrine.'

It was her pleasure to pronounce Heather's surname in that way. Heather thought it might be the only pleasure she ever had.

The great man rose to his feet as she entered. Manners were part of his weaponry.

'Well, well, this is a pleasure. A pretty woman among all this dust. What a relief! And not just a pretty woman, Heather. We never forget that. I hear you've been devilling away. How's it coming along?'

'I'll let you have the complete schedule next week, if I may.'

'Next week?'

The fine features eased themselves into a slight frown.

'Any particular reason?'

'Well . . . there are one or two things I'm not quite happy about.'

Sir Perry sat down and put his hands together as if about to pray.

'Not happy?' he enquired, raising an eyebrow (another well-modulated gesture, legendary in court).

'Our client's story bothers me,' she said.

'Simple enough, I should have thought,' said Sir Perry. 'He says it's a case of mistaken identity. He went into the wrong bar at the wrong time after buying electronic equipment. There are no fingerprints. Any further evidence is purely circumstantial.'

It seemed that Sir Perry, for all his elegance, had been doing some homework of his own.

'It's not quite as simple as that,' she said.

'Not simple? It is surely our business to make it simple.'

'The truth is simple, Sir Perry, but getting at the truth is another matter.'

'"On a huge hill, cragged and steep, Truth stands and he who will reach her, about must and about must go . . ."' quoted Sir Perry, rather surprisingly.

'That puts it very well,' she said. 'The fact is, the prosecution will make a lot of the fact that the shops had closed an hour earlier and that he was still around.'

'He could have been taking a stroll,' said Sir Perry, 'a pleasant evening, Battersea . . . or was it Clapham?'

'Clapham.'

It was doubtful whether Sir Perry had ever been to Battersea or Clapham or, having gone, would ever go again.

'It was raining,' she said.

'Well, then . . . there could be plenty of other reasons. You must dig one out.'

'I'll certainly try. But there's another thing . . .'

'Another thing?'

'He's really not the sort of person who would go into a bar like that. Or, if he did, he'd look in and look out again. And yet, by his own admission, he bought a drink. He was seen buying a drink. Someone says they saw him buying a drink. What was he doing? And what was he doing until eight thirty next morning when he was seen in Chelsea?'

'I think you're worrying too much,' said Sir Perry. 'I know this is important to you – it's important to all of us – but it really does seem quite simple to me. Ask the man again.'

'He seems curiously disinclined to tell me the full story.'

'I see . . .'

Sir Perry put his fingers together as though playing Here is the Church and Here is the Steeple.

'You don't think,' he continued. 'You don't think it might be your . . . over-zealous questioning?'

'I don't think so. No.'

'Or the fact that you're a woman?'

So there it was, out in the open, Arthur's little prejudice passed on to the boss. Or had it been there all along?

'Not at all,' she replied hotly. 'I think he particularly likes women.'

'Ohh.'

Sir Perry drew his fine brows together now and looked contemplative.

'Do you think he particularly likes *you*?'

She had fallen into that one.

'Not me particularly, no. A woman can tell if a man likes women. He's just a very attractive man.'

'And attracted, isn't that what you're saying?'

'Yes, I daresay, in a way . . .'

'Well, if he wasn't attracted to you he was showing it in a very odd way because Arthur tells me he saw him holding your hand.'

Sir Perry had wound her in and was now delivering his famous *coup de grâce*. She felt a blush rising from her neck upwards. Down, you wanton . . .

'That was a purely social gesture,' she said indignantly.

'Even so, we don't want our clients paddling palms and pinching fingers, do we? Bad for business, bad for the name. Stick to the facts, Heather, and don't worry too much about hypothesis. Soapy's very relaxed. Schedule next week, then. When's the trial? Do we know?'

'Not sooner than a month, Sir Perry. Around the end of April was the nearest I could get from them.'

'Excellent, a spring trial, get the old sap rising, eh? Just pass me that diary, would you?'

She reached across and handed him his leather-bound day-book, heavy as a church Bible.

'Wait a minute . . . I see I've a series of meetings with the Head of the Justice Department, over from the States, and our Inspector of Prisons, and others of the great and good . . . oh dear, we can't cancel them. Can't be helped. We'll just have to busk it, won't we? Throw you in at the deep end!'

'Yes, Sir Perry.'

She rather felt she was falling into the deep end already. The question was, was there any water in the pool?

'And watch out for the social gestures, won't you?'

'Yes, Sir Perry.'

Twenty-eight

As she walked home she came across a group of boys aged, she supposed, between ten and fourteen. They were breaking into a Jaguar.

Had they been older she might have walked on and telephoned the police from her flat, but they were so young she felt no immediate threat. They gave no sign of slackening in their endeavours as she approached.

'Hey,' she said. 'Stop that.'

'You what?'

She realized, too late, that two of the youths at the back were rather large for their age. The oldest of them – an oaf with the first fuzz of puberty hanging like a grubby swag over the horror-chamber of his too-large, half-open mouth – turned his gaze upon her with a kind of truculent incredulity.

'You what?' he asked again.

'You heard me,' she said, mustering authority, but beginning to wish she hadn't raised the matter.

'You fucking what?'

Heather sighed.

'I said stop that.'

'That's what I thought you said.'

'Well why not stop it then?'

'Oooze gonna make us?'

She tried an appeal to reason.

'You're doing this in the full sight of the street. People could be ringing the police already. Isn't that rather silly as well as wrong?'

The other boys guffawed at the word 'wrong' and repeated it idiotically among themselves, imitating her voice in falsetto. The eldest boy spat.

'Police? They don't bovver wiv us. We're juveniles, see? They can't touch us. But talkin' of touch . . . Nice tits you got.'

The other boys took up the refrain.

'Nice tits. Show us yer tits, then. Nuffin' wrong wiv 'er tits . . .'

They started to move towards her and she backed away, almost falling over the sloping bonnet of the car. She couldn't believe this. This was Kensington. Black-nailed hands fumbled towards her, a wrist brushed her breast. Just at that moment, however, the owner of the car, a large American who looked like an international banker, emerged from his door and shouted at them.

'An' fuck you, too, you fucking cunt, we'll fucking fuck you,' they yelled as they scattered like feral dogs confronted by a bear.

The American turned to her.

'They use the four-letter word for emphasis because they lack vocabulary,' he explained.

She thanked him warmly, not specifying whether it was for his insight or for his timely appearance. He gave a large, hopeless gesture, covering the country.

'It's like an army of occupation has just retreated,' he said. 'Like Britain after the Romans left, or Italy after the Germans. My father was there . . .'

'I'm sorry,' she told him, apologizing for her country, a thing one did rather often these days.

'There's no law any more,' he continued. 'So the night-creatures feel free to come out by day. Are you all right?'

'I'm fine,' she said. 'They were trying to break into your car. I hope it's all right.'

'I'll put it in the garage,' he told her. 'That's the third time this year. What are these children? Where do they come from? Where are they going? What happened to childhood here? This is Lewis Carroll's country.'

'They're universal wolf-cubs,' she said.

'Ah, I know that one.'

In the distance, far down the hill, the children were breaking into a Range Rover.

She could feel, suddenly, the tremor again, sliding the plates in the underground scullery.

'I'd better be on my way,' she said.

'They learnt it from us,' the American told her with his curiously baffled expression, 'but by God they're doing it even better than we did.'

Twenty-nine

She told Alan about the boys, and the episode was immediately drafted into the context of the series.

'"A sense of justice is the pillar that upholds the fabric of society. If it is removed, the great fabric of human society must in a moment crumble in atoms . . ." That's Adam Smith,' said Alan. 'But the trouble is, schools nowadays don't teach morality, which is the cornerstone of a sense of justice. They teach Discovery and Learn as you Like. Religion and learning taught people to look beyond themselves. Now people look at themselves . . . Caliban in the mirror . . . They don't like what they see, it makes them unhappy, but they're stuck with it . . . so they break the mirror and anything else they can find. Every tuppenny ha'penny little shrink is telling people to assert themselves, but nobody is teaching them how to think.'

She could tell Alan wasn't really speaking to her again but to unseen lenses which zoomed and glinted from every corner of her flat. He had been on tour with an Inspector of Schools, one of the old school as it turned out. The man had been despairing.

'The teachers' heads are filled with evil notions that are in plain contradiction to common sense and the nature of childhood. Where do they get these idiocies? The so-called education departments of the so-called universities where, it seems, the devil has taken root. It's as if they wanted to drive a deeper and deeper wedge between the haves and have nots. They don't even teach children to read the sensible way, phonetically. They regard it as bourgeois. It's like some kind of biblical prophecy . . . They grin like a dog and run about the city . . . and all the daughters of music shall be brought low . . .'

'Pitching it a bit strong, isn't it?' said Heather when Alan told her.

'He didn't think so. Anyway, what have you been doing?'

Heather looked at him. He couldn't possibly know that she had been unfaithful. She had changed the sheets, erased every vestige of Christopher from herself and from the flat, hoovered for black hairs, sprayed eau de toilette back and forth, and yet she still had this feeling that her infidelity shouted aloud.

'Oh, you know,' she said. 'Getting this case together, interviewing the accused, seeing my head of chambers . . . It rather looks as if I'm going to be doing rather more than a junior should at this trial. Sir Perry has a conference of bigwigs. But of course he'll be there to take the credit.'

'Or not,' said Alan.

'Exactly. If we lose he'll pass it off as his junior's mistake. He'll be nowhere around. I sometimes get the feeling that he actually wants to lose.'

'Rubbish,' said Alan. 'I've never met a barrister yet who wanted to lose.'

'It can happen,' she told him. 'Barristers have been known to be nobbled.'

'Not silks,' he said, 'surely?'

It was Tuesday, one of the nights they usually met, and she was being especially nice to him, to make up for her shameful indiscretion. She did like him, even though he didn't make her gasp like a guppy when he made love to her – which she didn't really want him to do but she couldn't refuse.

Now they were in her living-room with the curtains drawn listening to the classic recording of Handel's music for *Alceste*, played by the Academy of Ancient Music and sung angelically by Emma Kirkby.

'"Gentle Morpheus, God of Night . . .",' said Alan. 'The hard stuff, morphine and its derivative, has a rather different image these days. But this is a good disc. Where did you get it?'

'I just happened on it. No, I heard it on Radio 3. I had to have it.'

She squeezed his hand and they reclined in an approximation of happiness.

'Would you do something for me?' she asked.

The mention of the disc had reminded her of the chip she had put in the fridge again after Mei Noon's visit.

'Within reason,' he said.

It was one of the things she disliked about him – his reluctance to commit himself. No, she mustn't say dislike. She must be nice about him. She must stay well disposed towards him. What was it he used to say about his ex-wife? 'In marriage, you take on a permanent residential critic – only your best is taken for granted and your worst is never forgiven.' She mustn't be a critic or disturb any more the fragile span on which her life rested. Her moon was in a waning phase, doubtless it would wax in due course; but until then she must see the other person's point of view, and decision was to be avoided.

'Within reason . . . If you'll do something for me . . .' he continued.

Oh, oh.

'What's that?'

She took care not to betray by so much as an ear quiver her instinct that what would come would be untoward.

'You first,' he said.

'I've got something I'd like you to get analysed for me. You must know people in the advanced computer business . . . people you can trust . . .' she told him.

She had finally decided to confide in him; he was after all the person she knew best.

'I do . . . Where is this thing?'

She went out and returned with the chip. He examined it intently.

'Where did you get hold of this?' he asked.

She did not reply directly; something was urging discretion on her. It was only an absence of any more ideas that had made her turn to him. She still had doubts about his ability to keep a confidence. Still, needs must. The devil was driving.

'It might be evidence,' she said. 'On the other hand, it might be anything.'

'A sophisticated anything,' he said. 'I've only once seen anything like this and that was at a trade fair in Birmingham. It carried the instructions for a rather advanced new flight simulator. Odd, eh? Anyway, I'll get it looked at for you.'

'Discreet, please, Alan. If it's evidence, it could be important.'

'Very discreet. And talking of evidence, what about me interviewing your client?'

'No!'

The word was out of her mouth before she knew it, and Alan pounced forensically.

'No?' he asked. 'Just like that? You haven't got the hots for him, have you?'

'Of course not.'

She could feel the blush starting, and jumped to her feet – to fetch wine from the kitchen, to warm up the oven, anything to hide the tell-tale red.

'Just as well he's in prison or I might be worried.'

Oh God, what did she say now? Tell him the truth – the one that stands on a huge hill? Of course not.

'Of course not,' she said. 'Now tell me what you wanted.'

'Nothing so mysterious, I'm afraid. I've said we'd go down to Mother's on Sunday for lunch again.'

'Do I have to go?'

'She particularly asked. And now I'm particularly asking you.'

She just wants someone to bully, she thought, she's tired of poor old Daddy; it's no contest. But I shall be sick if I have to eat crème brûlée.

'I shall be sick if I have to eat crème brûlée,' she said.

'I'll ask for something else. Syllabub's another of her specials.'

The syllabub was if anything even worse, picking up the smell of fridge like a retriever. She remembered her resolve to be specially nice to him; even so, this was pushing it a bit.

At that moment the telephone rang.

'Saved by the bell,' she smiled.

It was her old tutor from Oxford, and what he had to say wiped the smile off her face in no time.

'Hullo, it's Dr James here.'

'Oh yes, I meant to call, thank you for sending Mei Noon. She was wonderful. She said she was no use, unfortunately, but she was really nice . . .'

'She's dead.'

He said it so flatly, so baldly, that she did not take it in.

'No, no. She can't be. There must be some mistake. She came to see me.'

'She was killed the night before last. Apparently she disturbed a burglar in her flat . . . Look here, I'm sorry to have to tell you like this. You hardly knew her, of course, but I thought you would want to know. We're all absolutely devastated here. She was a lovely person.'

Heather thought he might have been crying.

'Oh my God,' she said. 'A burglar? Why? In Oxford?'

'Oh Oxford's not the problem. The problem's Cowley. Twenty thousand jobs lost with the motor works closing, and nothing for most of them to do, nothing for the kids to look forward to. So they joy-ride and they thieve and they fight and they take drugs which the pushers are only too happy to supply, and then they have to thieve some more to finance the habit. The circle's so vicious it gives circles a bad name.'

'Why did he have to kill her?' asked Heather.

'And not just kill her, Heather. She was raped and tortured . . . would you believe that . . . in Oxford?'

Heather sat down with the telephone in her hand, suddenly weak. Alan was looking at her with concern tinged with journalistic prurience.

'What did they steal?' she asked.

'That's the odd thing. Nothing, but it seems they must have thought she had money or something.'

Heather couldn't believe what she was hearing. Could it be that someone knew Mei Noon might have had the chip? Clearly the thought hadn't struck Dr James in his grief. She thought it might be better not to raise it.

How strange that she should have had that premonition of the beautiful Mei's destructibility! That the girl should be tortured too . . . it was almost beyond belief.

'Who could do such a thing?' she said aloud.

'It is the abomination of desolation,' said Dr James. 'The funeral will be on Sunday if you should wish to come. We're having a short service in chapel first.'

It was the only good thing to be said for the whole sorry business. It provided an opportunity to escape from Mrs Haddenham.

Alan pounced, of course, as soon as she put the telephone down.

'Of course you must go,' he said. 'I'll come with you. Oxford funerals are becoming a depressing habit. I'll call Mother straight away and postpone . . .'

'Thanks, Alan.'

'Think nothing of it. I was going to do a piece on Oxbridge anyway . . . the ancient seats of learning . . . the Dark Ages up the road . . . this murder could be the nexus . . .'

'The broken nexus as it turned out,' she said bitterly.

But Alan was already calling his mother and explaining why they wouldn't be able to come. After a minute or two, he cupped the mouthpiece in his hand and turned to Heather.

'It's all right. She quite understands. In fact, she says she and Father will come too . . .'

Heather sighed to herself. The goodwill she had felt for Alan, the making up for her misdemeanour, seemed to be evaporating. And yet the guilt at her infidelity made her feel she owed him something. Let his dreadful mother come if it made him happy . . . Should she warn him about the chip, though?

The odds were, the Oxford burglars knew nothing at all about it, they were just thugs out for money or jewellery. But if they weren't, if they wanted something more, how could they possibly know that Mei Noon was meant to have it? And then she thought of the break-in at her own flat. No, they couldn't be connected. Could they?

'You will be careful of that chip, won't you, Alan?'

She felt better now it was going to an expert. Nothing would happen to Alan because he was a television personality. He had often spoken jokingly of the sanctity of the screen.

'Sure, sure.'

'And of yourself.'

She didn't want to make too much of an issue of it. If she were too anxious it would alert his natural nosiness. It could be prejudicial.

But he was thinking of his series again.

'Funerals in Oxford are becoming a depressing habit,' he intoned to camera.

Thirty

The chapel smelt sweetly and mysteriously of cedarwood, bringing back sweet and mysterious memories of being nineteen.

'"Man that is born of woman hath but a short time to live and is full of misery . . ."' intoned the chaplain while the Grinling Gibbons reredos writhed in oaken ecstasy behind him.

Trinity College chapel, though smaller in scale than some of its peers, is one of the glories of Oxford. Designed by Dean Aldrich, in consultation with Christopher Wren, it is essentially a perfect double-cube in the approved classical style with a fine painted ceiling showing Christ ascending. Below, the gallery with the organ, the lines of pews, and the black and white patterns of the marble floor, all combine to provide a cool but welcoming sense of order and benignity. As for the reredos itself – fifteen feet high and stretching at the top across the full width of the aisle – its strange colour, a sort of dusty, bony lightness which seems exactly to sum up the Anglican quality of the place, sets off its foliage, its particularly characterful cherubs, its plump acorns, with an inexplicable appropriateness.

Along the outside of the roof are stone finials sprouting flames of green copper, and on the four corners of the tower are the figures – etched by Oxford weather – of Astronomy, Theology, Geometry and Medicine.

It is acknowledged as a gem of the English baroque and it was fitting, thought Heather, that Mei Noon should be remembered in such a beautiful place.

She looked round at the congregation, composed mainly of graduates who had come up especially – term had not started yet – some undergraduates, and also a fair sprinkling of dons; and in one pew she noted a Chinese contingent, no doubt relatives. Somehow in Oxford, even the Chinese were in keeping with the cosmopolitan nature of serious learning. The one group that struck a discordant note was Alan and his parents.

There had been quite a problem getting them in. The chaplain had indicated that because of Mei Noon's popularity there was a shortage of space, but Mrs Haddenham would have none of it.

'But we are virtually family, Chaplain. Heather was a bosom friend of the poor girl.'

The chaplain, a mild, good man, murmured that poor Mei had had so many friends but Mrs Haddenham was not to be put off.

'And we'd like a place not too far from the door because Theo, that's my husband, you know, has a little problem.'

The chaplain looked nonplussed.

'A theological problem?' he enquired.

'More urological, actually.'

'Ah.'

'Hope you're wearing The Pants,' she hissed at her wretched mate.

'Really, m'dear . . .'

The chaplain looked left and right, stretching his long neck like a trapped emu, and seeing no escape, succumbed.

'Oh very well. We'll squeeze you in at the top of the north aisle . . .'

But squeezing was one thing that Mrs Haddenham drew the line at, with the result that the Chinese man at the other end of the row was obliged to leave his seat and take up a squatting position, which was a shame since he was a professor of biochemistry.

As the service continued, the woman kept commenting on the proceedings; the music, the congregation, the scent of the cedarwood ('too strong for my nose'), and the melancholy nature of the occasion, dabbing repeatedly with a handkerchief that reeked of some unspeakable scent reminiscent of stuffy rooms and cake essence.

'Hullo . . . who's he? . . . what's happening now? poor little May . . .'

Why didn't Alan just tell her to shut up? Instead he kept looking around for camera angles, professionally distancing himself from any involvement.

'Ave verum corpus' was sung, and finally, at her own request (it was said), because she was a creature of light and laughter, a small consort sang Morley's madrigal 'Now is the month of Maying' in her honour and to cheer everyone up.

'Really,' said Mrs Haddenham as they walked out into the cedary front quad, 'not at all suitable, I thought, the last anthem.'

'It was a madrigal, m'dear,' said Theo.

'Madrigal, then. "Each with his bonny lass, upon the green grass"! Apart from the fact that it doesn't rhyme, I should have thought it verged on the height of bad taste . . . Besides, it isn't May yet.'

Heather imagined Mr Haddenham thinking of the day long ago when he had laid Mrs Haddenham down upon a bank and crept over her like a fly on a sundew. The softness, inclined to the fleshy even then, had closed around him and he was lost.

'Why don't you go and find a gents while I talk to Alan and Heather?' she told him now.

Obediently he hurried off. It seemed to him, more and more, that she controlled his body. If she had willed him to be well, he would have flourished and his gland, now as big as a mandarin orange (his specialist told him) would have reverted to the desiderated chestnut.

The coffin meanwhile was being transferred to a hearse which would drive with the family to the crematorium. There was a pause while the great blue gates opened, and then the party moved into Hall where a reception was to be held.

Heather used the opportunity created by this diversion to mingle with the crowd and seek out Dr James. She found him surrounded by a little posse of students but, seeing her, he excused himself and took her into a corner.

'A melancholy business,' he told her, 'and one that makes me very angry, I must say.'

'Angry?'

'Such a waste of a good person. The sort that God spared Sodom and Gomorrah for.'

A white-coated scout approached with a tray of wine. They each took a glass. Heather kept swivelling her eyes to see if Mrs Haddenham was in the offing.

'Worried about something?' asked Dr James.

'About rather a lot, as it happens. Just at the moment, it's the thought of being buttonholed by my boyfriend's mother.'

'A large person with a bullying manner?'

'That's the one.'

'Why don't we go to my rooms for a few minutes?'

'Good idea. But look out for her . . .'

They made their escape through the Buttery stairway and out through the cellars to the Garden Quad. Heather thought she had seen Mrs Haddenham gesticulating at the other end of the hall, but didn't pause to verify the sighting. They had left their wine at the reception so Dr James poured her a glass of sherry, a drink that, rather in the manner of malt whisky in Scotland, always seems to taste its best in Oxford.

The room was panelled and hung with pictures owned no doubt by the college and portraying former members or distinguished connections of the place. There was a fine oil of Dr Johnson, and another (more severe) of Cardinal Newman. Outside, the golden stone of Wren's Garden Quad gave mellow reassurances in the sunshine.

Dr James himself was a man of rather over medium height, with a fresh complexion and a head of smooth, prematurely grey hair which made him look a little older than his fifty-five years. He was, apart from being a legendary history tutor and a master of wine, one of the wisest people she knew. One of his engaging characteristics was a slight and occasional stammer.

'What about these other problems?' he asked. 'I think we've dealt with the first. Let's have some more.'

'I'm defending a man on a charge of murder,' she told him. 'I don't think he's telling me the truth. There's something holding him back, some kind of organization he belongs to. He talks about cells. There's such a hole in his story at the moment, it's almost as though he wants to go to prison.'

Dr James was listening intently to her, fixing his eyes upon her face, her hands, as he took a sip of his Dry Oloroso.

'What about your silk?' he asked. 'Wha-what does he say?'

'He seems more interested in an international conference,' she told him. 'It's as though he's made up his mind and he's just using me to throw up a bit of dust.'

There was a silence as the sherry was sipped again. It was excellent – not your average Amontillado for Dr James.

'What is the name of the prisoner?'

'A fellow called Morbey,' she said.

'Morbey?'

She might have been mistaken but she thought she saw a flicker of recognition in his eye, or something more than recognition; or was it a reflection from his glass of sherry?

Dr James lit his pipe with all the ritual, the gestures she remembered from fifteen years ago. The whole scene now, as the Sobranie mixture floated out across the room, gave her the slightly dreamlike feeling that once again she was at tutorial, and that shortly he would give her next week's essay.

There was a long silence this time as he drew on his pipe, and at last he spoke, exhaling a fragrant cloud as he did so.

'What do we do with the folk of Woodpecker Leys?' he asked.

'Woodpecker Leys?'

'Up Cowley way . . . I don't just mean Woodpecker Leys, I take it as an example of the thousands of estates and places where people who live depressed and depressing lives, and who breed a savage underclass of criminals and unemployables? What do we do with them?'

'Well . . . we educate them, I suppose.'

'They don't want to be educated. They see education as at best a waste of time and at wor-worst like a devil who hates the light.'

'What is to be done?' she asked him.

'Oh, I expect you think of me as some kind of arrogant intellectual. I sit here in my comfortable middle-class way pouring scorn on the proles; but I assure you the working class were not always like that. They prized learning if they could get it. As for morality, it was the only way to survive. My father was a Welsh miner, you know.'

She hadn't known. Of course there had always been a slight lilt to his voice, Burton style, but his general deportment gave no hint of a two-up and two-down origin.

'They encouraged me, my parents, do you see? They thought it was great that I was interested in books, and when I won a scholarship to Jesus, the whole village celebrated.'

Dr James paused, lost in thought, the smoke curling lazily up past the book-lined shelves, the sun turning the sherry glasses to pools of tiger's eye.

'Was there no crime in the village?' Heather asked.

'Nothing to speak of. There was a boy caught thieving, but he didn't do it again. Everybody knew, d'you see? It was either stop or leave the village. The trouble is, now, reality's not real enough any more. That's what's behind morality, d'you see . . . reality. When everything's misted up with media of every kind, reality gets blurred – pleasure becomes a low thing, love becomes sex, sex becomes deviation, play becomes violence, energy to create becomes envy to grab. Thou Shalt Not becomes yes I bloody well will, if I can get away with it.'

Heather rather agreed about the media, which always seemed to her to be run for the media's benefit rather than the public's, although she didn't like to say such things to Alan. Sunday papers that were dropsical with unnecessary sub-information. Films that peddled violence as fashionably funny. Television shows which didn't even leave the laughter up to you. On every hoarding a picture, on every shelf a radio, in every hand a telephone which itself crackled with information . . . No wonder the truth of things, the fresh, the sometimes icy, the often uncomfortable wind of fact was getting shut out . . . But what to do about it?

She asked him.

'It is said that one can't put the c-c-clock back,' he told her. 'I wouldn't want to suggest that one could. We historians know the danger of trying to do that. However, the fact remains, as my mother used to say, that nothing worth while is achieved without effort. If the highest common factor is not to be dragged down by the lowest common denominator, some kind of effort has to be made.'

'You almost speak as if you knew that some effort was being made,' she told him. 'My mother used to say that too, by the way.'

'They did, they did, and they believed it,' said Dr James with some passion, and continued, 'There is talk, one hears talk at All Souls, cells of like-minded people . . . More sherry?' He filled her glass again.

'Cells?' she asked.

Christopher had spoken of cells.

'To see when my charmer goes by,
Some hermit peep out of his cell,
How he thinks of his youth with a sigh,
How fondly he wishes her well . . .'

sang Dr James.

'I have that in a song book of my mother's,' said Heather. 'You have a good voice.'

'That's the Welsh, d'you see. I must say you're looking very beautiful, Heather. If I were a younger man, I would become extravagant.'

'Thank you,' she said, smiling at him.

'Where were we?'

'Cells.'

'Ah yes. I know nothing of such things. I suppose that is the intention, if cells there be. And talking of cells, what do you think of prison?'

'Prison in general or in particular?'

'In general. What is the purpose of prison?'

'Well . . . it has two main purposes. Its social purpose is to placate the public, that is, to show as far as possible that crime does not pay and must be punished, otherwise there would be a free-for-all. Its purpose as far as the criminal is concerned is to punish him by depriving him of his freedom.'

'Good. And how do we do this?'

'We build prisons and subject him to the disciplines of being a prisoner.'

'And then of course he comes out and does it all over again. But while he's in residence, what keeps him there?'

'Gates, bars, prison officers, dogs, circuitry . . .'

'All this must be very expensive.'

'Oh it is.'

'Now what,' said Dr James, 'what if instead of building a prison of bars and spikes and wire and other grimness . . . remembering Richard Lovelace who told us that stone walls do not a prison make . . . supposing that we kept our prisoners in . . . with pleasure!'

'Pleasure?'

'It can be as much a prison as Pentonville. But it might be a lot cheaper. And they'd never w-w-want to leave. They'd never *have* to leave. Have you ever thought of that?'

'Well . . . no . . . It sounds like good lateral thinking. But how on earth would you do it?'

'Well, that gets a bit technical, I must admit. Though I have heard it expounded at high table and, indeed, elsewhere. We have some clever chaps here now. Virtual Reality is what it's about. Of course we know that we can create virtual universes within a personal computer – the quality, I understand, has improved unbelievably over the last five years. And yet nobody seems to have given real thought to the implication of these machines. They're in almost every home, but they're just used for games, for shopping with a virtual credit card, for selecting a holiday resort or looking round the *Titanic* . . .'

'But for prisons? I don't see the application.'

'It's always been said by some commentators that the danger is that people with limited social skills might start hiding behind their virtual personae and never emerge into the real world. But don't you see? That might not be a danger in prison. It might be a virtue.'

Heather thought about it. The idea did seem to have a certain logic to it but they could hardly be serious, could they? It was cynical, dehumanizing.

'I know what you're thinking, Heather. But the situation is serious. If we don't look out, there are soon going to be more criminals than honest citizens. It's the age of the new barbarians. Surely we have a duty to think of ways of restraining them or we ourselves will be overwhelmed and a new dark age will begin. Perhaps you don't see the people I do – undergraduates coming up who can't spell – I wonder if some of them can read – but we have to let them in because they're the best of a bad lot. If these are the best, what are the worst like?'

Dr James was smiling but she could sense his seriousness. She knew, of course, of the endorphin-stimulant feel-good games that had started to be released as long as ten years ago. No doubt the same – and more – could have beneficial effects on the prison population. But Dr James seemed to be talking of something more than this, something more like a long-term solution.

She could understand his despair. Some of the criminals she met were sunk so below the level which you would like to think of as human – so vicious, so weak, so lying, so conniving, so whining, so mindlessly violent, so self-helpless, so envious, so what her mother used to call low-grade in every way – that you felt degraded being part of the same race as they were: you felt bad about being a primate.

'I see some pretty loathsome people,' she said.

Dr James smiled at her again, measuring her, deciding he had said enough for the moment.

'The loathing that dare not speak its name. That is today's correctness. We'll talk about this another time,' he told her, glancing at his watch. 'My word, the wake will be nearly over. Come and meet a clever chap . . .'

But when they reached Hall again, the first person they saw was Mrs Haddenham who wasn't at all pleased.

'Really, Heather, what can you have been thinking of? Surely you know the simplest rules of hospitality. Do you usually leave your guests completely unattended?'

Heather didn't point out that it was Mrs Haddenham who had invited herself, but asked instead where Alan was.

'Alan is researching his programme. You know with Alan work comes first . . .'

Dr James gave Heather a wink and slid away into the thinning crowd, the rat.

'Where's Mr Haddenham?' she asked.

'Sitting on his air-cushion in the car. Well . . . aren't you going to introduce me to some of these clever people?'

Thirty-one

When the telephone rang, she knew it was going to be him, but she had made up her mind about something.

The enormity of what she had done, in meeting Christopher at home let alone allowing him to make love to her – no, that was the wrong phrase: making love with him – had begun to prey upon her almost as soon as he had left her bed, as he pulled his socks on and smoothed his hair.

Of course she had known it was against the code, not professional, a gross breach of etiquette in a profession where etiquette is everything, where even the fee is still called an honorarium – she had known that, but in the heat of the moment, in the lusty stealth of nature, it had seemed completely irrelevant. And in her forward mode, so it was.

Now, in her backward mode, it seemed total folly; for if she were found out she would lose the brief and (she was self-confident enough to think) he would lose the best chance he had of acquittal. So she had decided that, until the trial was over, and unless they had reason to meet at Soapy's or in chambers, they should not meet at all.

It was almost better that she did not talk to him.

She had already spoken to him more than most barristers with their clients. She had all the facts that he seemed prepared to give her. Anything more she must find out for herself. It was quite clear that Sir Perry wasn't going to exercise himself on Christopher's behalf. It was down to her.

'Hullo.'

Just to hear his voice made her knees go weaker than when she had been clobbered across the patella with a hockey stick at school, but she held on to her resolution. Apart from anything else, her line might be bugged. Nothing seemed innocent these days.

'Hullo,' he said again. 'Is that you, Heather?'

She wanted him so much – yes, she could now admit it to herself – she felt she would run mad like a Jacobean heroine, but she said: 'I don't think it's a very good idea for you to call me.'

Like many irresolute people, she could be adamantine when she finally made up her mind.

'I want to see you.'

'Not until the trial.'

'For God's sake . . . why?'

She tried to explain and she felt he understood, though he didn't like it. He rang off, downcast.

He telephoned again the next day to try to change her mind, but she wouldn't unless he could tell her something new about the case. This he would not or could not do. He appeared to be in the grip of some strange dark mood, talking of having things to do, of something he had to be and of somewhere he had to go. What exactly these things were he never exactly defined.

It simply reinforced her opinion, so to all his requests, even entreaties, she made the same reply.

'Not until the trial.'

It was too important to be jeopardized. Didn't he realize she had to get him off? And to do that she had to concentrate. She had sailed too close to the wind already. With people like Arthur around, you could never be sure you weren't being spied on. And then of course there was the prosecution. Soapy had left a message that he had heard it was to be led by a silk called Johnson Fyfe, well-known for his foxlike turns and twists, who could doubtless engineer a little scrutiny of his own.

Thirty-two

The next few weeks passed in a welter of hard and boring little jobs for Heather, occasioned (as Arthur didn't hesitate to point out), by her own over-zealous approach to the Morbey case.

She went through the schedule of the forthcoming trial with Sir Perry which gave him all the relevant facts and figures from the charge to the names of the witnesses to the times of Morbey's alibi . . . It was in the area of alibi that she still expressed her anxiety. The fact was, it seemed exiguously thin. No one seemed to have seen Morbey between the hours of 22.00 when he left the bar – he had finally agreed it was around that hour: he had been amused by the antics of the place – until 08.30 the following morning when he bought a paper, although they had found a bus conductor who said he *might* have boarded his No. 49 at 22.10 that evening but he couldn't be sure, they all looked the same. The girl Morbey had spoken of seemed to have vanished even from his memory. He did not refer to her again. Heather spoke to him on the telephone about her, in a hard, official voice, but he disclaimed all knowledge of such a person. He must have been joshing.

Sir Perry's view remained that it was up to the prosecution to prove he was guilty and there was no evidence – apart from circumstantial – to do so. Heather, on the other hand, liked to see round corners. The prosecution might yet come up with something more damning. Sir Perry was not impressed.

'Give her some more work, Arthur,' had been the general drift of Sir Perry's edict (according to Arthur), 'then she won't keep pecking away at it like a daft hen.'

And the cab-rank system which pertains in chambers – whoever's next in the queue gets the job – seemed to serve up some particularly irksome little numbers, involving travel to far-flung places and nights away from town. She even began to suspect that the cab-rank was not being fairly operated, but there was nothing she could do. However she did keep pecking away, at least in her mind, and her mind also kept wandering towards her client, not as a client but as a lover, but it was ridiculous and impossible and unprofessional, because Alan was in every way a more suitable person to be with; and besides, Alan trusted her, and was faithful to her, and she had been impossibly weak *and* foolish in deceiving him with, above all people, a client. If that ever got out, she would be a laughing-stock or worse. She could imagine what Arthur would say. It was only a degree or so better than a doctor bedding a patient. She would never practise again. No, she must stick with Alan because Alan was sticking with her, and it was where duty lay. Though unconventional in some ways, she did set store by duty – not an enormous amount of store but store enough. She was the daughter of a soldier, after all.

She did see Morbey again, very formally, at chambers where once again he repeated his story and provided no fresh explanation as to his movements on the fatal night. Every instinct told her that he wasn't telling the truth. And yet she knew – as certainly as she knew anything in these flickering days of spring as sun and rain strobed across the town – that he was not a murderer. He had made himself look villainous, true; but that was something else. Although . . . come to think of it . . . why had he made himself look villainous, slicking back the hair, hunching the shoulder, grimming the expression? It seemed a daft thing to do.

When she had talked and laughed with him, that wasn't how he looked. That wasn't how he looked in bed. He had made an attempt at re-establishing relations at the meeting but she had quite simply ruled it out of court. Why had he deliberately set out to look evil? And why was he doing it again? Someone would have to have a word with him before the trial.

Alan was busier than ever. Shooting had already started and a rough edit was billed for just before Easter, more or less when her trial was due to start. They were both busy and sometimes didn't see each other for days on end. Occasionally it occurred to Heather that they could have seen each other more, but she could understand, of course she could, how stressful it was for him. They planned, or rather she had planned for them, in more detail now, the little break together over the May Day bank holiday weekend to be taken at Chloe's cottage near Woodbridge.

A cloudy, windy spell had set in, and the days seemed driven by the same bustling urgency.

Alan had told her he had given the chip to a scientist friend of his who worked with a high-security artificial intelligence team on defence enterprises. It was locked in his office there. He would have a reply in due course, but it could not be rushed. She insisted that it should be rushed. He reminded her that the processes of the law were no more important than the nation's defence. It was maddening, it was frustrating, but there was nothing she could do. She found herself wondering about Christopher's vertigo. Something about it wasn't totally convincing . . . and things like vertigo were famously hard to prove . . . but maybe it could help . . .

Still she pecked away. She found herself missing Mei Noon – strange to miss someone you hardly knew – all the more tragic . . .

The South American continued to take an intrusive interest in her comings and goings, and sometimes she wondered if he was exactly what he made himself out to be. Surely no real South American would seem so South American in manner? Or be so tall? But why would he bother to pretend? She told herself she was becoming paranoid again. The telephone too continued to give her trouble, in spite of changes of number and monitorings at the exchange. It was almost as though a poltergeist were in it. It would ring for a second and then stop. Sometimes there would be a sound of distant music, or of a very old radio tuning up, or a humming, buzzing sort of static.

She could feel herself winding up. She burnt soothing oils, she went to Chloe's reflexologist, she tried acupuncture, but nothing really seemed to work. The face of Christopher Morbey kept presenting itself in her waking hours as much as in her dreams, returning to her on three subsequent occasions not as a lover but as the flying figure in the tunnel.

At last, one Thursday evening, when Alan was away somewhere filming – she had lost track of his movements – she knew what she had to do. She must go back to the bar in Clapham and see if there was any more to be learnt there. Of course she shouldn't be doing such donkey-work; it was the solicitor's job, but where was the solicitor?

She rang Joscelyn, who had given her his home number and taken her out to dinner once or twice, to see if he would like to go with her, but she was told he had been seconded to New York for a fortnight. There was nothing for it. She would have to go alone. After all, it was only Clapham, not the heart of darkness; hadn't the creature, what was her name, Mandy, hadn't she invited her to return? Tomorrow would be one of the nights she had said would be lively. It was just possible on such a night, when the regulars would be there, that someone might just remember something that might help.

She thought of telling Christopher she was going, but decided against it. She wanted him too much to want to hear his voice – and she had a scintilla of an instinct that he would not want her to go; which made her all the more determined. A dangerous place, he had said, but it had not seemed so when she went there with Joscelyn. The manager didn't seem a bad sort. Besides there could surely be no harm for a woman in a transvestite bar; she would be playing their tune.

With reasoning like this, perhaps affected by a gathering sense of unreality occasioned by the stress she was under, she assured herself of the good sense of the visit, and on Friday night set off in her Alfa: she was certainly not going to drink at Our Souls; equally she didn't want to be stranded out there.

Thirty-three

She found the High Street again without difficulty and made a little circuit to see whether any of the electronics shops were still open at eight. Indeed one was, Bronowski Electronics, and she stopped to ask the shopkeeper if he remembered a tall man with slicked black hair some months back – Christopher had said he had browsed for a while – but the little Pole shook his head saying he got all sorts, and offered her tea.

S&J Electronics was closed. But she had dealt with them some time back as part of her basic devilling. Her enquiries established that Christopher had indeed visited the shop and bought a chip (whether or not it was the one he wanted) and the till receipt confirmed that he had purchased it, as he had said, on the relevant day at the time he had stated, 18.45 – the shop closed at seven. The confirmation of his story comforted her more than she cared to admit. How trustless of her to doubt him!

The High Street issue being settled in her mind, she drove to the tributary road where Our Souls was already showing signs of animated activity. As she passed, she could hear the throb of music. Sounds of laughter caracoled in the soft spring air.

She parked a little distance away opposite a sign on a low garden wall which said 'Please Respect Our Slumbers' – only someone had crossed out the 'Sl' and inserted 'Cuc'.

Opening the door of the wine bar she was struck by a wall of noise. Girls, women, old bags were all talking at the tops of their voices, while in the corner an all-female ensemble of keyboard, guitar and percussion was doing its best to pile Pelion on Ossa.

A few people turned round when she came in – she had dressed in a style of low-key prettiness which she had supposed would be suitable for such an establishment without provoking either condescension or jealousy. It was actually impossible to allot the sex of everyone present. Some were obviously men, others had a delicacy of feature and smoothness of skin you would swear marked them out as female; but she had been told that in this strange land you could never tell.

She made her way to the bar, relieved to find it was Mandy behind it, not her colleague, the witness Walter. Mandy immediately recognized her.

'Hullo, dear,' she said. 'What brings you to our little corner of paradise? Look, Val, see what the cat's brought in.'

The unforthcoming barperson grunted into a pint she was filling with Bass. Heather wondered what made her tick.

'I thought I'd come and see how things were in the evening,' Heather said.

'Noisy, dear. What you drinking?'

'Orange juice, please.'

'Ooh, being careful tonight, are we? Your time of the month or something?'

Heather didn't answer. She supposed that roguishly intimate questions were more or less *de rigueur* in transvestite circles, and looked mildly disapproving. It was a mistake.

'You can't look down in the mouth here, you know,' said Mandy reprovingly. 'What's wrong? Got your tampon in a twist? Go on, have a vodka. That'll cheer you up.'

'No,' she said. 'I'm driving.'

'Have a vodka,' said Mandy in a voice that brooked no denial.

Heather supposed she'd better humour her if she wanted to get anything out of the evening.

'All right, thank you,' she said. 'Just the one.'

Mandy appeared mollified as she measured out the spirit.

'Ice and lemon? There you are, dear. On the house. That'll put the oomph in your oestrogen. I see you've left your adorable hunk behind. Were you looking for something?'

'No, no,' said Heather hurriedly. 'No, I was just wondering whether anyone else would remember the night of the murder . . . whether anyone would have seen my client leave . . .'

'Evil-looking bugger.'

'Maybe. But he didn't do it.'

'Ooh. Fancy him, do you?'

Heather could feel herself starting to blush again. Luckily the creature's attention was being distracted by a red-faced wench at the other end of the bar.

'Of course not.'

'Excuse me, dear, someone wants a suck. I'll be back.'

Heather tucked herself into a corner and looked round. The strange thing was, once or twice she fancied she recognized someone, but only in a flash, then she would look again and decide that she didn't know them at all. It was odd, though, that other eyes, looking at her, seemed to recognize her too.

Mandy was engaged in conversation at the other end of the bar. Just as well. Heather enjoyed being on the outside of a party; the sound of many voices was particularly lulling. She regaled herself with a close examination of the gamut of costume in the room. It ranged from high fashion – with long split skirts and jackets revealing the latest corsetry – to the most extraordinary approximations of Highland lassie. There were gym slips, of course, and a few ballerinas, but most of the punters were wearing everyday women's clothes, with a preponderance of twin sets and pearls, and floral prints from mail order catalogues, and there were one or two absolutely stunning creatures in party frocks, with long legs in the sheerest of tights.

There were also some men around. Several of them were clearly bouncers, but some of the others were there for the market. It slowly dawned on Heather, also, that some of the creatures who looked like women *were* in fact women, and they were there for the market too.

'There's one person who could help you,' a voice said beside her ear.

Heather turned with surprise to see Val leaning over the bar next to her.

'Val,' she exclaimed. 'What . . .'

'Shh. Don't tell 'er I told you. See that little punter over there?'

'Where?'

She pointed at an exquisite young creature in high heels and a black frock.

'She was 'ere that night. She saw your feller leave. I know because she told me. I used to go with 'er and now she's gone with someone else, so that's why I'm telling you, innit? I really fancy you, you know that.'

'Oh, er . . . thank you.'

What sex was Val? It was quite unsettling.

'Val . . .'

It was Mandy giving the barmaid a very beady look.

'Coming, Mandy.'

'Can't you keep it in till later, dear?'

One or two punters around the bar guffawed. Mandy was in vintage form tonight. Mandy smiled on all concerned and primped her hair. Her success distracted her from investigating Val's whisperings.

Heather moved through the crowd towards the girl Val had indicated.

'Hello,' she said.

The creature looked startled, almost as though she had been warned to be on her guard and keep shtumm.

''Ere, who you?' she said, Italianly.

'My name's Heather. What's yours?'

'No interested.'

'That's a nice name.'

'Look, why not piss off?'

'Is that another of your names?'

'I'll call Mandy if you not leave off. She no like that.'

So it was Mandy who had supplanted Val in the creature's affections!

'Look,' said Heather, 'I think you're incredibly beautiful.'

If flattery didn't work, it wouldn't be so popular, she thought. The creature's eyes lit up.

'Would you like to come upstairs?' the creature said.

'What?'

'Oh come on. Don't be so coy.'

Heather thought hard. It seemed the only chance to talk to the creature, and yet it was fraught with all manner of danger. Still, she was such a little thing, she hardly seemed to pose much of a threat.

'What about Mandy?' Heather asked.

'Oh, Mandy doesn't mind. As long as you pay?'

'Pay?'

'Of course.'

'Oh no.'

'Mandy!'

The girl signalled furiously at the manageress.

'With you in a shake of tits, dear.'

'Oh dammit,' said Heather in a panic. 'How much?'

'Hundred quid. Up front . . .'

'Oh very well.'

It was fortunate that she had brought the money with her, grabbing it only that evening at a cash point on her way there.

The creature led Heather out, through a side door and upstairs onto a landing. She opened a door and ushered Heather in. The room was not large but it contained a five-foot bed, a chair, and in the corner, a shower recess. It smelt of secretions and gardenia. The door closed and the creature put her arms round Heather.

It seemed the right moment for some kind of explanation.

Thirty-four

'Look,' she said, 'first of all. What is your name?'

'First the money.'

Heather counted it out into her hand.

'Graziella,' the creature said. 'My mother was Italian. I'm usually called Grace. Kiss me.'

'My God,' said Heather, 'you're a girl.'

'Yes. Kiss me.'

'Yes, but . . . wait a minute. I thought this was a transvestite bar.'

'Well, what are you doing here? We like to play double-bluff, no? Kiss me.'

'No, Graziella.'

'You don't like me, you think I am no good? See, I am good.'

The girl started to take her dress off, revealing breasts of the utmost delicacy and the tops of white thighs cordoned off by expensively tenuous underwear.

'You are wonderful, Graziella. You are fine. You are perfect. Though I don't know what you're doing here.'

'I not know what *you* are doing here.'

'What I'm doing here is easy to explain. I'm a lawyer.'

'You are the law. Oh, my God. Sapristi! HELP!'

'Shhh! Not the law . . . I'm a barrister, an *avvocato* . . .'

'Ohhh . . . *un' avvocato*. Naughty *avvocato*, should not be here, not . . . respectable!'

'I'm not here for myself. I'm here for my client.'

Heather had brought copies of his photograph with her and

she showed the girl one. There was a long intake of breath. Graziella looked at her with fear in her eyes.

'Who say I know him?'

'I didn't say you did. But you do, don't you?'

There was a long silence.

'Yes, I knew him,' she said at last in a small voice. 'He was with me the night of that murder. We came up here. I no sleep with many men but he was special. But I cannot witness. That is what you are going to ask me, yes?'

'Yes. But why can't you witness?'

'Because they send me back to Italy . . . in a box . . .'

'Who will?'

But the girl wouldn't say.

'Don't say anything about this to anybody. When the trial comes, it won't be long now, I'll come and collect you and we'll keep you absolutely safe. No sending back to Italy in a box or otherwise. They're just trying to frighten. This is London, not Palermo.'

'I no like.'

'But you wouldn't like that, what did you call him?, that special man to go to prison for life?'

'GRACE!'

'That is Mandy,' the girl said. 'What we going to do?'

'ARE YOU UP THERE?'

'Quick,' said Heather. 'Get in.'

She tore off her skirt and sweater and pulled Graziella into bed, giving her as steamy an embrace as she thought would serve the purpose. The girl's body was wonderfully cool and lithe. The door opened and Mandy loomed at the lintel.

'What's going on?'

She peered more closely, recognizing Heather.

'Oh, it's you, is it? I thought you were after a bit of the other. Not very respectable, though. I don't suppose you'd want the papers to know.'

Heather got up, pulling her clothes back on.

'I don't suppose you'd want the police to know some of the

things that go on here. Didn't I see a needle under the bed?'

Mandy opened her mouth and roared.

'CHARLIE! LAZARUS!'

There was a rushing of feet and two enormous bouncers appeared.

'This lady thought she saw a needle in here. Disabuse her, will you, boys?'

The two men picked Heather up, holding her stiffly between them and took her downstairs again and into the bar. The crowd fell silent when they saw her. This was clearly part of the sport of the place.

'This lawyer person . . .' said Charlie.

'This personage . . .' intoned Lazarus.

'Says she thought she saw a needle upstairs.'

'A NEEDLE?' roared the crowd.

'Not a knitting needle . . .' said Lazarus.

'Nor yet a pine needle . . .' replied Charlie.

'BUT A FUCKING GREAT HYPODERMIC,' shouted the congregation.

'Must have something wrong with her,' said Lazarus.

'She's over-heated,' agreed Charlie. 'So what do we do with her?'

'WE TAKE HER FUCKING CLOTHES OFF AND WE WASH HER DOWN.'

Yes, thought Heather, it had been a mistake to come. She had underestimated the undercurrents in the place, to say nothing of the over-currents. Of course she should have known. It looked as though something horrible was about to happen to her, a sudden reminder of the sharpness of things, the madman at the door, the terror that walketh by night . . . when suddenly a little voice spoke in her ear. It came from a small woman with a beehive hairdo and a *Come Dancing* gown with bees-bottom petticoats.

'I'm going to create a diversion. Meet me round the back as soon as you get out.'

The face looked familiar but she couldn't place it just at the minute.

'Quick as you like,' she said.

The crowd was drawing round with soda siphons at the ready. Hands were beginning to pull at her clothes.

'THE MOON SHONE BRIGHT ON MRS PORTER AND ON HER DAUGHTER,
THEY WASHED THEIR FEET IN SODA WATER,'

chanted the motley crew, spraying her legs, her breasts.

It was cold and frightening and humiliating. But suddenly there was a cry of 'Police!' and there was instant turmoil. Lights went out and there was a frantic rush for the back, which was well supplied with exits. Heather found herself carried along with the crowd which, once out, scarpered in all directions. She found herself standing alone in the chill night air, bruised, wet and shivering, trying to work out which exit she had come out of so that she could re-orientate herself.

A little voice said: 'Over here.'

She looked across and the beehive nodded in the gloaming.

'It's me,' said the voice, 'don't you recognize me?'

It was Theo Haddenham.

'Do you want a lift?' he asked.

'My car's round the corner,' she told him.

But it wasn't at the 'Please Respect Our Cucumbers' sign. It wasn't anywhere.

'I'll drive you.'

The journey back had the quality of something out of *Alice in Wonderland.* Theo in a beehive hairdo looked curiously like the White Queen. He said nothing for most of the way and Heather thought it was better not to ask for information unless he proffered it. Occasionally he consulted her for directions. She was busy meanwhile with her own thoughts. Why hadn't Christopher told her of his alibi? She knew what he would say – to protect the girl – but was that an excuse?

Shortly before they reached Kensington, Theo spoke.

'I'm sorry about that place. It's my first time there. I usually go to Twickenham. There's a very jolly little scene going on there, I can tell you. But someone said this had to be tried. I won't go back again. I say,' he turned to her, 'you won't tell Daphne, will you, m'dear? She thinks I'm at the Rotary Club. I change in the loft above the garage. It's very secluded. Daphne never goes there. I've told her there are bats. She has a phobia.'

Heather promised not to tell, and when they arrived at her flat she asked Theo in for a coffee, but he shook his head.

'I won't if you don't mind. Alan might be there. I couldn't bear that.'

'He won't be, Theo.'

'Got to get back. Really. Thanks most awfully. No one really understands about anything, do they?'

He drove off into the night and back to his monster wife. No wonder he liked to escape. At least his monster was tangible, though, she thought; not like mine that I can only see through gaps in the mist, whatever it is, wherever it may be leading.

She towelled herself dry, too tired to take a hot bath, too tired even to report her stolen car, and fell into a deep sleep shot through with strange images and perturbing incident.

Thirty-five

She woke with sunlight flooding her room and with a strange feeling as though she had taken some kind of pill, or had 'flu, both light and heavy at the same time.

Alan was away. This time he had gone to the top, interviewing the ageing Prince of Wales on the subject of the monarchy, another institution shaken by change, perhaps even the prime example. At any rate, Alan had gone down to stay with friends in Gloucestershire close to Highgrove.

She lay in bed for some time enjoying the luxury of not having to do anything, not having to go anywhere, pitying the smart drudges who had cottages in the country, two households to keep. It was all she could do to keep her two frontal lobes together.

As she lay, she let the curious events of the night before filter through her mind. In the light of day, they seemed scarcely credible. It couldn't be, could it, that she had in some way, dreamt or imagined the scene? Certainly the feeling in her head seemed post-narcotic. Had Mandy put something in that vodka? She wouldn't put it past her. Or had it happened before that? The Pole who had given her tea? The coffee she had had in the Kings Road? The Afternoon Easer herb tea – which tasted of wee-wee but was said to lift stress – which she had drunk in her own flat?

Had she imagined the whole Clapham incident? Impossible. You don't imagine 'Please Respect Our Cucumbers'.

And when she at length got up, she found her clothes of the

night before hanging over her chair, crumpled and damp, mute and insubornable witness to an eccentric evening, though exactly what form it took they could not say.

Such reassurance as it brought, however, turned into alarm when she looked out of the window and saw her car parked outside. This was ridiculous. The only person who could verify the night's proceedings – apart from the people at Our Souls, who couldn't be trusted – was Theo. And yet, if it were some kind of hallucination of hers, would he not be mortally offended if she asked him about it? Of course he would.

She made herself some breakfast and felt a little better after eating. Then she went downstairs to the car to see if it had been broken into. Everything seemed perfectly in order. It was locked. The alarm was on. There were no dents, no scratches. It was almost suspiciously pristine.

She decided to drive to Clapham there and then, to see if anything there would confirm her last night's visit.

Bronowski's was open, but there was an Asian cleaner there who said she knew nothing of the Polish man. S&J Electronics was still closed. Heather then drove round to the street where she had parked the car, but there was only a notice which said 'No Parking' to which some wag had added an extra semicircle so that it read 'No Barking'.

As for Our Souls itself, it looked if possible even deader than it had when she visited it with Joscelyn. There was no answer when she rang the bell. The upstairs windows seemed more office-like than bedroomy.

Finally she gave up and went to have a coffee in a large American-style Pizza 'n' Donut in the High Street. She bought a tabloid newspaper and read it from cover to cover. It was like eating mock-meat made from a tiny relative of the mushroom. Just as she was finishing it, something made her look up from behind her paper and she saw Graziella with two men sitting at a table at the other end of the room.

With beating heart, she put the paper down, got up from the table and walked across. Graziella looked up and saw her, and her face (Heather could have sworn) went momentarily pale; then she spoke in a low voice to the two men, who turned round as Heather approached.

'Good morning, Graziella,' Heather said. 'I don't know what happened but I was here last night. We did talk. You did say you had been with my client. I did give you £100 . . .'

''Ere,' said Graziella. 'Who d'you think you're talking to? Who's this Graziella when she's at home? I don't like your tone. Give me money, did you? What for?'

All trace of the Italian accent had gone. This was straight South London.

'I think you got the wrong person, darlin',' said one of the men to Heather.

'She's going to be a witness for the defence in a murder case,' explained Heather patiently. 'I spoke to her last night. We went upstairs to talk. I gave her £100 because . . .'

'You were trying to bribe 'er, is that what it was?'

'Certainly not. She thought I wanted to sleep with her but I didn't. We just pretended to be in bed together because of Mandy . . .'

'I've never 'eard anything so disgustin' in my life,' said the first man.

'I dunno who she is,' said Graziella. 'She never give me money or nothing.'

'You're a fucking lezzie, that's what you are,' said the second man, a hulking brute with a chinful of stubble. 'We don't 'ave to stand for this. Piss off. 'Ere, miss . . .'

He summoned a waitress who ambled over. She was large and black.

'What is it?' she said.

'This woman's annoying us. She's propositioning our friend 'ere. Says she give 'er money.'

'Open your bag,' said the waitress to Heather. 'Go on. Let's see what you got in there. You have her money?'

'*I* gave *her* money,' Heather expostulated, 'it's my money I'm talking about.'

'You just shut your mouth, missus,' said the waitress. 'I'm in charge here.'

Heather sighed and opened her bag. To her astonishment, the £100 she had given Graziella was still inside, neatly folded. The waitress triumphantly reached in and handed the bundle to Graziella who accepted it uncomplainingly.

'Here,' said Heather, 'wait a moment.'

'No,' said the black woman. 'I wait. You go.'

'But . . .'

There was no recourse. Naturally there was no policeman in sight, and even if there had been, the explanations would have taken all morning. Better to cut her losses . . .

As she passed the window she saw her precious witness dividing the spoils with her accomplices. Heather climbed into her car and cried.

Thirty-six

Notice of the trial had now been given. It was to be heard in Court Three at the Old Bailey on 20 April, two weeks away – rather sooner than Sir Perry had expected. It coincided exactly with the arrival of his VIPs. Heather was called up by Sir Perry to be given the news.

'It's very inconvenient, Heather,' he told her, 'but what can I do? We can't have all these bigwigs attended to by someone like Fentiman.'

He was referring to the head of a rival chambers.

'Would that be on the cards?' Heather asked.

She was rather anxious that Sir Perry should play some part in the proceedings; so no doubt would Soapy be. It was too big an occasion for a junior to handle alone.

'Fentiman would be only too happy to dance attendance,' Sir Perry told her. 'There'll be a great deal of coverage for the conference. The whole relationship of British law, European law and International law . . . If I'm not there, I might as well kiss goodbye to my peerage . . .'

Tough, thought Heather. And what about the poor bloody client? But instead she said: 'I'll be able to handle it, Sir Perry, if you can do the first cross-examination and the closing speech.'

'I'll be there, I'll be there,' the great man said vaguely, his voice patting her shoulder.

'Perhaps we should go through the schedule again?'

She didn't want to tell him that she'd found – and lost – a witness. It was too delicate at the moment. Her activities in

Clapham must be kept strictly under cover. If only Graziella had agreed to speak up, it wouldn't have been a problem, but in circumstances of failure her exploits would be unacceptable to say the least.

'Plenty of time for all that,' said Sir Perry airily.

He was relaxed as a surgeon before a heart transplant, thought Heather. The only trouble is, the heart in question seems to be mine.

'Oh. Right,' she said.

'Keeping you busy enough, are we?' he asked.

'Quite busy enough, thanks,' she told him. 'In fact, I'd like more time to put the Morbey case together.'

'Come, come,' said the great man, 'you've had the best part of six weeks. You've got to catch the moment, you know. Cases go off. It doesn't do to brood. Anyway, well done, keep it up. 'Bye.'

It might not do to brood, but still she thought of Christopher – whether she was in court, in chambers, drinking wine with Alan or alone in her bed.

In the end, she weakened just a little, deciding that her silence was too strict – it was, after all, only strictness with herself she needed if she was to hold out – and was perhaps unfair on him. He had stopped calling up. So she wrote him a letter.

Dear Christopher,

I think I love you, I can't stop it, I'm glad we made love, but I'm perplexed. No let's be honest, I'm frightened. Ever since I first became involved in your case, there seem to have been attempts made to unsettle and confuse me.

Do you know anything about this? I can't ask you these questions to your face because there are too many long ears at my chambers at the moment. Tell me what is going on. I don't want you to go to prison. You will be there for at least fifteen years, probably more.

The trouble is, every time I try to explore what happened to you in those vital hours that night, I seem to come up against not a brick wall but a sort of web of fantasy. It's like something out of a Celtic romance, the Forest of Falsehood.

'I met a lady by the meads, full beautiful, a faery's child . . .' Her name was Graziella. Does that mean anything to you?

We had an extraordinary evening together, I think. She told me you had one too, and that she would be the magic witness.

Then I met her next day and she was someone different. Do you see what I mean about the Enchanted Wood?

Do you want to go to prison? I can't help you if you do, though I can't think why anyone should wish to do such a thing. Can you? Or do you have an urge to retreat from the world and from me? Why didn't you tell me of your alibi? At all events, it now seems it's no good.

I have decided, as you may have noticed and regardless of what *you* may wish!, that we should not meet except in chambers or at Soapy's until your case is over. I think Alan needs me in his strange way, and I hate the idea of deceiving him. Everything seems to hang upon this case.

When it's over, either way, everything will be resolved.

I'm sending you this letter by special delivery, to be signed for by you only. Please destroy it when you have read it. It is highly compromising.

More love than I can really afford,

Heather.

He did not reply, but three days later a strange and beautiful flower arrived, unlike anything she had ever seen.

Thirty-seven

Alan had been more elusive than usual for some time now. She sometimes broke the rule and rang his office but, though the girl said she would give him messages, he seldom called back. The girl said he was busy on the series. Heather knew Alan when he was immersed in a project; this was very much the way he worked. He communicated by postcards and cryptograms.

However, one night he rang to say he was back in town; could he call round? She set herself to receive him with mixed feelings. Guilt, pleasure, curiosity, irritation . . . and annoyance with herself. Why had she let a perfectly good affair down? Alan was far more her sort, her friends' sort, than the enigmatic Christopher who, if one looked at the worst scenario, could be described by ill-wishers as a homosexual rapist-murderer. Not that either reason or instinct went along with that. Why else would they give him bail if they thought he was dangerous?

Alan, even if her mother hadn't entirely endorsed him, was in almost every way more suitable. He was good-looking, educated, successful, intelligent, from her own kind of background, a good lover . . . And there was a part of her, too, that felt almost protective towards him, as though he needed her back-up if not in presence at least in emotion. What would she be missing if she allowed herself to let it all go? And yet her heart was still resolutely, wilfully intent on destabilizing the situation . . .

She had resolved to give it one last try. During the May Day bank holiday, she would take Alan away as she had planned.

They would go to the woods, or what passed for it these days, and frolic as they had of old.

As soon as he arrived – looking, she thought, a little frayed round the edges – he launched into an account of his latest forays with the establishment, this time with the Royal Family itself.

'Royalty by its nature must be apart,' he said. 'We keep trying to see its warts with our telephoto lenses, then when they're revealed on the front page of the *Sun*, we have a good look and say how shocking. Royalty, it seems to me these days, must be resolute. It must be kingly. The Prince of Wales, on the other hand, still seems to want to be loved. The trouble is, those who want to be loved seldom are. It's no use showing your doubts and humanity in public if you're a King. Look at Hamlet. Look at Richard the Second. Look at the Duke of Windsor. And yet . . . are we expecting too much? These days, expressing one's feelings is a disease, it's a sort of emotional dysentery. Nothing's held back. How can we expect a prince not to catch the amoeba?'

He paused, rhetorically, and she took the opportunity of reminding him of her plan.

'Alan. You'll still be able to go somewhere for a few days over May Day? I think we need a break.'

'What? Yes, yes, of course. But what d'you think?'

'I think there's no mystery any more. I think we are in rats' alley. Everything has to be gnawed,' she said.

There was no point in pursuing the holiday idea when he was like this. At least he had said yes.

'That's good,' he said, 'rats' alley.'

'Not mine,' she said. 'Eliot.'

'Oh.' He sounded disappointed. 'Oh well, we could use it as the title for the royal slot.'

'It's your fault,' she told him.

'Mine?'

'Television, journalism, the media, the hungry screen. It's got to be filled with what passes for life, served up in tasty bite-sized nuggets with monosodium sauces because life, real life, is on the way out.'

'What d'you mean?'

'You know in the "Te Deum" when it talks about the sharpness of death? Well, what's happened to us today, we've lost the sharpness of life. Pleasure was to be a reward hard-earned after a day, a week of struggle and toil. Pleasure was something you could taste, you could sing, you could dance to forget the hard world. Now we think our world is softer and we can have pleasure on tap, all the time, but we're wrong. The world isn't softer, it's harder if anything, but it's changed its approach for the moment like the devil. And the pleasure we have isn't pleasure at all. It's gratification, and that's a prison.'

She was to some extent quoting Dr James to see how Alan would respond. And how was he responding? He was looking at her appreciatively.

'Well said,' he told her. 'No wonder you're a barrister. You could talk the hind leg off a journalist. And talking of prison . . .'

She knew what was coming next. An Alan interview with Christopher was the last thing she wanted.

'No,' she said, finally.

'Hm. I think you're hiding something. Come on, Heather. Tell Uncle Alan . . .'

'For God's sake, Alan. Stop it.'

He looked surprised, a little hurt.

'What's got into you these days?' he asked. 'Working too hard?'

'Fat lot you'd know about it,' she said. 'You're never around.'

'Now that's not fair. You know how I am when I'm working. I was talking to some of the more intelligent MPs last week and you can imagine how hard they are to get hold of. I can tell you, they're seriously concerned – both parties . . .'

He was off again. She seized the tangent gratefully.

'Concerned? Why's that?' she asked.

'Something of what you were saying. Public apathy is so great, the life force if you like is so weak, the bureaucracy so strong, that democracy itself is in danger. Only those with strong feelings make themselves heard – and strong feelings these days usually means anger – a deadly sin if you remember but now used as a righteous justification of any act however murderous – so we end up with tyranny by minority and a very suspect minority at that. Why do we let them do it? Because the majority's sitting at home watching videos or playing interactive games. Britain today – a triumph of never mind over it doesn't matter. Discuss.'

She looked at him with affection. This was the Alan she knew and loved in her way; boyish, tousled, spooky-toothed, enthusiastic. Something in her eyes must have stirred a response in him because he suddenly dropped his presenter's bravura and spoke with genuine and vulnerable feeling.

'I do need you, you know, Heather. I don't know what I'd do without you.'

It reminded her that Alan too must have his doubts, however strong the presenterly façade might be.

She held out her hand; love and guilt, protectiveness and inconstancy made a curious mayonnaise of emotions inside her. This was both what she wanted and didn't want to hear.

'I know,' she said, and kissed him on the temple like a child. 'We'll go away for the Bank Holiday and forget about everything and everyone.'

It was a somewhat slender hope, but she owed it to him. The kiss seemed to please him, and he kissed her in return.

'Any luck with my chip yet? The trial's in a couple of weeks.'

She had been saving the question for a propitious moment, but she couldn't disguise her anxiety.

Graziella had seemed to provide such a strong alibi for Christopher that she had put her interest in the chip temporarily on ice. Of course, even the remote possibility that it might have been the cause of Mei Noon's death was enough to make her anxious for a solution. It had been simply a question of priorities between the dead and the living. And now, since Graziella had shown herself to be a backslider, to say the least, the hunt was on again in earnest for an answer. Was the thing relevant? Was it crucial? Or ludicrously unimportant? Or was she going to have to pin her faith to something as notoriously unpinnable as vertigo?

A slight frown crossed his brow.

'You know how busy I've been.'

'I know, but I would be grateful. I would be bloody grateful.'

'I've left it with the top man.'

'It's rather desperate, Alan.'

'He's on the case, Heather.'

'I know. I know.'

Bzzzzzzzzzzzz. Surely he could feel it? Zmmmmmmm.

She felt impotent, nightmarish. It was like trying to hit someone with no bones in your arms.

'Please,' she begged. 'Don't let me down.'

'But I can't hurry the top man. You know how it is,' he said.

Thirty-eight

They had been digging up the road again outside.

The sound of the new super-silent drill was marginally quieter than the whispering jumbos overhead; but it was still louder than the amorous blackbirds in the cherry trees that fringed the street.

The approaching trial weighed heavier on Heather now, more so than with any brief she had ever known. But it wasn't the trial itself, of course, it was the other things; the mystery, the uncertainty, the shifting sandy nature of the pitch she was playing on; even the goalpost seemed to have sprouted legs. And then there was this business of love. It would have been so helpful to have been sure, to have surrendered herself to the drug of it, or to have been absolutely positive that she was out of love. That would have been at least a calm thing. As it was, she was in love without any of the benefits. Sans man, sans sex, sans company, sans everything but a sadness at the heart and an absence in the body. Oh yes, it was self-inflicted; but where would she have been otherwise?

She hadn't realized what a craving the absence would set up in her. It was almost embarrassing. And then there was Alan. Her sense of self-preservation could not bring her to let him go; and there was something else, too; her sense of Alan-preservation. She knew he needed her. It would be madness to tell him that she no longer wanted him, while he was in the middle of his series and she was in the throes of her trial. Better to wait; to have your cake and eat it was the sensible if ignoble course. But who cared about ignobility these days? Well, yes, she did for one.

She remembered her mother had once said to her:

'Nice people do horrible things. That is the difference between literature and life.'

And here she was doing the horrible thing; holding onto one lover while the other held onto her. It all added to her curious sense of dislocation . . .

The telephone rang in the early evening at the violet hour. The human engine wasn't throbbing like a taxi but taking some light refreshment in the shape of South African Chenin Blanc which was slipping down a treat. Perhaps she was drinking a little too much these days – but who wouldn't in the circumstances? Life was so bloody, a glass or two of wine was the only sure palliative. Only it wasn't a glass or two, it was a glass or twenty-six if she felt like it. No Christopher, precious little Alan, colleagues behaving strangely – oh yes, she had noticed: glances in the corridor, sniggers behind the computer screens – and no friends she wanted to see. Susannah, Lisa, Hebe . . . those jolly half-friends at whose flats she had had dinner, with whom she had holidayed sometimes in the past, who used to call almost every week, now no more, mysteriously dried up like the River Alphaeus in the heat of the last two months. Chloe, she knew, was out of London, press-ganged for early sea-trials in King Farouk's yacht. That left the Chenin Blanc and the steely Chardonnay . . .

The telephone rang, but she was in no hurry to answer it. Anything it could bring would be meagre or worse.

'Why don't you shut up?' she told it. 'I'm sick of you, the way you think you can interrupt people. We *are* living, you know.'

But it rang and rang as telephones will, mewing and mewing like an unwanted cat, and in the end she reached over and grabbed it, knocking over a small and much-prized pedestal table.

'Oh fuck,' she said to the telephone.

'And fuck you too,' it said, rather to her surprise.

'What?'

'It's me, stupid.'

'You?'

'Graziella.'

Good God, it couldn't be. She was suddenly sober.

'Why didn't you talk to me at that place?'

'I did. I said I didn't know who you were.'

'I don't mean that.'

'You don't think I was going to tell those pigs what you were after.'

'Why not?'

'You people don't live in the real world.'

'Why are you calling me, Graziella?'

'I don't like to see him set up.'

'Who by?'

'I can't say.'

It sounded like Graziella, but which Graziella was she going to be this time? Italian, South London or something altogether cooler, more controlled?

'Why can't you say, Graziella?'

'You people don't live in the real world,' the girl said again.

Heather sighed. Which real world was she talking about?

'Will you give evidence?' she asked.

'That's what I'm calling about, stupid. I like Christopher. I don't like to see him put away for something he didn't do.'

'How do you know he didn't do it, Graziella?'

'I was with him, wasn't I?'

Heather's heart was suddenly beating like a maraca.

'Look. I'm not really supposed to talk to you about your evidence. Will you speak to the solicitor? Then they'll pass it on to me.'

'I only speak to you.'

Heather had been expecting the reply. Too bad – proper procedure would have to take its turn. Better a witness ill-obtained than no witness at all.

'Look. Can you come over?'

'Okay.'

'You know my address?'

'Yes.'

'How do you know my address?'

'The same way I know your number.'

'How do you know my number?'

'You gave it me, remember?'

Heather didn't remember, but supposed she must have slipped her a card at Our Souls. Everything had happened so quickly.

Fifteen minutes later, Graziella rang the bell. Heather let her in by the entryphone and heard her stop on the first floor for the inevitable invitation from the rumba merchant. Finally she was there, sitting with a glass in her hand and explaining just what had happened that night. Strangely, when she heard again that Christopher had slept with the beautiful creature, she felt no jealousy, only a kindling of her own desire.

'Yes,' Graziella told her, 'I will be a witness. I cannot say more, but I will do it. Then I will have to go away.'

'I'll help you,' said Heather, 'pay for you. Anywhere.'

'Sure, sure. And now I would like to go to bed with you.'

The suggestion was made as though it were the most natural thing in the world, like fruit after dinner.

'That's not part of the deal.'

'Certainly not.'

Heather thought it almost certainly was, but she desperately needed the witness; she was rather drunk; and the growing confusion, even anarchy, in her mind drove her to recklessness.

She could not see now beyond the trial. The days before it seemed storm-racked, cloudy; the days after cloaked in darkness. Was this what the psalmist called the valley of the shadow of death? It was a phrase that had always seemed to her potent with sadness; and yet disturbing, fearful, weirdly attractive. It was odd to find herself here at last, in a place she half recognized.

'Good,' she said.

'Let's do it, then,' said Graziella. 'I don't think I can wait.'

It would have been easy to say yes.

In fact there was more than a certain attraction in the idea. She was lonely, frustrated, in need of a cuddle, in need of love. And a certain desperation, even anger, encouraged in her a tendency to feel that if any traces appeared they should be kicked over.

Of course it would be disaster for her bar career if she were found out. But did she care now about professional suicide? She had metaphorically slashed her wrists a number of times already.

She had decided to resign anyway when the case was over.

More importantly, though, it would prejudice her defence of Christopher if she were found out. And there was too a selfishness, that sense of self-preservation – a reluctance to become involved with yet another individual – which finally drove her to refuse.

Even as she shook her head, she felt guilt towards Christopher. It was perhaps a sacrifice she should make; but she was damned if she did and damned if she didn't. She was reminded of her mother's story of the old Oxford don who, when an undergraduate told him that he had got a governess into trouble, said: 'You're a fool if you marry her and a blackguard if you don't.'

She would rather be a blackguard, but on this occasion it seemed she would have to settle for the fool.

'Sorry,' she told Graziella. 'Bad timing, I'm afraid.'

At least she could try to hang on to the girl's goodwill with the time-honoured excuse.

Graziella's eyes widened and she looked at Heather intently. Did she believe her? It was impossible to read any meaning in the brown eyes.

Thirty-nine

There was the sound of a minor riot coming from the Strand as she walked down St Martin's Lane towards Fleet Street, so she turned back and threaded through Covent Garden.

The marches and attendant disturbances were becoming so common now that you simply tended to regard them as traffic nuisance, and listened to the radio in order to avoid them. It was not so good to be caught up in one. Your car could be set on fire, or you could be abused and assaulted with a placard, or merely trampled, or vandalously brickbatted or knifed or even raped if you took the wrong turning. The sound of anarchy was still in the air as she turned into the Temple, but it was soon shut out when she reached the perennial imperturbability of her chambers. Here she found Arthur looking obsequious. This was a rare demeanour for the head clerk but she soon discovered it was not on her account, because when he ushered her into Sir Perry's room she found Soapy there as well. She was surprised to see him. Arthur had not mentioned that the solicitor would be present – which meant he intended the surprise to be in some way disturbing or unpleasant. And then she noticed Christopher sitting quietly in the corner. She almost fainted.

The room smelt the way rooms used to smell when she was a child – of polish and newly-lit crackly fires and hyacinths and spring sunlight. Every March or April, between the ages of six and nine, she used to go down with a streptococcal throat and be sent home from school to convalesce. It was this smell that reminded her of it, making her almost feel weak again as she had been all those years ago, and there was something else too that went with it, her grandmother's calm voice reading *Pilgrim's Progress.* The memories helped her recover her composure.

'You look as though you had seen a ghost,' remarked Sir Perry, smiling at her. 'Surely it isn't the unwonted but nevertheless desiderated sight of Mr Protheroe here? Or of our client Mr Morbey?'

Soapy had risen to his feet and was extending a hand. Heather took it and tried to look pleased at its cool, slightly oleaginous touch. Christopher half rose and sat down again.

'Hullo, Mr Protheroe, good to see you,' she said. 'I was remembering my childhood. The smell of the fire and the hyacinths . . . spring smells . . .'

'Did you like your childhood?' Soapy asked.

'Yes I did, as a matter of fact. I got on rather well with my mother.'

'Didn't see much of your father?'

'No. They were divorced.'

The two men exchanged a glance.

'A tendency of the times,' said Soapy. 'But even divorce seems almost old-fashioned these days. Did you know that something like forty-five per cent of all births are now out of wedlock?'

The conversation reminded her of one she had recently had with Alan who had included The Family in his list of failing British Institutions.

'I did, actually,' she said, and told them about her boyfriend's forthcoming television series.

They seemed peculiarly interested. It was both exciting and disturbing, she found, to do all this in front of Christopher. Although the client, he seemed almost the voyeur.

'Things fall apart,' said Soapy, 'and the centre shows no signs of holding. And yet when we were young, such a situation would have seemed unthinkable. It's as if we had been born to riches and chosen instead the midden heap.'

'What do you think of that statement, Heather?' asked Sir Perry, watching her closely, handing her tea.

It was like some kind of bizarre interview, she thought. Then, suddenly, there it was again. A perceptible vibration, stirring the surface of the tea into concentric ripples, tickling the lampshade, feathering the dust. Why did the others not notice it? Or perhaps they did notice, had known about it all the time. What did she think of that statement? What did she think of herself today?

'I think . . .' she began and stopped.

She was confused by the tremor and their lack of response. Perhaps it was considered bad form. Maybe they were just testing her. She knew what she thought. She knew they were in rats' alley.

'Take your time,' said Soapy, irritatingly.

She collected herself. If they didn't want to comment on the shaking, it was their prerogative. Let this house fall about their ears.

'I think things are going wrong, yes . . . but perhaps they've always gone wrong. It's part of some law or other, isn't it?' she said.

'Law?' asked Sir Perry, raising his patrician eyebrow.

> *'Law, say the gardeners, is the sun,*
> *Law is the one all gardeners obey,'*

she quoted, laughing nervously. It was almost a giggle.

'Ah, that sort of law,' said Sir Perry. 'A law of nature.'

'Entropy, I think it's called,' she said. 'Everything gets worse.'

'But does that mean we should excuse it?'

'No,' she said. 'No. I don't think so.'

'What if I told you, Heather, that some of us have got together in a . . . venture . . . to try to see that things do not get worse, to try and see, in fact, that things get better? What would you say?'

'I suppose I'd have to say . . . good,' she replied, rather mystified at the direction the conversation was taking.

It was a slightly odd line for Sir Perry, but you couldn't argue with his general drift. Things should be better. But what things? There were so many of them. And what was better for some wouldn't be better for others. Objectively, of course, there were things she believed in: literature, learning, art, beauty, the freedom to explore the walls of one's own personal prison; these were the things, in part, which she understood Sir Perry to be wanting to protect. But there was more to it than that. This was old men's talk. What did they really want? And who did they think they were?

She was aware, of course, of a growing tendency for lawyers and judges to think of themselves as above the law, above the jurisdiction of a legally elected parliament; but she was used to the arrogance of the profession. Was this another plan to flout the government? And why not, since the government seemed so eminently floutable?

'I'd have to say keep going,' she told them.

'Excellent,' said Soapy. 'We felt we could count on you. Now, tell us about the case.'

'I gave Sir Perry the schedule, of course, and really the facts are there. To my mind,' she said, 'our client's case really seemed far too weak. He didn't have an alibi. He seemed almost not to be disposed to help himself.'

'It is sometimes the situation,' remarked Soapy, sagely. 'A sort of lethargy prevails.'

'But he is not a lethargic man,' Heather protested. 'He is . . .'

'Yes?' the Sir Perry eyebrows enquired.

'Well, he is intelligent, vigorous . . .'

'We are glad he has this effect on you, Heather, but you have to admit he looks like a villain. He has sapped his strength in unsavoury pursuits, I daresay.'

At this, Christopher did at last show some emotion, raising his eyebrows like startled rooks.

'I disagree,' she protested. 'And, to prove it, I have at last been able to find a witness who will say she was with Christopher . . .'

'Christopher?'

'Christopher Morbey.'

'Ah. A witness?'

Another exchange of glances with Soapy.

What the hell, she might as well tell them.

'A Miss Graziella Fortezza,' she told them.

'But this is . . . extraordinary . . .' said Sir Perry. 'You said nothing of this on the schedule. What is going on? I insist on being kept informed.'

'I only found out about her a short time ago . . . and then she wouldn't testify . . . but it seems she's changed her mind.'

'Well, I must say, it's all very sudden,' said Soapy.

Neither of them seemed in the least excited that their client had what might very possibly prove to be a lifeline to grasp at. In fact they both seemed rather put out.

'Aren't you pleased?' she asked, mystified.

'Pleased? Yes, of course we're pleased. We're well pleased, Protheroe, aren't we? She will have to be proofed, of course.'

'Of course, we're pleased,' said Soapy, the firelight spinning on his bald dome. 'She will probably have to be summonsed.'

Heather couldn't help feeling that she had earned a black mark. Sir Perry changed the subject.

'Heather will be taking some of the minor interrogation for me,' he told Soapy as if he had told him already but this was for Heather's benefit.

'I know you have some important visitors, coinciding with the trial,' Soapy said. 'I shall be very happy with Heather, I have no doubt. What did you say that new witness's name was?'

'It's all down in the revised schedule,' Heather told him. 'I have a copy for you here. Oh, and I've also noted that the client suffers from vertigo and could not have climbed down from the victim's second floor window . . .'

Sir Perry and Soapy exchanged glances.

'Good, very good,' said Soapy.

For some reason or other, he didn't seem all that pleased.

'Hard to prove, that sort of thing,' said Sir Perry. 'I've known a man put on cerebral palsy just for a trial.'

'We will of course get medical evidence,' said Heather.

'And the prosecution will get another quack to shoot him down. No, let's stick to the alibi. That's your best bet.'

'I'd go along with that,' said Soapy.

The two older men exchanged glances again.

'We shan't need to keep you any longer, Heather,' said Sir Perry. 'I have a few things to cover off with Mr Protheroe and our client here.'

'Oh . . . right . . .'

Soapy tried to look up her skirt as he climbed out of his seat, but it was only ritual; his heart wasn't in it. There was something he urgently wanted to say to Sir Perry, and he was saying it almost before she was out of earshot.

As she closed the door behind her, she caught the one word 'bar'.

Bar (to paraphrase Sir Perry), what sort of bar were they talking about? She pondered the matter as she walked slowly through the hall towards her coat. Was it bar as in The Bar? Or was it a bar to progress? Or an MC and bar? Or a harbour bar that there must be no moaning at? Or was it a bar where alcoholic drinks are served to persons over the age of eighteen, just possibly in the district of Clapham in the many-towered Borough of Lambeth?

She wished she could talk to Christopher about it – why the whole thing seemed so veiled, as if she were missing some vital part of the story – but there was no chance of that at the moment and no peace of mind either. She was rather piqued about the way her vertigo angle had been put down; still, perhaps Sir Perry was right. Graziella would certainly make a stunning witness. No point in clouding the issue.

'Off now, Miss Semple?'

It was Arthur, eyes hard and bright as the dog-star.

'Going anywhere in particular?'

'No, I don't think so. Home, I should think.'

'Oh, I thought you might be heading for a breakdown.'

There was an explosion of mirth somewhere behind a

computer. Heather's face hardened. She hadn't become a barrister for nothing.

'Come, come, Arthur. This is *before* lunch, remember. Surely you can do better than that?'

The laughter died as if a switch had been thrown.

Forty

She met Alan for lunch one day in the week before the trial. Neither of them could make an evening – there was too much work, he was too tired – it seemed to her indicative, but she couldn't blame him because it was as much her fault as his. The trial dominated her attention.

He had telephoned to say that he had news about the chip that could be helpful.

'Can you talk?' she had asked.

'Not now.'

There always had to be a mystery with Alan. So they arranged to meet at a restaurant near the BBC in the Turkish quarter of Great Titchfield Street. Dark-haired, plumpish waiters, heirs of the victors of Nicopolis, moved sleekly between the tables carrying shashliks and kebabs and bottles of Buzbag.

'He says it's a chip,' Alan told her.

'I know that.'

'Well, it's nice to have confirmation, isn't it? It's interesting, he says. Some kind of interactive game, he thinks, but much more complex than any he's seen before. Could be from one of those simulated learning devices. He hasn't been able to crack it yet. It's one of those things that needs time, and he's a busy man. But he's really intrigued, so he's promised to let us have something next week.'

'But the trial's next week,' Heather wailed. 'It could be evidence.'

'I hardly think so,' said Alan. 'I don't see how an interactive game could be central to a murder trial. You know these rent-boys, they live like dung beetles and have state of the art electronics.'

'Even so,' she said. 'I would be grateful. My client would be grateful. A life sentence for something you didn't do concentrates the mind almost as much as the gallows.'

Her pressure brought out, as it sometimes did, a little burst of private petulance from the public man.

'Leave it, Heather, for God's sake. I'm doing what I can.'

'All right, all right.' She put on a placatory smile. She wanted him in constructive mode. 'Sorry, just anxious. I always get a little adrenalin going before a big trial. Tell me about the series.'

'The thing just gets bigger all the time. We're thinking about a second series already. Things like the British mealtime. We don't sit down together any more. And British stiff upper lip – one of the triumphs of our civilization – we gritted our teeth and carried on. Now the American shrinks say we have to "let it out" . . . with how many shaming and disastrous consequences . . . and childhood . . .'

'Childhood?'

'That was a British institution, a Victorian one. They practically re-invented childhood. Look at it now – disappearing before our eyes – with little streetwise burglars of eight, and girls of eleven and twelve going around mugging pensioners. I'll have that.'

'Like Burglar Bill,' she said.

'What?'

Alan evidently wasn't so well up in childhood literature.

'Oh nothing,' she said.

And then he came out with the bombshell.

'I won't, alas,' he said . . . she was already nervous when he said alas – alas always seemed to precede shifty news . . . 'I won't alas be able to come to Suffolk for the Bank Holiday.'

'What?'

'Alas.'

There it was again.

'Not come? But you promised.'

He looked discomfited. She thought he was going to say alas a fourth time.

'Don't say it again,' she told him.

'What?'

'It doesn't matter.'

'I've just got so much on,' he said. 'The Bank Holiday's the only time when I can really get away from the office and admin, and visit locations. I'll be writing as I go. We have to have scripts and the hacks just can't get their heads around this one. We'll do it later, darling. Why don't you go anyway? It'd do you good. Go with a girlfriend.'

A vision of taking Graziella to Suffolk assailed her. She shook her head, plying the mental Magnadoodle.

'We'll see,' she said. 'I'm just rather disappointed. For us, I mean.'

It was true. She had set such store by this rope round the mooring of her past. If only she could go away with Alan again, she could recreate the comfortable safety that had surrounded her before she had pushed out on this dark tide. That, at least, had been the idea; but it was not going to work. She could feel the quay receding even as the waiter put down the Imam Bayildi and salad and poured the sinful wine, and Alan looked across at her over his forkful of garlicky chick-peas and smiled his crooked smile.

'Sorry, darling. But you know how it is.'

But did she know? And if she did, what was to be done about it?

Forty-one

Heather had her last briefing meeting with Christopher, Soapy and Sir Perry at Soapy's office this time, a large Victorian building off the Strand.

Sir Perry was slightly distant, obviously thinking about his bigwigs, and once or twice Heather had to repeat her questions to him. Neither Soapy nor Christopher seemed to mind. She had the strange feeling that she was enacting some pre-ordained role; that they all were; and that nothing she could do or say would make the slightest difference.

Christopher looked withdrawn, crestfallen, almost shifty – which he had never looked before. It didn't diminish her feeling for him; almost increased it, in fact, for she couldn't but understand how anxious he must feel; how her continued refusal to see him must lower his spirits.

Don't worry, she wanted to tell him. We're going to win; we have to concentrate on that. Afterwards things may change. Alan may not need me so much . . . I may not need to be whatever I have been.

'You're quite sure?' Sir Perry had asked in between memorizing the first names of his important visitors. 'You're quite sure that this witness of yours, this Graziella Fortezza . . .' here he adjusted his spectacles energetically, '. . . you're quite sure that she's reliable? We don't want any foul-ups, Heather. This one's all down to you . . . She does exist?'

'I'm quite sure she exists, Sir Perry,' she said.

'Have you checked her out?' Sir Perry asked Soapy.

'As far as we can. I sent young Joscelyn up and he took a proof from her. No negatives came back as far as I know.'

'Fine, fine.'

Christopher turned at last and gave Heather a profound, sad and meaningful look which she could not interpret.

'Happy then, Mr Protheroe?'

'Quite happy, thank you, Sir Perry.'

'Happy, Mr Morbey?'

Christopher paused.

'I don't think happy's quite the word,' he said, looking fixedly at Heather again.

'Of course not, of course not. You're anxious and quite right too,' said Soapy. 'As happy as circumstances permit?'

'I'd go along with that,' said Christopher.

'Right, then. See you all in court.'

'Just one thing.' Christopher raised his hand, stopping the general exodus. 'Do I get the chance to see my counsel before the trial starts?'

'Certainly you do,' said Sir Perry. 'I, ah, unfortunately can't be there first thing, but Miss Semple and I . . . we speak as one, don't we, Miss Semple?'

'Absolutely, Sir Perry. I shall be there.'

She smiled professionally at Christopher, closed her notes, and walked through the door, held open with superficial gallantry by the solicitor.

Forty-two

On Sunday evening, the day before the trial, Heather was sitting at her desk in the living-room going over her notes, thinking about Alan, missing Christopher, when the telephone rang.

'Miss Semple?' said a half-remembered voice.

'Yes.'

'I'm the Sister who was in charge of your mother's ward.'

'Ah . . .'

The mention of her mother brought an extra dimension of loneliness. She was over the shock of her death, but not the loss. It was strange; she had had a presentiment when she picked up the telephone that her mother's voice was going to say 'Feather?' with that little lift on the second syllable.

'I'm so sorry,' continued the caller. 'I've been away on holiday for three weeks and then I had a course. I should have done something about it before I left but there was some trouble with the tickets and . . . there wasn't time. I tried . . .'

'I'm sorry . . . but what are you talking about?'

'That telephone call. The person who rang and told you there was no cause for alarm that night your mother had a heart attack.'

Of course. How could she not have thought of it?

'Right,' she said. 'I'm with you now.'

In the confusion of the last few weeks, she had put the false call out of her mind, classifying it as just another item in the sequence of unpleasant oddities that seemed to be dogging her path.

'Have you found out who did it?' she asked.

'Well, no. When I asked the night sister, I found that the card with the telephone number we had been told to contact – the false one – had been thrown away. Your mother was dead, you see. That's what usually happens when . . . that happens. It was my last day before going away so I wasn't able to check it out any more myself. In fact, I was only able to do that today.'

'Did they keep the number?'

'No. But one of the nurses said she was almost certain she could remember it. She has a sort of photographic memory. We rang the number today but there was no answer. Anyway, we thought we should pass it on to you. Hope it's the right one.'

Heather found she was shaking very slightly, the profound engine starting somewhere again underground.

'What is the number?' she asked.

'Got a pen?'

'Of course. I mean, sorry, yes.'

Why didn't the woman get on with it? Perhaps no one was tunnelling in Oxford.

'It's 0181 076 4161. Got that?'

For some reason the number sounded familiar.

'Yes, thank you,' she said.

'You will let us know if you want to do anything about it, won't you? You know, prosecute or whatever? It was such a shitty thing to do. And why? What for?'

'I'll let you know,' said Heather. 'Thank you so much. It's very kind of you.'

'The least we could do. Goodbye. Take care.'

'Goodbye. And thank you again.'

Heather put the telephone down and sat looking at the number she had written, trying to think why she knew it and feeling the tremble in the floor. A new tunnel for a cyclotron line, a bunker for the Armageddon squad? . . . What was that number? Why did it fill her with a sense of foreboding? Her subconscious must know it all right. Why didn't it pass it on? Didn't she want to know who it was who had diverted the hospital's calls and stopped her being by the bed when her mother died? Yes, of course she did. How dare they? Quite apart from the cruelty of the thing, it was illegal, it was actionable, she would have the law on them. But did she really want to open all that up again? Oh well; might as well.

She lifted the telephone and dialled no-trace, followed by the number. It rang for a moment or two, and then she knew why the number seemed familiar.

'Hello?'

She couldn't speak. Bile rose in her throat. She could feel the tremor now, rocking her shoulders, shaking the nation.

'Hello? Who's there? Anyone there? I can have you traced, you know . . .'

Heather put the telephone down. She could hear again the rustle of leaves, see the worms dropping out of the corner of the eyes.

The voice, now loud and clear, belonged to Mrs Haddenham.

She called Alan at the editing suite, and a girl's voice that she hadn't heard before answered. Yes, he was there. It was a rare thing to call him at work – not part of the agreement – and he wasn't pleased at being disturbed though he tried not to show it.

'It was probably the night sister confusing the numbers. Mother used to ring up the hospital and ask how your mother was. She was very fond of her, you know,' he told her with exasperated reasonableness. 'She liked to be involved.'

Alan, in spite of his irritation, set about pouring oil in his usual way. He didn't like trouble. It interfered with filming. Changing the subject adroitly he told her now that he was widening his brief to include the British Mother (funny she should mention mothers).

'Do you know that forty-five per cent of babies born today are to unmarried mothers? That thirty-five per cent of young women don't want to have children?' he said.

'Fuck the unmarried mothers,' she said, refusing to be soothed.

'That's just the trouble, Heather,' said Alan seriously. 'They have been. And because the family's collapsing, childhood itself – that great Victorian institution, we touched on it the other day – is collapsing along with it. The unmarried mum can't cope, wants her kids to get out of her hair and grow up quick so she can get back to grazing and viewing. So the kids go out on the street, play truant, sniff glue, mug, burgle, murder – and the law stands by and says tut, tut . . . it's too bad . . .'

It was rare for Alan to repeat himself; it was almost as though he were rabbiting.

'It doesn't alter the fact, Alan, that what your mother did was inexcusable,' she said.

'You've always had it in for her a bit, haven't you, love?'

'Had it in? I had it in for her – after all those crème brûlées – after she gate-crashed that funeral?'

Heather was speechless with indignation.

'Yes, come on, admit it,' he told her.

'Alan, I don't want to talk about it. Not now.'

'But you did want to talk about it.'

'I only want to register a protest. A strong protest, Alan. She stopped me seeing my mother before she died.'

'She was only trying to help. She only wants to feel part of things.'

'I don't know about that. Did I ever tell you I had a dream about her once? She was coming out of the ground, clutching at me, saying, "Call me Daphne that's Greek for laurel, you know". My subconscious was trying to tell me something. She wanted me to die.'

'Now, now, Heather. Dreams and superstitions. You'll be studying chicken entrails next.'

It was always the same with Alan. Why couldn't he look at the facts for once instead of endlessly talking about them? If only the trial wasn't so close, if only everything wasn't quite so on top of her, she'd go over and have it out with the woman, once and for all.

'Don't take it out on my mother just because I can't get away, alas, for that weekend you were planning.'

It struck her that Alan had known it was his mother all along.

Five minutes later the telephone rang again. It was the duty clerk. Christopher's bail had been revoked; his surety had been withdrawn. No reason was given. It was too late to do anything about it now. She was to see him in the cells of the Bailey before the trial next morning.

Forty-three

She breakfasted on hope and adrenalin washed down with a cup of coffee, and arrived at court an hour before proceedings were due to start. She went straight down to see him, going through the 'decompression corridor' where you're locked in before you're allowed through, feeling she could use some de-pressuring device herself. She knew that no one from the solicitors would be there yet. Why had the surety been withdrawn?

She could see him sitting at a table in the conference room ready for her, moodily playing patience under the watchful eye of a large officer hovering outside.

'Morning, miss,' said the officer as she briefly introduced herself. 'Hope you can cheer him up a bit.'

He held the door open for her as she walked through. Christopher did not look up when she came in. She saw that it was not after all patience he was playing: the pack consisted of tarot cards.

'Perhaps I should have brought some chicken entrails for you to look at,' she said, remembering Alan's jibe.

'I've just dealt myself the Hanged Man,' he said.

'Well, whatever happens, it's not going to be as bad as that.'

She felt at least she should be cheerful for him.

'It is as bad as that,' he told her, lifting his startlingly black eyes towards her at last.

'Don't be so defeatist. I think we have an excellent chance of winning. Why didn't you tell me about Graziella early on?'

'I didn't want to make trouble for her. Or for you.'

'For me?'

'We'll see,' he said.

She couldn't understand his gloom.

'Are you cross with me?' she asked. 'I just had not to see you till this was over. Do you understand that?'

'Of course I understand. It's myself I'm cross with. Myself and . . .'

'And what?'

'Just . . . the whole thing. There's things I can't tell you because I don't really know them. But I do know you're wasting your time.'

'With you? I'm wasting my time with you?'

'Not with me exactly; no. I love you. Do you understand that? Can you understand that? I've never loved anyone the way I love you – and yet I'm putting you through all this and I can't stop it.'

It surprised her now to hear him repeat the words she had often imagined him saying. Did he really love her? Or was it just momentary? Was he simply in a low-lying pocket of love or was it a genuine pea-souper?

And how was it for her? Her sense of growing isolation made it harder for her now. It's difficult to love when you're fighting for survival. It seemed to her that she had swum out to rescue someone who actually wanted to drown. The question was: could she rescue him, or was she going to drown as well? Did she love him enough to want to risk drowning? She supposed she must or she wouldn't be here.

It was just that she was beginning to lose touch with her feelings which frightened her more than anything. Of course she was in love with him. It was the one thing, surely, that she could hang onto. But she didn't understand the last part of what he was saying.

'I don't know what you mean,' she said. 'Tell me what you mean.'

'I can't. I don't know . . . Christ, I wish I could make love to you.'

The man at the door, just out of earshot, looked in with good-natured attentiveness.

'It'd give him something to talk about,' she said. 'Liven up his life a bit. Make Justice jangle her scales.'

'Justice? That's a funny word to use. Let's see if we get Justice.'

He started dealing his cards again.

'Justice would be the Woman with the Sword, Venus . . . There we are. Pick up a card. Maybe you'll have more luck. Ah . . . Tower of Destruction.'

She could feel the vibration again, deep down under the Bailey.

'You'd think cracks would open up the walls,' she said.

'They are,' he told her. 'Only you can't see them.'

'Oh my darling,' she said.

'I'm so sorry.' There were tears in the black eyes.

She ruffled his hair unobtrusively to make him look blackbirdy. It was the slicked hair that made him look evil. Somewhere a bell rang. She looked at her watch.

'I'd better go up and find Sir Perry. He'll have had his devilled kidneys with the bigwigs and be pawing the ground to get back. Mustn't miss his peerage.'

She touched his shoulder as she left.

'See you in court,' she said. 'Buck up.'

'Buck down,' he said. 'Buck very down indeed.'

She couldn't think why he was so dejected.

'Good luck, miss,' said the man at the gate. 'Break a leg.'

But it wasn't the leg she was worried about; it was the heart.

Forty-four

After two days, the trial, she thought, was going well.

The jury looked mostly like reasonable people – if there was such a thing. Christopher had given his plea of 'Not Guilty' in a firm, clear voice, and you could see a couple of the matrons in the jury glancing sympathetically at him.

Johnson Fyfe had given the outline for the prosecution in a rather bad-tempered way, not endearing himself to the matrons, making much of the strands of material found at the scene of the crime which matched fibres in a jacket belonging to the accused. He rested on these slight filaments as though they were pillars of stone. They and the evidence of the manager of Our Souls – a name which did not endear itself to the matrons – were the basis of the prosecution's case. He stated that there were no issues on the medical evidence since the defence had indicated they did not intend to contest the nature or indeed the hour of the deceased's death . . .

Sir Perry was looking as eminent as a QC should. A slightly donnish vagueness mantled the purposefulness of his eyes which, she noticed, swivelled constantly from judge to prisoner to jury and back to prosecution. All impression of wanting to be with his bigwigs had vanished – though she knew he would soon be slipping off after the first and most important witness, Walter Muscott from Our Souls, was called. Even the judge, Mr Justice Hardiman, seemed a reasonable sort of fellow and was so by reputation – if a little inclined to have his jest.

No, everything was fine. She couldn't understand Christopher's gloom but she supposed it was the accumulation of weeks of uncertainty, coupled perhaps with his impatience and frustration at not seeing her. He seemed to understand the reasons for that, but there was still something that worried him. Well, it would soon be over. Somehow or other she must make her choice between him and Alan. Somehow or other she must decide what to do with her life. It was becoming clear that the bar was not for her; and yet what else was there for her? Someone, probably Alan who was full of good worldly advice, had told her you should never make a big change at home and at work simultaneously. You must hang on with one hand while you scrabbled for a hold with the other. And here she was contemplating letting go with both . . .

The first witness was being called:

'Walter Muscott.'

And that was the first surprise. Heather's heart leapt sickeningly up to her mouth, ricocheted against her teeth. The man was Mandy; Mandy in a man's clothes. Walter Ego! She broke into a cold sweat. How could she have been so stupid?

'You are Walter Muscott of 42 Plumstead Road, Wandsworth?' asked Johnson Fyfe.

'Call me Walter,' said Mandy, camply.

'Mr Muscott,' ordered the judge. 'Answer the question. Or we may call you Wally.'

A polite ripple of appreciation passed through the court.

'Give a dog a bad name, my lord,' said Mandy, simpering. 'Oh, never mind . . .'

Now the cat was out of the bag, Heather thought. I've done it now – talked to a prosecution witness. I should have known, of course I should have known, transvestites can have two personalities, can mislead themselves, let alone anybody else, into thinking they are two people. What happens now? Do I tell Sir Perry? Or do I hope no one will find out?

She looked beside her at her head of chambers. His fine features were turned earnestly towards the witness as though hanging on his every word. She tried to catch his attention once or twice but it never seemed the right moment.

The morning wore on. Mandy/Walter vowed he had seen the accused leaving with the deceased at ten o'clock that night. He had particularly noticed the time because one of his regulars had asked if he could watch *News at Ten* in the office.

Heather nerved herself to broach the issue with Sir Perry at several further points, but somehow the timing was never quite right.

When Johnson Fyfe had finished, Sir Perry got up to cross-examine. His slightly dithering manner put Mandy/Walter instantly at her ease. He felt at home with people like Sir Perry. Indeed a number of his customers were very similar to him; and so counsel led him gently on until, almost as an afterthought, he asked him whether Our Souls was full that night.

'It's full every night. That night it was crammed.'

Sir Perry pounced like a panther.

'Then how could you possibly see them go out of the door together? Let alone walk off in the same direction?'

Mandy/Walter floundered and flustered, but there was no doubt who had come off the winner.

At this point, Sir Perry whispered to Heather that he must be off for a short while, giving her a mobile number to call if anything urgent came up. She wanted to tell him about her débâcle with the witness but there was plainly no time. By now anyway it was far too late . . .

After he left, a considerable hiatus in the proceedings followed, with the judge finally deciding that he too had had enough and ordering an adjournment, during which he would no doubt take his coffee.

Heather wondered whether to go down and see Christopher again but decided that she needed to keep emotion at bay for the moment. A clear head would do more for him than tortured conversation in the cells. She went and had a cappuccino, and thought about the morning.

She was impressed as always with Sir Perry. He played the amateur, he might act in private like a mandarin, but he was a killer in court. She wondered about him. What did he mean by that curious conversation the other day, almost a deliberate digression from the forthcoming case – with the client present – to talk about the country and 'some of us getting together'. She had noticed a certain flinching at the present state of things in people of that generation who had been young before what Sir Perry called 'the beaded curtain of the sixties', but she had put it down to the usual distaste of the old for the new.

The court still not having reconvened she glanced at the newspaper and looked through her notes, while her thoughts turned back to the earlier proceedings. Quite apart from her gaffe with the witness, perhaps she should have told Sir Perry about Val saying Mandy/Walter was jealous where Graziella was concerned. That would have cast the gravest doubt on Mandy/Walter's evidence. But she hadn't wanted to introduce mention of Graziella to him until she could produce her as her ace witness – a 'late witness' now, of course, so late the police had not had time to check her out, and the judge's leave to call her had been needed.

Anyway, Sir Perry had done for Mandy/Walter without Graziella. In fact it seemed Sir Perry was going to leave Heather's witness to her. That was an unexpected gesture, a sign of real grace in the man. Many another QC, a vain breed, would have wanted to handle the crowning moment of the case, but not Sir Perry . . .

'You have worked hard, Heather, perhaps too hard,' he told her on his return at lunchtime, the adjournment having been extended until two o'clock.

Here he paused and surveyed her under his bushy grey eyebrows.

'I don't mind hard work,' she had told him, 'as long as it's appreciated.'

'It's appreciated if we win,' he said. 'We're never appreciated if we lose. That is the barrister's burden. At any rate, this is your star witness. I think it is only fair that you should handle her.'

Was there a slight emphasis on the penultimate word, or was the stress merely in her mind? Everything seemed to have a cloaked or double meaning as if sense itself had turned transvestite.

His general theme, however, encouraged her and she decided to tell him now of the embarrassment into which she had unwittingly put herself.

'There is one thing, Sir Perry.'

The great man turned and cast a dubious eye on her.

'One thing? When people say one thing it usually means one big thing in my experience,' he said. 'What is your one big thing?'

'When I visited the locus,' she said, taking the plunge, 'I talked to the person who ran the wine bar. The clerk from the solicitors was with me.'

'Go on,' said Sir Perry.

'The manager of the bar told me she was not a witness but . . .' It sounded foolish now. '. . . I didn't realize she was a man. She told me she was not a witness.'

'Let me get this straight. She told you that she was not a man?'

'Not *the* man, no.'

'Not which man?'

'The witness.'

'She told you she was not the witness? But she was a man.'

'She was the witness man. She called him Walter. Walter Ego.'

'But the name is . . . let me see . . . Walter Muscott.'

'That was her way of telling me she was two people. I should have seen.'

Sir Perry looked very put out. He placed his lips together, puffed his cheeks, and blew out with a loud whoooo.

'Oh dear, oh dear,' he said at last. 'We *are* accident-prone. Why did we not say this before?'

'I only realized it when the witness appeared.'

'You should have told me then and there.'

'I tried but . . .'

'You tried? Really, Heather, we have to do harder than try when procedure is at stake. Anyway, nothing to be done about it now. Damage limitation is the name of the game at this point. I will have a word with the judge and with Johnson Fyfe. I don't think there will be a problem. But, please, Heather . . . no more foul-ups, eh?'

It didn't exactly serve to bolster confidence.

He told her he would not be in court that afternoon but she should call him after it adjourned, at six.

Forty-five

After the police evidence and the pathologist's gruesome testimony, the witness Johnson Fyfe called next was a forensic scientist named Dove who explained how he had found these fibres from a blue jacket or blazer of popular make caught on a slight splintering of the wood in the deceased's cupboard. It matched exactly a jacket of the same kind found in the accused's wardrobe.

When the moment came for Heather to cross-examine, she made much of the fact that this was a popular jacket.

'Boss, I believe?' she asked.

'That is correct.'

'Do you know how many Boss blue jackets are sold in a year?'

'I have no idea.'

'I have asked them and it runs into tens of thousands.'

'There was a frayed end to one of the arms on the accused's jacket.'

'I daresay there are thousands of frayed ends, Mr Dove, hanging in the wardrobes up and down this country.'

'Or as Mr Pooter would put it, I'm frayed there are,' said the judge.

'Thank you, my lord,' said Heather, as another murmur of respectful mirth circulated the courtroom.

'Yes,' said Mr Dove, 'but not with a little blood from the same rare blood group as the accused's on it. It seems the owner of the jacket also caught his hand on the splinter. It was difficult to do an STR-type DNA test since the sample was too small, but analysis suggests a very high likelihood of the blood being of the same rare rhesus negative type as the accused.'

'I . . .'

Heather was momentarily at a loss for words. This was surely not in the prosecution's bundle that she had received? No one had mentioned blood before? Or had she overlooked it in the throng and press of the last month? Surely not. The Defence scientist had said nothing about blood. Why had blood not featured in Johnson Fyfe's questions in chief? Reality seemed to blur and tremble for a moment. It was as if in one dimension it rang a bell, and in another it had no existence. She wondered whether to challenge the prosecution on the point but feared she might only look more foolish.

'Well, Miss Semple?' asked the judge, not unkindly.

It was like being on stage and forgetting your lines, or finding that you had neglected to put your clothes on. She reached for the nearest straw and grasped it.

'May I have a ten-minute adjournment, my lord?'

'Very well, Miss Semple, if you must.'

She sat down, gratefully, breathing hard, blushing in spite of every effort to stop it. A slight buzz of curiosity ran round the gallery, a faint crowd noise of humanity sensing blood whatever group it was. She glanced at Christopher sitting white-faced under his black thatch, expecting to see anger or mortification at her lapse but all she could discern was a curious expression that seemed almost one of shame – or sorrow. Zmmmmmm.

Ah well, she thought, we needn't worry. Whatever his blood group or his torn sleeve, there are hundreds of others like it. It will mean nothing when we produce our alibi. However, when the court reconvened, she had to concede that she had no further questions, and in due course the prosecution finished calling their witnesses, and closed the case.

When the court adjourned she called Sir Perry and told him of the new evidence. He listened gravely and, much to her surprise, told her he recalled mentioning the blood group to her in one of their discussions.

'I thought you had covered it off, Heather,' he said.

'Well, I . . . er . . .'

She couldn't very well say she had forgotten everything about it.

'I hope you're coping all right, Heather. We did think we could leave most of this in your capable hands. We can, can't we? I'm very tied up at the moment, as you know. It's cleared with the judge, of course. I had a word. He gave leave for us to adduce our evidence of alibi with some reluctance, I may add. Sure you're all right?'

'Absolutely. I'm fine. Just looking forward to introducing my witness.'

'That's the spirit. Catch 'em on the hop. Don't let us down now, Heather. Counting on you, you know. Safe pair of hands. 'Bye.'

'Goodbye, Sir Perry.'

Wandering thoughtfully down Fleet Street, she bumped into Johnson Fyfe, a bumptious little man with a big head and glaring eyes, hurrying round a corner from the other direction.

'Caught you there, didn't we?' he said, spitefully. 'Better luck next time – if there is a next time.'

He hurried on before she could reply. What did he mean by that? There was always a next time in a court of law, and she could show him when that next time would be.

Forty-six

As it happened, the timing of the trial would have fitted in very nicely with her plan to take Alan away for a break.

It looked as though they would even get a verdict before the Bank Holiday weekend. There might of course be an adjournment if the jury couldn't decide. In which case, sentencing – not that there would be sentencing, but if there were – would be carried out following the verdict on Tuesday. She had a last surge of desperation for the past; a final clutch at the jetty. She would have another go at Alan when he called in – whenever that might be – and insist he come away with her, if necessary, not taking no for an answer. They owed it to each other. You couldn't just wash four years down the drain. She had got the key from Chloe who had called in at chambers before she left for Scotland; Primrose Cottage would be waiting on the banks of the Deben . . .

She tried to telephone him that night but there was only his answerphone. She tried the editors but again there was a machine. Apart from anything else, she wanted any more information he could give her about the chip. After today's fiasco with the blood group, she was feeling sensitive about evidence, although she knew the chip was a slender vessel to pin any hopes on. Still, it would be good to have it. She left a message to that effect, asking also for the telephone number of the expert, the top man, even though she knew he wouldn't give it.

Next morning she tried again but there was still no answer.

No matter; this morning was the big one; the case for the defence was to open.

Some puckish instinct made her wear stockings and frivolous underwear. It amused her to go to court in such things. She looked at herself in the full-length mirror, ran her hands over her body, remembering the sudden feeling yesterday of nightmare and nakedness. Today, she would be better underpinned.

Putting on the court suit with the shorter skirt, she walked down the stairs and out into the street feeling altogether prepared for victory.

There was a message from Sir Perry waiting for her saying he had been detained but would arrive later in the day. She was to go ahead with the case for the defence.

In the cells, Christopher was sitting with his tarot cards again. He had been reading them for the officer outside. It was strange to see him sitting there, almost incredible that he had made love to her, as if it were a sequence from another set of dreams.

'Mr Goggin comes from Banbury. He tells me it's a local name. He has a very interesting set of cards here, particularly strong in wands. But I don't like his Magician.'

'What's that mean?' asked Mr Goggin.

'You have everything within your grasp, Mr Goggin, but you must beware of trickery.'

'I'm selling my car this weekend,' said Mr Goggin. 'Thank you for that. I'll bear it in mind.'

'May we talk?' asked Heather.

'Certainly, miss,' said the officer. 'A very interesting prisoner we have here.'

'Very interesting,' agreed Heather.

'Please go ahead, don't mind me.'

Mr Goggin wandered away with his *Autocar*, and Heather sat down opposite Christopher in the cell.

'I'm sorry about yesterday,' she said.

'It wasn't your fault,' he told her. 'They haven't got it in for you particularly. It's because you're representing me. They want me inside.'

'Well, it's my job to see that doesn't happen.'

'I'm sick about it, to be honest with you,' he said, 'but my hands are tied.'

'Metaphorically speaking,' she told him. 'Soon you'll be out of here.'

'We'll see,' he said. 'Don't count my chickens. Oh Christ, I wish I was a thousand miles from here.'

'You will be soon,' she said.

'Would you come with me?'

'Oh Christopher, I don't know. Let's leave it till this is over.'

There was a tap on the window. It was Mr Goggin saying they were wanted shortly in court.

'Fingers crossed,' she told him. 'I'll do the best I can for you.'

'You're wearing sexy underwear, aren't you?' he said.

She was completely astonished.

'How on earth do you know?'

'I could think it,' he said. 'Remember the first time you came to see me?'

'You were extremely rude.'

'Still am, darling.'

They smiled at each other, making love with their eyes.

''Ere,' said Mr Goggin, 'there's a Fiesta just like mine, 70,000 on the clock, for £5000. What d'you make of that? Magic.'

Forty-seven

She had arranged to meet Graziella in the public restaurant on the second floor of the court. Joscelyn should have been there too but was, inevitably, delayed again. Anyway, it was a relief to see her sitting there in her trim blue suit and white shirt, looking so businesslike and credible – not at all like the wayward creature with whom she had been invited to share a bed.

'Why you look surprise?' the girl asked. 'You think I not going to come?'

'No, no,' said Heather, hurriedly. 'I trusted you implicitly.'

'We are lovers, no? Why should I betray lover? I betray enemy, yes, but lovers no.'

She was becoming quite what Heather's mother used to call agitato.

'Shh,' Heather warned her. 'We don't want the whole Bailey to hear.'

'Why not? You ashamed?'

'No, no. Of course not.'

'That's good because if you ashamed I go away.'

'You can't go away. You're summonsed.'

'I bloody can. I do what I like. No one tell Graziella what to do.'

Oh God, thought Heather, make me patient. Now she had seen Christopher she felt nothing for the girl – no, maybe a touch of embarrassment. She hoped she wouldn't make trouble.

'Just . . . just do it, Graziella. Remember, you liked Christopher.'

'Maybe. But I do it for you. You like to go to bed after?'

'Er, no, I don't think so, Graziella.'

'Why not?'

'I have work to do here. We have a case to win. There'll be time for all that . . . later . . .'

She didn't want to turn the girl right off; not yet at any rate.

'I no think you like me any more,' said the girl sulkily.

'Of course I do – very much.'

Heather leaned across and patted the girl's hand. It was a mistake. Graziella seized her hand and pressed it to her bosom.

'Feel,' she said fervently. 'Feel how I love you.'

'Er, not now, Graziella.'

She withdrew her hand and looked furtively around. A policeman, opening the door, gazed over at them curiously.

'Why not now?'

Heather lost her temper.

'Because you're giving evidence at a fucking murder trial, that's why. It doesn't get more serious than that.'

At last Graziella seemed to see reason. She withdrew into herself, pouting a little.

'You do not love me any more,' she said.

Oh God, thought Heather, why did I get into all this? But aloud she said: 'Of course I do.'

Graziella seemed unconvinced.

Forty-eight

The court rose, formalities were ended and it was Heather's turn to present the case for the defence. All memories of her embarrassment yesterday were behind her. She looked good, she sounded good, and she couldn't help noticing Johnson Fyfe looking more and more deflated as, with admiring eyes upon her, she eloquently drove home the points for the defence.

The judge himself seemed quite captivated, and when she said that the prosecution hadn't got a leg to stand on, he couldn't refrain from interjecting: 'Happily, that is certainly what one cannot say about the counsel for the defence.'

There was an appreciative murmur from all sides at this sally, although Johnson Fyfe immediately sprang up with an objection.

'Sit down, Mr Fyfe, we are not commenting upon the case, merely the counsel. Pray continue, Miss Semple.'

Heather intended to show that the case for the defence rested upon one simple point: nothing so intricate as that he didn't strike the fatal blow or tie the fatal knot or that his blood group might or might not match that found on the thread . . . but that he wasn't there at all that night and therefore could not have committed the murder. In order to prove that point, of course, he needed an alibi. And it so happened that a witness was to hand who could vouch for the defendant's presence with her from ten that night until seven next morning.

As if in anticipation, Johnson Fyfe was looking really sick, and Heather revelled in the effect she was about to make. Success like this had an almost sexual quality to it. She could feel herself move in the silken thinness under her skirt.

'Call Miss Graziella Fortezza.'

Heather looked round triumphantly, smiling at the judge, at the jury, finally at Christopher. She was astonished to see that, alone in the court, he was actually looking dejected, almost hang-dog. She smiled at him again, encouraging him to be cheerful. But what was this? Why was there a commotion over by the witness box? Why was Johnson Fyfe grinning all over his big head?

'There seems to be some problem with your witness, Miss Semple,' said the judge, kindly.

'The problem is,' said Johnson Fyfe, springing bumptiously to his feet, 'the problem is, there is no witness.'

And it was true. Graziella, whom Heather had scrupulously checked out, briefed, organized and embraced beyond the call of duty, had simply vanished.

There was of course a great deal of commotion. Heather was called into the judge's room where he questioned her closely about the witness, questions to which Heather gave what answers she could. The witness had been summonsed. Where was the witness? She had spoken to her that morning, she knew about her court appearance. She had checked with the usher again that Miss Fortezza was present. But she was not present – at least, not now.

At length the judge, much to Johnson Fyfe's objection, decided on an adjournment.

'No, Mr Fyfe, it is not partiality. Justice must be done if a man's freedom is at stake; it must be done always. If a witness is missing, we must try and find the witness.'

'If there *is* a witness,' said Johnson Fyfe snidely.

'That remains to be seen. I shall give you, Miss Semple, until the day after tomorrow. If you cannot find your witness in that time, Miss Semple, we shall have to proceed without her. I hope you manage to track her down, tell her of the penalties of non-appearance, and persuade her to keep faith with her barrister. Semple fidelis, eh?'

While Johnson Fyfe ground his teeth, Heather thanked the judge and assured him she would look for Graziella, but a little toad of doubt had begun to take up residence in her heart.

Forty-nine

She called Graziella at the number she had been given but the line was discontinued. She tried Our Souls but no one had seen the girl. Mandy spoke to her and seemed moody and unhelpful.

'No, I've not seen her and I'd give her stick if I had. What does she want to go poking her nose in for anyway? None of her business.'

'It is her business if she spent the night with my client.'

'I wish I had sixpence for everyone she spent the night with. She can't remember who she spends her nights with. It'd be like asking a flea how many people he's bitten.'

'Ask her to call me, will you? She's been summonsed . . . subpoenaed.'

'Sub penis more likely. And I didn't like your chum, Sir Wotsisname. I reckoned he was right out of order.'

That was all Heather could get out of her. She went round to the address Graziella had given her, but the woman who lived there had no knowledge of her. She went to the Pizza 'n' Donut in the High Street and spoke to the woman who had been there before, supervising the transfer of money from her bag.

'I remembers you,' said the woman. 'You's a conman.'

Heather didn't waste time arguing.

'Those people I was talking to last time. Do you know where they live?'

'No.'

'Do they come here often?'

'No.'

'You're not being very helpful.'

'You goin' to rip 'em off. Why should I help?'

'I'm a barrister, a lawyer. I'm not going to rip anyone off.'

'A lawyer? Not going to rip off? That's a good one, man. Hey, Christabel.'

Another large black woman appeared from behind the counter.

'This woman's a lawyer and says she ain't going to rip no one off.'

The other woman approached; mountainous, implacable.

'I don't like no lawyers,' she said.

'I tell you what, man,' said the first woman. 'If you's not going to rip no one off, how come you's a lawyer.'

They stood over her like Fates. It was a question she could not answer. She returned to her flat and sat hunched, staring at the wall and feeling the floor shake.

Later, it seemed hours later, she had a call from Sir Perry.

'I've been talking to Soapy,' he told her. 'His junior says you failed to produce your witness. Bad, Heather, very bad.'

'I know,' said Heather. 'I've been trying to find her.'

'You'd better do that.'

There was none of the usual affability. Sir Perry was hardly ever tight-lipped so when he was, he was very tight-lipped indeed.

'I shall be in court on Thursday, day after tomorrow, Heather. I strongly advise you to have your witness by then.'

'I'll try, Sir Perry.'

'You'll have to do more than that.'

When she had put the phone down, she poured herself a glass of wine. It helped a little but not very much. She stared at the wall some more, and then she realized that the answering machine had been blinking. My God, it might be Graziella, she thought. She almost ripped the thing from its socket in her haste. But it wasn't Graziella, it was Alan.

'Hullo, darling,' he said. 'Sorry to be so elusive, had to go up to Scotland, State of the Union and so forth. That's really cracking up now. And sorry about the weekend. I'd really have liked to have done that. Maybe another time. Now, about your chip. There's something rather funny about it, in fact the top man says it's quite extraordinary. I think if he's right it might have quite a bearing on your case. He's just running another test or two, and I'll call you tomorrow. Anyway I'll see you next week. Get ready for some jolly juice, hm?'

And that was it. Typical Alan; totally infuriating. Why should he think her job could wait and his couldn't? Why hadn't he got on the case before? That chip was important, perhaps more important than Graziella. Where was that man? She called his office and his home again but no one answered.

Fifty

That night the tunnel dream came back again.

It was so simple, she should have seen it all along, but she knew that in dreams the obvious is often astonishing while the impossible is taken for granted. The man was of course Christopher. And yet he wasn't Christopher. The answer was, he was two people in the same body.

His cough was worse now. It made her heart bleed to hear it.

He turned a corner and there was something almost completely blocking the path, another roof fall, must have only just happened because there was still dust, it was like living in Japan down here, or California, there was an earthquake going on but the authorities weren't telling anyone, they thought they could keep it quiet.

His breath was coming in painful wheezing gasps now as though he had sharks' teeth in his lungs, and his side hurt like buggery. How long had he been running like this? Was it day or night? What were the people doing up there where there was still a life to be led, where there were men he could have mugged, girls he could have fucked, lagers he could have lifted, football fans he could have kicked?

He stopped to listen and there was that slithering sound behind him again, louder, more insistent . . .

The tunnel had been sloping for some time now, making the going easier. He knew he couldn't run any faster. Unless a miracle happened he was in the shit – even deeper and worse shit than the shit that surrounded him, and that was shit enough for anyone's book of shit.

He rounded a corner and ran slap into a great grille that straddled the tunnel. Beyond it came the sound of water pattering onto shingle and the scurrying light of the river. He turned without hope. There had been no side tunnels for a while. The sounds were too close to go back and look for more. He sank down beside the grille with his face to the light, feeling the earth shaking.

What would they do with him now? Heather had the feeling that he was going to die and she was sorry for him even though he was a thug.

They held him down and rolled up his sleeve to give him an injection. Brutishly, he asked them to kill him there and then; and they said no, it wasn't part of the plan. That was not the idea at all.

He told them to put him in the river which he could hear lopping along beyond the grille, the urgent noise of water bristled by the wind, the fret against the current, and the whoop-whoop-whoop of the emergency swans.

They took him back to the white room and put him into the mask. His mind floated out again on the tide.

When Heather woke she found she had been crying, even though the man in the tunnel wasn't Christopher or even half Christopher at all.

Fifty-one

She did not find Graziella in the day allotted to her. She had known instinctively, from the moment of the girl's non-appearance, that she wasn't going to find her – ever. Graziella, delinquent, delicious, was back in Italy; she was in America; she was in a concrete trouser-suit; she was gone. Heather called Sir Perry and told him the bad news. He took it badly, saying it was the worst thing that had happened to him in all his thirty-five years at the bar.

When the court reconvened, the judge sent for her and asked if she had found her witness. She said she had not. She was sorry. There was something else, though, she told him.

'And what is that?'

'A chip.'

'A chip?'

'I found it when I was looking round the deceased's flat.'

'Did you not tell anyone?'

'I thought at the time it wasn't important. There was a lot of junk there.'

'A chip, d'you say?'

'Yes. Rather like a computer chip.'

'You feel that it may throw light on the case?'

'I do, my lord.'

'Where is this chip? You realize you cannot be your own witness?'

'I don't have it. It's at my, er, friend's. He has a computer expert who's looking at it.'

'What is on this chip that you think may be important?'

'I'm afraid I don't know.'

Something seemed to be going on behind the judge's kind old eyes, something like a dawning realization; a weariness.

'We have heard enough of these chimeras of yours, Miss Semple. Enough of chips. End of discussion. I'm afraid we really cannot have another adjournment while you institute yet another search. You should have got your material ready. I will really have to speak to Sir Peregrine . . .'

And so the trial entered its final phase. Johnson Fyfe gave a spirited and vindictive conclusion, painting a picture of Christopher that made him out a monster of vice and cruelty; and she in her turn (no sign of Sir Perry) endeavoured to make bricks without straw. It wasn't very convincing and the fact was noted in the judge's summing up.

'You may think,' he said to the jury, 'that the missing witness would have proved beyond doubt the innocence of the accused; the impossibility of his being in that grim flat in Poynter's Road. But we did not have the witness. And without her, the prosecution's case, though to some extent circumstantial – a rare blood group is just that: it is a remarkable coincidence, but no more – may seem to you overwhelming. After all, we can all produce a missing witness. It is the tangible, the manifest, the three-dimensional, red-blooded witness *in the flesh* that prevails upon our judgement. Absence, though it may make the heart grow fonder, is hardly likely to carry the day in a court of law, so we must not speculate on what the witness might have said . . .'

It was not surprising that the jury returned a verdict of guilty, after spending only an hour to consider it.

'The court will reconvene on Tuesday next for sentencing,' said the judge, anxious to get away for the long weekend.

'All rise,' said the usher.

Johnson Fyfe sprang to his feet with a show of arrant triumphalism which was tantamount to punching the air, while tears sprang to Heather's eyes as she bowed her head, not bearing to look as Christopher was led down to the cells.

Fifty-two

Heather retired to the Ladies to lament awhile, undisturbed, at the duplicity of people and the unfairness of things and the strange determination of Christopher to be found guilty in spite of all her efforts, and then she went down to the cells to say goodbye.

There was a new officer outside, unforthcoming and saturnine. Goggin must have been taking his tea-break. Christopher was sitting alone with a resigned look on his face. It was strange how her love grew in the bitter dust of defeat. She knew now that the break with the past would be total.

'You did your best,' he said.

'We'll appeal, of course.'

There was only one sentence for murder: life.

'I think not,' he told her.

'Well,' she said. 'If you want to go to prison, that's what you'll get. A good long spell. I suppose you're happy now.'

'I'm not happy,' he said, without looking at her.

'Well, why then? For God's sake, Christopher, what have you been doing? You've lost your freedom. I've lost a . . . friend . . .'

'Not lost,' he said.

'Yes, lost,' she told him. 'You'll be inside for at least twelve years, and I don't think I could wait that long. Why did you do it?'

He was silent for a while, and then he turned to her.

'They're not recording this, are they?' he asked.

'Why should they?' she replied bitterly. 'They've got what they want, too, haven't they?'

'All right,' he said. 'I'll tell you. But you must swear not to repeat this to anyone. Not for my sake, you understand, but for yours.'

'Mine?' She laughed. 'I hardly think . . .'

'You must promise me.'

'Very well, then. I promise.'

'You deserve an explanation,' he said, 'God knows you do. But I simply wasn't able to tell you before. It would have been even more dangerous for you to know. You would've . . . given the game away.'

'The game away? What game?'

'Spilt the beans,' he said, 'blabbed, let the cat out of the bag.'

'I don't understand,' she said again.

'The Plan,' he told her. 'It's at a very critical stage. There's still some fine tuning to be done, and it's still vulnerable. Give it six months and the thing will be on the road.'

'Will you tell me what you're talking about?'

His features seemed to sag momentarily as if he were once more shouldering some burden that had been put aside. She felt a wave of pity for him in spite of her own frustration and sense of failure.

'You know that I'm a mathematician,' he said at last.

'Yes. So?'

'I've been working with an outfit, very big it is . . . I stand to make a very great deal of money . . .'

'Yes?'

'It's associated with Interfood. You know – SupaBread, Stella Hotels, Snackanory, Choc-a-Box, Jollity Brands, Eurovin . . .'

'The wine importers? I suppose they own the wine bar?'

'They do. But they're only part of the plan. They just provide some of the funding. It's a pilot scheme in association with the Prison Service. The whole thing's still unofficial. If you asked the Home Office about it they'd deny all knowledge.'

'That's nothing new. Even if they knew they'd still be ignorant.'

She was feeling bitter this afternoon.

'It's a pilot scheme,' he said again.

'But what's it got to do with mathematics?' she asked.

'Artificial intelligence,' he said. 'That's what makes virtual reality work. You know how far it's come in the last few years. Well, we've been working for some time on the notion that . . .'

'Yes?'

'Iron bars do not a prison make.'

'Stone walls, actually,' she told him. 'It's the cage that iron bars don't make.'

'I stand corrected. The point is, with the growing prison population and the endless trouble it makes, one or two people have been working on the idea of prison by pleasure.'

'What?'

She would have laughed if he hadn't looked so serious. Dr James of Trinity had obviously been talking to someone. These dons get around.

'It's true,' he told her. 'Prison by force is expensive and inefficient. Prison by pleasure, on the other hand is irresistible.'

'It's an idea; perhaps a good one. But why is it so secret?'

'There are ramifications that might be considered undesirable.'

'So you show these criminals endless violence and porn and get Interfood to provide gourmet feasts?'

'Only in virtual reality, if that's their particular idea of pleasure. You let them live their every fantasy in virtual reality, and Interfood will provide pabulum . . .'

'Pabulum?' Where had she heard that word before?

'Pabulum is a kind of vitamin, protein, starch and bran slurry tasting of almost nothing which will deflect as little attention as possible from the virtual feasts in front of them. With some bacterial addition, it can be largely self-renewing.'

'Is this possible?'

'It's more than possible. It's happening. At the moment, of course, we're using chips but soon we'll switch to a highway. It's already in place.'

It was almost too much to take in. Enormity was too small

a name for it. And yet in a curious way it made some kind of insidious sense.

'And where do you come in?' she asked.

'I have to go into prison with every semblance of authenticity to fine tune the system from the inside. It is impossible to get it right without doing that.'

'Did you have to go in for *murder*?'

'Killing a homosexual is good for prestige in prison. It'll help me move around without hostility which could undermine the programme. I need all the help I can get.'

'But you *didn't* kill a homosexual.'

'No.'

'Well, who did?'

'My twin brother.'

'Your brother?'

Surprise was being piled upon astonishment. His brother? This was the sparky lad who had procured him a transvestite in Singapore. Of course, it had all been in the dream . . . it was like having someone telling you your thoughts.

'My brother was, is, evil. He's always been in trouble. I was supposed to keep an eye on him, but there's bad blood there. I took him to Singapore with me because I thought it might help him to be with me. But he was violent, wayward even then. We had to leave in a hurry or he might have been flogged . . . or worse . . .'

Once again there was that sagging look of fatigue and even guilt.

'He was in trouble here again, nearly sent back to prison, but I got permission to see if he could help me with . . . this project.'

'Did you force him to?'

'Not likely. No one forces Greg. It was a doddle for him. Just what he wanted. Nothing but drink, sex and violence. Said it would suit him fine. Better than prison anyway. The only thing was, I didn't have a back-up in case of a power failure. It was fine for six weeks, then there was a cut and it all went wrong. He escaped for some reason and killed someone – that boy from the wine bar. The only good thing to come out of it was an opportunity for me to take his place . . . switch jackets and so on. He looks like me. Mandy was telling the truth so far as she knew.'

'So where's he now?'

He paused for a moment, looking, she thought, curiously hunted himself. Extraordinary, beyond the experience of any dreams she had had, that the tunnel one should be so prescient. It almost made one doubt reality. Was this the true, the incontrovertible onset of breakdown – or some kind of terrible prophetic poisoned chalice?

'Oh, he's been taken care of,' Christopher said wearily.

'And what about Graziella?'

'She was lying when she said I was with her. We needed her to make it look like a strong case for you. But of course we couldn't win. I have to go inside to do the job properly.'

'I see . . .'

Her mind was in a complete turmoil, but anger was taking over from astonishment. So this was what it had all been about! She had been a stooge, a fall guy all along. She had slept with him as part of their plan. They must have known about it. God what shits. But there was something else, something she still didn't understand. Soapy and Sir Perry . . . did they know about this too? Was that what they had been talking about?

'You could have told me this before,' she said. 'My God, you could, you bastard.'

'I couldn't, you know. It had to look authentic.'

'I suppose it was the money,' she told him bitterly.

'Strangely enough, no,' he said. 'It was the loyalty.'

'Not to me.'

'I could not love thee, dear, so much, loved I not honour more,' he said.

'Honour?' she laughed. 'That's rich. I don't think Sir Richard Lovelace had that sort of thing in mind. Mind you, loveless just about sums it up, doesn't it?'

'Not so,' he protested. 'That's one thing that was true from the start.'

'You've made a fool of me,' she said. 'You and my own people. How could that be? What did they have to do with it all?'

She was crying again with anger and humiliation.

'They knew about the experiment,' he said. 'They simply wanted a junior to carry the can. They said it wouldn't reflect on your career. Quite the reverse.'

'Do you believe that?' she asked.

They could stuff her career, and theirs.

'I did when I was told about it. I didn't know you then. I'm sickened by the thought of it now, but I was powerless. You see, they were after Greg, my brother.'

'You mean . . . to arrest him for the murder?'

'I don't know. There are some funny people in the organization. He caused a lot of trouble. I think they might have . . . done something. God knows I feel ashamed of him, horrified by what he's done, but . . . he's my brother. I can't feel indifferent. I had to agree to do things their way in return for his safety.'

It seemed there were people in the organization who would stop at very little.

'And is he safe now?' she asked.

He paused again as if momentarily uncertain.

'Safer than he would have been if I hadn't gone along with them.'

'I suppose it was they who helped you get bail,' she said. 'It was so unusual as to be almost unethical.'

'I suppose it was,' he said. 'But I needed to be outside for a while longer to finish things off.'

'Does that include me?' she asked.

'Yes,' he said, mollifying. 'That was the most important thing of all. But that was just a beginning . . . I will be out soon, you know.'

She didn't feel mollified. Let him come out tomorrow and she wouldn't have him. Let them both go back to their tunnel.

She was beginning to see below the surface now; things swimming in the dark lake of his personality that were better unsummoned, fears and deceptions . . . How different from Alan who had always been so scrupulously honest with her, Alan whom she had deceived and whose virtues now shone by comparison. Loveable, open, engaging, spooky-tooth; how have I deceived you!

'Do you know who Interfood's lawyers are?' she said.

He mentioned a firm whom she knew had affiliations with Soapy's. So her instincts had been right! There was a connection. The question was, how far did it reach? Into her bedroom, perhaps? Into her answering machine? Up Jarn Mound? Was that what it had been about – they didn't trust her on her own to cock the case up? They had to unsettle her as well? They had to make her fall in love? It was a compliment in its way, she supposed. Well, she would go and talk to them about it.

She stood up, smoothing her skirt, her short one for court appearances, put on with such desperate hope that morning.

'I must go,' she said.

'Please don't.'

'Things to do, places to go.'

She was surprised to find that she was crying again.

'Please don't,' he said again.

'I'm not going to carry the can for this,' she said. 'Whoever's behind your organization and whatever it thinks. Not for all the money Interfood thinks it's going to make. I'm going to see the head of my chambers. I'm going to talk to the press.'

He looked concerned.

'I wouldn't do that,' he said. 'Talk to the head of your chambers first.'

They both stood there, looking miserable. Then she stepped up to him and gave him a kiss.

'Goodbye,' she said.

'I won't be in long,' he told her. 'But come and see me.'

She shook her head.

'Goodbye,' she said again, and turned on her heel and left.

Fifty-three

London was already beginning to clear for the bank holiday weekend and traffic was lighter than usual. She hailed a taxi and told the man to take her to the Temple.

'Quick as you can, please.'

'In a hurry, are you?'

The man was obviously *Mastermind* material.

'Yes,' she said, 'I'm in a hurry.'

'Everyone's in a hurry these days,' said the driver, reprovingly, 'but for what? However far or fast you go, you're still locked in your body.'

She restrained an urge to shake his scrawny shoulders, pull his cap down over his watery nose. The man was trying his best, however. Buildings flew past, cyclists scattered. She felt she should show her appreciation.

'The trouble is, too many people are standing and staring,' she told him. 'Staring at their screens, gawping at their videos, twiddling their Gameboys . . .'

'That's sitting and staring,' the old boy said. 'Oops . . .' He nearly clipped a bollard. 'Yes, that's sitting and staring. Sitting and staring's no good,' he continued. 'What we need is more *standing*. Remember that feller used to go up and down Oxford Street with that placard: Passion Protein. Excess lust from fish, eggs, butter, cheese, meat, sex, and SITTING.'

'Before my time, I think.'

She couldn't help smiling. It was the old people who knew what was what, but they couldn't stop the rot, could they?

'That old feller, he knew what was what. Too much sitting, you see. It breeds fantasies and stirs the loins. Mind you, I do a lot of sitting in my job . . . But I don't get turn-ons. I get piles . . .'

She was grateful to the old boy for a breath of old-fashioned normality. He reminded her of the josser at the end of *1984*, sitting in the Victory Café drinking watery beer and complaining about litres.

When they arrived at her chambers she tipped him generously. Then, squaring her shoulders, she walked in.

Arthur was back from lunch. The news of the fiasco in court had already reached him. If he knew about Interfood and the new plan for prisons, he didn't show it.

'Ah, Miss Semple. I hear we managed to snatch defeat from the jaws of victory.'

Just as the tittering was starting behind the computer screens, she said what she had been wanting to say to him for some time.

'Fuck off, Arthur.'

No one, it seemed, had ever spoken to him like that.

His face whitened, throwing the tiny broken veins around the nose into relief. The tittering stopped this time, as if a guillotine had descended. Really, she should have said it to the man long ago.

'There's no call for that kind of language,' he told her, embarrassed to be thwarted in front of his staff. 'I shall have to have a word with Sir Peregrine.'

'You can have a word with his backside if you want. Isn't that usually the place you creep up to?'

She had gone too far, but she didn't care. This part of her life was over and the future could look after itself. Noises that sounded like amusement were now coming from behind the computer screens. It was a sweet noise when it was not against you.

'Be quiet. How dare you? Are you drunk?' Arthur hissed.

'That's rich, coming from you.'

Before Arthur could say any more, the door to Sir Perry's room opened and the great man looked out. Mirth instantly subsided and the keyboards reverted to their impotent clacking.

'Any sign of . . . Ah . . .' Seeing Heather, he raised a bony finger and beckoned. 'This way, please, Miss Semple. I have someone here who'd like a word with you.'

Fifty-four

Hyacinths were long over and it was orange-red tulips now, tipped with yellow, bursting from graceful vases in the corner of the room in gentle conflagration.

The windows were open; the sun was just setting – tinting little fluffy clouds, such as putti might play with, the most delicious blood oranges and flamingo pinks – and the gardens in the centre of the square still basked in the warmth of it, the varied green of its trees and bushes so fresh and shiny that they seemed almost foliaged with mirrors. Song-thrushes warbled like divas among the purring of the pigeons.

It was strange, Heather thought, that in the most important moments one always seemed aware of the irrelevances.

There were three other men besides Sir Perry in the room. One was Soapy, looking grave but by no means displeased. The second was a man with a thin, ascetic face and an air of privileged information. The third was a very tall, lean, bony, youngish man with large hands and an academic air – he had an interesting reddish-sallow complexion which, with his beady dark-brown eyes, made him look like an Aztec sun priest. She could imagine him with his dagger poised over the heart of a sacrificial maiden. He looked wild to her, unconfined, dangerous. She recognized him immediately as her South American diplomatic neighbour.

'Miss Semple, Heather, let me introduce Mr Tunnicliffe from the Home Office and Mr Tate who is in Security.'

The two men, who had been standing near the window,

moved forward and made themselves known. They did not shake hands. The Aztec did not refer to the fact that they had been neighbours.

Soapy was already seated. He made a very slight move upwards to indicate that he acknowledged the necessity of some formal display of politeness, and then sank back into his armchair to show her she merited no further elevation.

The deportment of all three men indicated that they were prepared to deal with her if she wished to deal with them, but they would not care very much if she didn't.

'Shall we sit down,' Sir Perry said to the rest of them.

They all sank respectively into armchair and deep sofa. Heather, conscious of her short skirt, crossed her legs, folded her hands and waited. Soapy's eyes wandered just a little towards the tantalizing proscenium arch of her hemline.

'Now, Heather,' Sir Perry began, 'I think an explanation is owed to you.'

She said nothing but her eyes said: I should think it bloody well is. The man from the Home Office took notes. Somewhere doubtless the voice processor was recording.

'I understand you know something of what's been happening already. I am not pleased that you know. None of us is pleased, particularly Security . . .'

The Aztec frowned slightly and put his bony hands together in a sun-god praying motion. Heather could feel the point of his stone dagger already on her breast.

'However, I understand that you yourself have so far been discreet, so we can let that pass. What we are engaged upon is at the experimental stage. That is why we have to be so careful. I am telling you this in the strictest confidence, Heather. If you should divulge any of this to anyone – I understand your boyfriend was a journalist . . .'

'Is,' she told him.

'Ah, of course . . . *is* a journalist . . . but if any of this gets out, above all to a journalist, I cannot answer for the consequences. Do you understand?'

'I understand.'

'I cannot emphasize that enough, Heather. The consequences would be very dire, possibly fatal.'

The Aztec cracked his fingers as if to underline the point. It was a neck-breaking noise.

'There is a move to equip some of our most violent gaols with virtual reality machines. This in itself will not occasion much public suspicion. After all, they have television, videos and interactive games already.'

'I understand that,' Heather told him. 'But what I don't understand is the need for all the secrecy, the subterfuge.'

'Subterfuge is an ugly word, Heather,' said Sir Perry, also pressing his fingers together but mercifully not cracking them.

'There are times when subterfuge is expedient,' said Soapy. 'Once in place in certain prison recreation rooms, there will be moves to put these machines in special cells where inmates will deem it a privilege to be allocated. Soon every inmate will want one. And they will get them too, Heather, make no mistake, for it is far easier to secure a prisoner happy in his machine than to control a loose cannon – truculent, anti-social, usually ignorant, vicious and vindictive. It is a truism, Heather, that crime is rising, the prison population is growing, prison itself is corrupting ... Isn't that right, Mr Tunnicliffe?'

The man with drawn features now chipped in.

'Of those who go in, something like forty per cent will return at some stage. The expense of these places is simply horrendous. The cost of keeping a prisoner in, say, Parkhurst for a year is something like £60,000. We have around 100,000 people in prison and remand homes at any one time ... we have 80,000 prison officers. You can compute the burden on the Exchequer for yourself. These machines now work out at just £2000 each. The programs can be provided at perhaps, for the average prisoner, £10,000 a year. Guards, food, recreation can be slashed. We reckon we can halve our running costs ...'

'But ... isn't there something rather ... degrading about all this? Putting people into machines? It's like battery-farming.'

'Not a bit of it,' said the man from the ministry. 'They actually ask to go in.'

'But it's still degrading.'

'They've degraded themselves. After all, the battery hen has done nothing wrong. It's innocent. It hasn't killed, raped, mugged, assaulted, burgled, terrified and generally committed affront to the average law-abiding chicken. I could feel sorry for a battery hen. But these people. We are not degrading them. They have degraded us. What we are giving them is a civilized and pleasurable cul de sac.'

'But that's just the beginning of it, Heather,' said Sir Perry.

'The *beginning*?' she exclaimed.

Sir Peregrine put the tips of his fingers together and continued.

'Democracy's at an end, Heather. You know that. We all know that. It's only a word now, a placebo to keep the people happy. What we seem to have, if we have anything, is tyranny by minority. As the poet says – Belloc isn't it? "The more offensive make the greater mark". Well, our plan is to have a little tyranny of our own. Benign, of course. We have only the country's interest at heart.'

'Of course,' repeated Soapy, and the man from the ministry nodded while the Aztec cracked his knuckles again.

'The trouble is,' said Sir Peregrine, warming to his theme, 'there are too many people. And because of the pull of cheap labour in the Far East, there's increasingly little for them to do, and so many of them – the worst of them – make trouble. Drugs, violence, litter, the despoliation of the countryside . . . and of course babies.'

'Babies,' echoed Soapy as if the word were a plague of locusts. 'It's always the worst who have the most. And of course we now have proof that violence is genetically determined. Did you know that the percentage of unmarried mothers has risen to something like fifty?'

Heather had heard the figure quoted rather often but she wasn't going to admit it.

'Really?' she murmured.

'And these children, of course, are brought up without a father's controlling influence, the stability of a family or the faintest concept of morality. They are violent but alas not sterile drones whose only concept is self-gratification.'

'So our concept, Heather,' went on Sir Peregrine suavely, 'is to give them what they want in virtual reality. The technology is there now. We will turn them into happy battery chickens who don't have to lay any eggs, where they can enjoy sex, violence, indulgence of every kind without stirring from their chair. A capital notion, eh?'

'Basically, we're running down the population,' said the man from the ministry. 'You have to admit it makes sense.'

Soapy made agreeing noises and turned again to Heather.

'There are some of us in this country who feel a radical solution to our society's problems is called for. It is a truism to say the country's going to the dogs. But why is it going to the dogs?'

She knew the answer to this one.

'The rate of technological change is making our institutions collapse,' she told them. 'They are in a state of shock.'

'Very good,' said the man from the ministry. 'Where did you get that from?'

'My boyfriend is doing a television series on the subject.'

'Of course,' said Soapy.

Why of course, she wondered. She had told them about Alan's project. Now she suddenly wondered if he was in this too?

'It is this technological change that interests us,' said Sir Perry. 'You can't fight it. You have to use it to your advantage. Tell her, Hugh.'

The man from the ministry took up the story.

'From the end of the last war, for forty years,' he said, 'the old efficiency was to keep inefficiency at a properly high level, thus ensuring full employment for nearly everyone. But computers have changed all that. Now only the best people will be needed. The rest will have to have something to do. So instead of unemployment we will have leisure . . .'

'And instead of people kicking their heels and getting into trouble on the streets, we will use the new interactive fibre optic cable channels and superhighway to provide virtual reality in every dwelling,' said Sir Perry. 'There will be magazine-fed chips to provide day-long entertainment.'

'What about Europe?' Heather asked.

'What about it indeed?' snorted Sir Perry. 'Europe's tired. But even the busiest of bodies can't complain if we're giving the people what they want. Europe will follow in due course.'

'There will be virtually no crime because everything you want, however vicious, can be done at home,' Soapy explained. 'Chips will be handed out, even delivered, as part of state benefit. The totally immersive hardware will already be installed.'

'Bad for solicitors and barristers,' said Heather.

'Not necessarily. There will still be work but it will not be dross. And knowledge, wit, culture, wisdom – those things hated and despised by the Calibans – will once more assume their rightful place in our society.'

'So, very briefly, that's the picture then, Heather,' said Sir Perry. 'I have of course been painting with an absurdly broad brush. What d'you say?'

She was momentarily lost for words. What they were describing was a conspiracy; but a conspiracy of what, of whom? She put the question to him.

'This is a broad association, Heather. You have heard of the Secret Army? It is involved. There are all sorts, all ranks; politicians, civil servants, dons, business men – though by no means all business wants the public confined to barracks as it were. Many other people don't. But the beauty of VR is that it is almost irresistible. Once it is generally available, people – especially the uneducated – will gravitate towards it as they have to television and to video. Only this time it's not a pastime, it's a way of life.'

'If it's unstoppable, why did you bother with me?' she asked. 'Why did you go to all those lengths to set me up?'

'Just at the start, the thing is vulnerable. If anyone thinks deeply about VR, they may see the downside of it, the – what did you call it? – the degradation issue. We don't want any disruption. Softly, softly, Heather.'

She didn't like the answer and she knew she wouldn't like the answer to her next question.

'Talking of degradation, did you raid my flat?'

'We were looking for that chip, Heather. It had been dropped by the murderer. You should have declared it.'

Just because she knew the answer didn't make it any better.

'And did you try to unsettle me, put frighteners on me? Make obscene calls?'

She couldn't bring herself to ask them if they had intended her to fall in love.

'We needed you to be . . . perhaps . . . on edge . . .'

Heather exploded.

'On edge! My God, you were pushing me *over* the edge.'

There was a silence.

'I must impress upon you, Heather,' said Sir Perry, gently, 'the magnitude of what lies ahead. Great issues are involved. The very fabric of democracy is tearing apart. Instead of tyranny by minority – what is the phrase: "the best lack all conviction while the worst are full of passionate intensity" – we must institute an oligarchy. We must have the best full of passionate intensity. And in that we would like you to join us. We understand you are fond of . . . our ex-client, Christopher Morbey, one of our technical people . . . Join us and you join him. What d'you say? No, don't answer straight away. Take your time . . . And, by the way, there were no obscene calls, Heather. That must have been someone else.'

Heather got up and went to the window. Everything seemed perfectly normal outside. An old woman feeding the pigeons; a pair of duck flying over; a couple holding hands beside the garden railings; the trees, oblivious of tremendous issues, quietly shooting moisture up their vascular bundles . . . everything seemed normal. But it was the computers, the artificial intelligences, which were alive now, gathering and passing on information, improving with every generation, using humans to propagate them as flowers use bees – and already preparing to put the bees into hives . . .

She should have felt sympathy with Sir Perry and his people. Her instincts were to conserve, to cherish learning and beauty, to enjoy the past and not to wipe it out with an impatient present like a child at a blackboard. There was some sense in what Sir Perry had said. He was merely formalizing a tendency that would, through trial and error, probably blunder sooner or later to the same conclusion. But the cold-shouldering, the fostering of paranoia, the under-handedness, the clinical formulation of the idea were surely not to be condoned. She turned at last and looked at them.

The clock ticked on with a strangely liquid sound today – drip drip drip – as if it were leaking seconds.

'Perhaps you would like to go home and think about it,' offered Sir Perry at length.

Heather hesitated. It would still have been rather easy to say yes, she could see quite clearly all the pressing advantageous reasons for acquiescing, but she couldn't quite bring herself to do it. 'I don't think so,' she said.

'I'm sorry you feel that way, Heather,' said Sir Perry, gravely. 'But if we cannot persuade you, perhaps there is someone who will.'

'There is no one who will,' she said. 'It is the tempting nature of the idea that makes it so disgusting.'

Sir Perry made a light motion with his hand, the door opened and Dr James walked in. Somehow he was the last person Heather was expecting – although of course, as he appeared, she knew she had been expecting him all the time. This was their most subtle attack on her determination.

'Hullo, Heather,' he said. 'I'm sorry you had to get involved in all this.'

'She has done well,' countered Soapy, unctuously.

'I imagine she doesn't think so,' replied her old tutor.

'I've done badly,' she told him.

'Perhaps not as badly as you think,' he said kindly. 'Now do sit down.'

She perched on the edge of the chair, warily.

'Please don't ask me to do what they want,' she said.

Even as she spoke, she knew the situation was hopeless. He was in it up to his curly Welsh eyebrows. She knew now that he had been sounding her out at Mei Noon's funeral. Her heart sank; she remembered just how persuasive he could be.

'Consider, Heather,' he said reasonably. 'How can there be any harm in a concept which actually increases the sum of human happiness?'

'There is a difference, surely,' she argued, 'between happiness and gratification.'

'Intellectually you may be right. But try spelling that out to the people at the receiving end of the idea. To them happiness *is* gratification. Art, religion, honour, self-fulfilment, integrity, truth, honesty . . . all these are merely words to be hissed and booed at. Beauty? It is something to be raped. Don't condescend to them, Heather. Don't believe they are something they are not and never will be. That's the Karl Marx mistake. And in his day the working class really did have some virtues; not as many as he thought, but some. Anyway, it's all gone now. Now it's every man for himself. And that means *into* himself.'

She knew that in a way he was right.

'But there must be some good people out there,' she protested. 'Even in Sodom, there was Lot and his wife.'

'The modern equivalent, Mr and Mrs Lot, are very welcome to opt out of such an arrangement, just as they can opt out of any other welfare benefit. They don't have to do it. Their children can attend good schools while the parents can work productively and enjoy the fruits of civilization. Our idea is purely for the benefit of those who have nothing to offer society, who *wish* to have nothing to offer, the job lot as you might call them . . .'

Heather could feel herself giving in. Dr James always had this way with him. And yet she could remember him now, rather drunk, at a party somewhere when he had surprised her, kissed her, in somebody's kitchen. Strangely, she had put it out of her mind – perhaps she had been drunk too – or had she dreamed it? The memory, or the image, brought her up short. Perhaps indeed even he, old friend, was not all he seemed to be.

She got up again and looked out at the gardens. A small-breasted, slatternly woman was walking in front of a tiny snot-faced boy, presumably her son. The mother seemed glazed, wrapped in vacuity, while the son played a private game, making circular motions with his hands and turning round, crouchingly, as he went, bringing the hands into an approximation of a weapon-like mode. He was no doubt playing at killing something or somebody, and quite possibly he would grow up to accomplish the real thing.

'That mother and child out there, for instance. Doubtless the father has long since absconded. What use will any of them be to society out on the loose? The mother will go on the game and spread disease. And the child will grow up to do what his absent father does. Get drunk, take drugs, beat up old women and beget more children.'

Normally Heather might have agreed with him. The boy certainly looked like a thug in the making if you could see through the snot on his face. But somehow the vision of the child, so intent on his play, and the mother so indifferent, stirred something else in her today. How was anyone to know what other people were thinking or what they were like or would grow up to be? She could see that the mother would grab at the Perry Plan as if it were a life-raft. Anything would be better than the life she led. But what about the child? If Sir Perry and his friends had their way, that thug in the making would be bracketed as a no-hoper, another candidate for the unconcentration camp and the deep mines of indulgence. Surely it would be the greatest kind of betrayal, the worst kind of hypocrisy, to agree to a servitude just because it was pleasurable? Perhaps after all there might be good in the boy.

She suddenly had the feeling that her decision had momentous importance, that the fate of the world – absurd of course – trembled upon her answer. She thought of Cranmer and those two who had been burned, Latimer and Ridley, only a few yards from the gates of her old college, refusing to take the easy way.

She could feel the answer growing and glowing within her, the uncut cocaine of conviction. It was wonderful after so much hesitation, so much doubt over these last months, to come again to certainty and decision.

'No,' she said.

Dr James seemed to have aged. His pink face was drawn and pale, and his fine white shrubbery of hair looked thin as a winter tree. He gazed at her sadly.

'Is that your final answer?'

'Yes,' she told him.

'I'm so sorry about that, Heather,' he said.

The mother outside had turned and was shouting something at the boy. He took no notice but, glancing upwards, he saw Heather looking down at him. As if to reward her for what she had done – and doubtless quite out of character – he gave her a beatific smile.

She was surprised to find tears in her eyes.

'It goes without saying that there would be a role for you in the new dispensation,' said Sir Perry, betraying his impatience by stating the obvious.

But there was a question she had to put to him.

'Did you have Mei Noon killed?' she asked.

No one spoke. The Aztec cracked his knuckles.

'Heather . . .'

Dr James began to speak again, gesturing as though a regrettable slip-up had occurred, but she stopped him.

‘No,’ she said, absolutely certain now, ‘I don’t like your methods. They seem to be those of the people you want to put in your machines.’

‘You can’t make an omelette without breaking eggs,’ said the Aztec, speaking for the first time and stirring a memory of Alan making the same remark.

She walked out into the roadway and took a deep breath of Fleet Street air. Full of diesel though it was, it felt good after the Temple. Who needed omelettes anyway?

Fifty-five

When she reached home, she half-expected rumbas to be playing from the South American's flat – she was beginning to credit these people with almost supernatural powers – but there was silence. That at least was good news. It was in a way a comfort, too, to find that her original instincts about him were correct. He had never seemed right. No cause for paranoia there.

There was no Chardonnay in the fridge either, so she drank it warm; this was not the moment for niceties.

She had been aware as her taxi drove back towards Kensington that she was now being followed. Insultingly, there was little attempt at concealment; the large, dark-windowed, gunmetal-grey BMW simply tucked in behind and, when the taxi drew up at her door, parked fifty yards down the street in good view of her window. It was still there. Was it a good thing to exchange paranoia for tangible threat? She filled her glass again.

What was she to do now? She had an instinct to get out of London, to go without Alan if necessary (as it seemed was the case) to Chloe's cottage on the Deben and leave all this mess behind. She had a curious feeling that life was at an end, and yet cars passed, aeroplanes flew overhead, dogs crapped in the street. Maybe it was just *her* life that was at an end.

Warm Chardonnay was rather nice. Maybe, she thought, this whole thing is an elaborate hoax. She warmed to the idea with the help of the Chardonnay, and then she thought, what would be the point? To make me look a fool? That could surely be achieved much more cheaply. Give Arthur a *pour-boire* and he'd manage it any day of the week.

She went to the window and looked out again. The BMW was still there. She tried to diminish the man behind the wheel. He wore dark glasses . . . and panty-hose . . .

Good Chardonnay, this; Hunter Valley, all of 13% alc vol. Too good to drink warm; put another bottle in the freezer. Suddenly felt terribly sleepy. Couldn't possibly drive to Suffolk like this. Better wait till tomorrow.

It was only six o'clock but she had been up since half past five and it had been a long and extraordinarily taxing day. She double-locked the front door and went upstairs to bed.

She sat up in the middle of the night, shockingly awake. Two things impinged on her consciousness. The telephone was ringing, and she was suddenly aware of the bottle of Chardonnay in the freezer. It must have cracked. Oh shit. She picked up the telephone.

'Who is this?'

And it was the voice again.

'You filthy bitch. Thought you could change your number, did you? Well, I'll tell you what I'm going to do. I'm going to come and knock you about. Nothing violent, Heather. Just for starters. Then when you're lying on the floor helpless, I'm going to rip your bra off and squeeze your breasts hard, oh yes, Heather, you like that don't you?'

Heather said nothing but she didn't put the phone down because there was something about the voice that caught at the edge of her memory. She leant over and put the answer-machine on to record.

'Are you listening, Heather? You're excited, aren't you? I can hear that. You're wetting yourself. So then, when you're helpless with pleasure, Heather, I'm going to pull your drawers down and . . .'

It was vile to hear this gross act being played out by a stranger who presumed to think such things – which ought to be thought in private or between friends or not at all – about your body. And there he was again coming all over her with his organ of speech. But the worst was yet to come.

'And then, Heather, I want you to remember this, this is the good bit, Heather ... I'M GOING TO CUT YOUR THROAT ...'

It was vile; but not as vile as it had been before; because, yes, there was definitely something about it she recognized.

She made no sound but, as the caller put the telephone down, she wound back the recorded message and listened to it again. The more she listened, the more she felt she would know at any moment who it was. Enough for now. She would try again in the morning. It was strange how this time she felt no fear. What did worry her, however, was the bottle in the freezer.

She went downstairs and found it, cracked, with a little bubble of pure alcohol in the centre which, even as she looked, shivered as something deep underground stirred and twitched at its cloak of earth.

Fifty-six

A brilliant sun woke her, banishing the night and almost obliterating yesterday.

Looking out of the window, she thought for a moment that the BMW had gone; but then she spotted it parked nearby. The driver's window was open, and she noticed that the man at the wheel had an unmistakably red-brown cast to his skin . . .

There were strangely few cars in the street – almost as though the world were drawing away from her, as though she had some contagion, had become a pariah. And then she remembered; London would be almost empty because of the holiday.

She looked out again. The man had not moved. She had to tell someone about all this – but who? – and if she did, was she brave enough to put up with the consequences? Doubtless her telephone was tapped. Sir Perry's threat had not been idle, nor would the Aztec be when retribution came. He seemed as dangerous a man as one could ever hope not to meet.

There was, of course, Dr James of Trinity; in the old days she could have talked to him about it, but now there came the disturbing recollection that this old friend was one of the dons in league with Sir Perry, had treated him with more than ordinary respect. One by one, the pillars of her world were being removed.

Normally, if she were going to tell anyone it would have been Alan. He would know what to do about it, how to nip the thing in the bud or expose it to the chill blast of publicity. They wouldn't dare to threaten such a well-known figure; but where was he? There was no answer to her call, and still his office gave its infuriatingly recorded message.

'We're not in the office right now,' said the priggish little voice which sounded as if it needed a lobster in its briefs.

And then of course there was the matter of the obscene telephone call. She was going to have to sort that one out, indeed she almost had the answer this morning, but it was gone again. Could it be Arthur? No, somehow it wasn't his style. She doubted whether he ever used some of the words the caller had pressed into service.

Where was Alan?

She hated the idea of doing it, but the only person who might be able to help was his mother. Maybe she should ring up the old monster. She had a strange knack of keeping tabs on her son, far beyond Heather's ability. With sinking heart, she dialled the number, and waited, and waited, looking out of the window at the BMW.

Finally she realized that the telephone was making none of its usual noises. She dialled again. The line was dead. Shit! There was nothing for it but to find a call-box. Or, why not, since there was no traffic, drive to Richmond and ring her doorbell? Half of her was repelled at the notion of seeing the dreadful woman, but the other half suggested that even Mrs Haddenham was better than nothing. Suddenly, badly, she needed company.

On an impulse she ran downstairs, got into her car, and swung out into Kensington High Street with the grey snout of the BMW pointing attentively up her exhaust pipe like a lurcher following a bitch, or a shark after a seal.

Richmond too was comparatively empty and she began to wonder whether the Haddenhams themselves might have absconded to the country, but when she turned into the laurel-fringed driveway on the hill, she saw their car in the garage, and there was a flicker at the window of the loft above where doubtless Theo was trying on a tutu.

She sensed the BMW gliding to a halt somewhere just

beyond the hedge, as she walked over the gravel, wrinkling her nose in anticipation of the peculiar smell of the Haddenham menage compounded of talcum powder, gin, the particular cloying perfume Eau Fade that Mrs Haddenham affected, overfull refrigerator, cat's pee (or Theo's, perhaps: they didn't have a cat), and old mackintoshes.

She rang the bell and waited. Somewhere in the womb of the house a lavatory could be heard flushing – why was it people always chose to be on the loo when you rang? – and in due course footsteps could be heard approaching. A beady eye was pressed to the peephole. Bolts were slid back. (Mrs Haddenham believed you couldn't trust anyone these days and she was probably right.) And finally she appeared in a housecoat, hair less carefully coiffed than usual, blinking crossly into the sunlight. Heather realized that it was still only nine o'clock, early for retired folk.

'Yes? Who is it?'

'It's me, Mrs Haddenham.'

'You? Heather, is it? I couldn't quite make out. What on earth are you doing at this hour? Is Alan with you?'

There was something slightly desperate about the woman this morning. Her eyes seemed reddened. Her face was only sketchily made up. It was like wheeling out a World War II bomber before it had been properly rebuilt.

'No, he's not, Mrs Haddenham.'

She didn't even correct her and tell her to call her Daphne. Something must be up.

'You'd better come inside,' she said.

Heather would rather have stayed in the driveway. She could sense the house-smell coming out in billows but there was nothing for it, and she followed Mrs Haddenham obediently into the kitchen.

'You'll have some coffee.'

It wasn't an offer, it was a command. Heather knew it would taste of contaminated slurry.

'Thank you,' she said.

'So what brings you here so bright and early?'

'I was wondering if you'd seen Alan.'

'My God.' The woman's face had turned paler than the powder she had put on, making it look like dust on a teapot. 'Nothing's happened to him, has it?'

She trembled visibly and had to clutch at a chair for support.

Now at last Heather saw it all. She was not merely proud of her son. She was not just possessive. She was obsessive.

'Nothing's happened, Mrs Haddenham. I think he may have gone north. He's working very hard on his series, you know.'

'Oh my God,' said the woman. 'I think I'll have to sit down.'

And indeed she looked awful; perspiration was breaking out behind the powder and making little snowballs of it.

'I'm sorry, Mrs Haddenham,' Heather said. 'I didn't mean to upset you.'

The impossible had happened. She felt sorry for the woman.

At the perhaps unexpected words of sympathy from a woman who had previously not taken enormous pains to hide her dislike, Mrs Haddenham uttered a low groan and dissolved into tears.

'Alan, Alan,' she sobbed. 'I should kill myself if anything happened to you.'

It was the low groan that did it. Heather suddenly knew who it was who called her last night. She had looked the wrong way. She had thought it was a man, but it was a pathetic old woman, madly jealous of the girl who was taking away her son. She couldn't even feel the anger to reproach her with malicious, crazed interference on the night of her mother's death.

Mrs Haddenham mopped her eyes, playing further havoc with her powder which was now coagulating into a sort of pastry.

'I talk to him every day, you know,' she croaked. 'It's when I can't talk to him I get desperate.'

Heather knew now why the obscene calls came intermittently. They simply coincided with a lapse in communications between mother and son.

'It's not me, you know, Mrs Haddenham,' she told her. 'I'm not taking him away. I'm not taking him anywhere.'

It was hard to believe the pathetic old thing was capable of the kind of filth she spewed down the telephone, she thought; but who knew what dark dreams hid behind lace curtains? A career at the bar had made her all too aware of the thin enamelling of respectability.

The old woman looked at her gratefully. She knew that Heather knew, and that she would say no more. They both understood, there would be no more calls.

The back door opened and Theo appeared. He looked at Heather anxiously to see if she had spilt the beans about his nocturnal activities, but relaxed when he realized there were no recriminations. He knew that tears would not have been his wife's response if she had learnt he was a cross-dresser.

'Heather!' he exclaimed with genuine pleasure, 'what a delightful surprise.'

'Hullo, Theo,' she said.

The little man circled his wife warily like a bird around a crocodile.

'Anything the matter, m'dear?' he enquired.

To his surprise, she didn't try to bite his head off, though Heather noted that he instinctively stepped back when she opened her mouth.

'It's Alan, Theo. None of us seems to know where he is.'

'He's a big chap now, you know, m'dear. Long out of shorts, if you know my meaning.'

'But I miss him so,' she said.

Theo put his hand on her shoulder, something he had probably not done for years. Heather left them in the kitchen, a picture of curious and doubtless fleeting tenderness, and made her way quickly across the gravel before Mrs Haddenham remembered her offer of coffee.

She felt strangely relieved, healed almost by the rapprochement with Alan's mother. To add to her relief, there was no sign of the BMW. She wondered how long it had been gone.

As she edged the car out onto Richmond Hill again, she knew where she had to go next. It was strictly against the unwritten agreement she had with Alan, that she should ever go to his flat unannounced or uninvited – he said it would be an infringement of his space, though he didn't seem to mind so much about hers – but she was going to have to break it this time.

For some reason, she felt that the answer to her problems, either in the shape of Alan himself, blithely unaware of the concern he was causing his mother and indeed herself – immersed as he was in the pilot for his show – or in the shape of the chip and its revealed contents, would be provided if she could but open its polished oak door. And happily she was in a position to do this since Alan, at the height of their affair, had given her a set of his keys.

Admittedly they were more for his benefit than for hers, since he had a habit of mislaying his own set, but she had taken the precaution of bringing them along with just such an outcome in mind.

And now, whether he liked it or not, they were going to be pressed into service.

Fifty-seven

The sun was already high when she reached the street where Alan had his flat, a quiet dead-end on Campden Hill, lined with substantial Edwardian red-brick mansions. Alan's apartment was on the top floor of Number 20. She paused outside, feeling the pavement tremulous under her feet.

A brisk breeze had got up, swirling the remains of last year's leaves and this year's faded-sepia cherry blossom in an excitation that the ginger cat at Number 19 across the way did not share. He looked at the circular commotion resignedly, perfectly aware that it was not a mouse.

She hadn't been here, she realized, for at least three months. She had an instinct that Alan didn't want her here, that it would not be good for their relationship. No matter, needs must, the devil was driving hard today.

She put a hand over her eyes, feeling momentarily faint. She had had no breakfast today, not even horrible coffee. The shocks were coming faster. Plaster was falling from the portico and dust eddied like smoke in the street. A storm was coming.

She turned her key and went in. The hall was dark and smelt of polish and privilege. She climbed the wide stairs, thinking again that she had never done this before without telling him. They had agreed that this should be so. They needed their freedom, their creative privacy. Yes, yes; it was more, perhaps, for his benefit than hers, but she went along with it, why not? They trusted each other, didn't they, even if she had let the side down with Christopher. That was all over now.

She opened his door with the latch key. The other two locks were already open. He must be in, or near at hand. At first she thought he was in the flat. She could hear his voice quite distinctly.

'Alan?'

No answer.

Advancing into the living-room, she saw that his video was on and that it was playing what must be sequences from the pilot of *A State of Shock*. Alan was standing in front of Buckingham Palace and talking to camera as the title rolled to the sound of kettle drums.

'There's an earthquake going on,' he was saying. 'It's even shaking this old place. You can't see it, you can't touch it, it won't make the ground open at your feet and the buildings fall on you . . . at least not yet . . . But it is in its way an earthquake . . . and it is in its way every bit as alarming as the real thing . . .'

'Alan?' she called.

She was sure he was in the flat. Funny man. Why had he lied to her that he was away?

'It is caused by the rate of technological change – never before has science so completely overwhelmed us with innovation of every kind – think back only thirty years – computers of any power had to have rooms built for them. Now they fit on your desk. Think back twenty years earlier. They hardly existed. And yet these machines are as important to the human race as the wheel . . . And may yet be our downfall . . . No, cut that. We're getting too far from the central idea. I'll do that bit again . . . And yet these machines are as important to the human race as the wheel. The trouble is . . . it's all going too fast . . . Not for us . . . we're highly adaptable creatures as *creatures* . . .'

The picture cut now to Alan in flying gear going through the sound barrier as passenger in an RAF fighter. Everything was shaking.

'But for our institutions,' he continued. 'This speed of change is shaking them to bits . . . they're going into shock . . .'

At this point, the picture changed to Alan in a white coat, speaking from a casualty ward. He talked forensically about the clinical symptoms of shock as doctor and nurses fought to save the victim of a road accident. Heather thought it was in rather bad taste, but such considerations had never put Alan off a good angle.

'The whole fabric of our country, those things which have held us together for centuries, democracy itself, is in need of intensive care,' he was saying. 'Transfusions, drips, wonder drugs, cardiologists, dedicated nursing, what you will. Is the situation terminal, is the writing on the wall? Has the state coach finally run out of road? Join me on Wednesday night for the first in our series as I put the spotlight on our institutions, and make up your mind for yourself. *A State of Shock* . . . Wednesday, nine-thirty.'

The final image of a stretcher case being given heart shock treatment seemed a bit strong even for Alan, but perhaps this was merely an experimental tape. At any rate, the screen faded at this point, and Heather turned her attention to the rest of the flat.

On the desk in his study, she found an undated letter he had started to write. 'Heather,' it read, 'This chip really is extraordinary. The top man has told me what's on it, though he has no idea what it means. But I think I do. I won't write it down – you never know these days – but I'll post it special delivery today and you'll get it on Tuesday. Hope it's in time for you. Call me then and we'll meet. Love, Alan.'

There was no sign of the chip. Where was the man?

Perhaps he was upstairs in the loo, 'adjusting his expression' as he called it. The bathroom was in a little passage off which the two bedrooms also opened. She tried the door and it swung open to her touch. Clearly he wasn't there, but she walked in, she had no clear idea why, an instinct perhaps, and the first thing she saw was a condom still floating in the loo. It had a rather unpleasant pinkish colour and looked like an anemone suffering from North Sea blight. The next thing she saw was a girl's make-up on the shelf under the mirror. It was a brand she did not use. There was a pair of knickers on the bath rail.

For a moment the images did not register, and then she had to sit down – on the loo, as it happened, the nearest thing to a seat under the circumstances. A state of shock wasn't in it, she thought. She just couldn't believe what she had seen. Alan? Unfaithful? It had never crossed her mind. He was so much older than her, she thought inconsequentially. It seemed to have something to do with him being lucky to have her. What really rankled, however, was the fact that she had given up Christopher in order to stay faithful to this man; that she had tried so hard to persuade him to have a relationship-healing bank holiday weekend with her, and he had lied. She wondered how often he had done so.

She sat there for several minutes, poleaxed, feeling more wretched than she could ever remember. Her career was a shambles, her lover was in prison, and her boyfriend had been quietly fornicating on the side. Doubtless he joked or complained about her to his floozie.

Below her, the condom seemed almost animate, gently flapping in its porcelain rock pool, until she could bear it no more and sprang up, stupidly flushing the thing down – it wouldn't go and she had to do it twice – and made her way, half blinded with tears, almost by habit to the bedroom.

Here she found Alan. He lay, as if in repose, across the double bed with his head horribly beaten, cheeks smashed, skull caved in. He was obviously quite dead, and had been for some time. All his words were spilt.

Her legs gave way again and she sat on the floor. It was her fault. He had been killed before he could pass the evidence.

It was as she was sitting there, tears still streaming down, unable to cope with the latest enormity, not sorrowing for Alan yet, thinking about the strange stage-prop-like quality of the corpse, that she heard the noise. It was the creak of a floorboard in the passage, and she knew that whoever had killed Alan had come back.

The sound concentrated her mind, though in her state of shock it kept repeating the same message; she dared not use the telephone; she knew she had to get out. She forced herself to think further. The only escape was down the passage and the murderer was there. She looked at the window. That was it; there was a fire escape on the other side of the roof which served the other top floor flat as well as Alan's. They had spoken of it in the past. That was where she had to go – but quietly.

She took her shoes off and very softly began to crawl across to the window. Mercifully it was not a sash but a quiet-opening casement. She opened it as far as it would go and began to wriggle through. She was almost out when the door opened and a tall, thin, bony man came in. He had a baseball bat in his reddish-brown hand and he broke into a run as he saw her.

With a desperate wriggle, tearing her dress, she managed to throw herself through just as the bat made the glass explode in a vindictive fountain of splinters.

She knew the man would find it harder than she had, getting through the window, but that was the only good thing to be said for the situation. She set off round the parapet as fast as she could, tripping and swaying perilously near the edge, scattering slates to steady herself. As she came in sight of the fire escape, she could hear slates falling from the direction of Alan's window. The man must somehow have got out.

Her feet ran down the stairway too fast for her mind, and twice she half-fell, saving herself on the rusty railing and cutting her hand as she did so. And, as she reached the bottom, she could hear the man's feet, relentlessly padding down after her.

An elderly man was walking his dog on the pavement as she jumped down in front of him and he stared at her open-mouthed. She presented a wild sight, her dress with half its front torn off, her face streaked with tears and blood from her hands.

'Wha'?' was all he could manage.

'Call the police,' she shouted as she ran past.

He was still staring in astonishment as her pursuer appeared and knocked him over.

Heather threw herself into her car and fumbled for the keys. The face was almost at the window when she found them. Groaning, whimpering to herself, she started the engine, letting in the clutch almost simultaneously so that the Alfa bucked and squealed like a guinea pig. Thank God, she was away.

Her relief was short-lived, however. Looking in the mirror, she could see the man jumping into a grey BMW with a strange communications dorsal which leapt forward in her wake as she turned the corner . . .

Fifty-eight

Too fast. She must be doing eighty. Even the milder bends made the car skip and slither on the greasy roadway, but she dared not slow down.

Any minute now that heavy gunmetal shape would be showing in the mirror.

A truck came towards her, hooting furiously. She pulled the steering wheel and swung the car back onto her side of the road.

With a fresh surge of panic, she wondered whether the keys to the cottage would be in her bag. Hadn't the secretary come in with a question just as she was taking them out of the envelope? . . . How could she be so stupid?

She fumbled across to the passenger seat and tried to undo the clasp. It was always a stiff one. She had meant to have it seen to. Too late now.

Damn the thing. It wouldn't open. Another bend was coming up, with beyond it the bridge over the estuary.

She checked the rear mirror, looked ahead, and saw a van stopped – the idiot – at the roadside just as she rounded the curve. Even that would have been all right but just at that moment the shaking began again, and the bridge started to bend and writhe as though it were a living thing. She slammed on the brakes and the car began to ski in slow christies, first left then right. It clipped the side of the van – she could see the driver's white face inside – and skidded on.

This was it, she thought. The moment so long dreaded. No

way out. Funnily enough, it was almost a relief. Time seemed to go in and out like potter's clay. Up and down went the bridge in serpentine undulations.

Left . . . right . . . a car came towards her . . . she could see quite clearly a woman with children in the back . . . please God, not the children . . .

The cars passed as if they were waltzing together.

She heard herself making noises but it was as though someone else was doing it.

She gripped the steering wheel as if it were life itself but she could do nothing with it. She saw her face white in the mirror. She could feel her heart racing. Where were her careful systems of behaviour, her useful arms? Everything was happening fast now.

The car went up onto the bank, slid down, up onto the other, hit a thorn bush, turned over and started cartwheeling as it dropped from the carriageway down a gentle incline towards a miniature ravine. Trees, grass, and pebbles flew in front of her, and as the car rolled, lines she had learnt at school filled her mind.

> *'No motion has she now nor force,*
> *She neither feels nor sees.*
> *Whirled round in earth's diurnal course*
> *With rocks and stones and trees . . .'*

A flock of little birds fluttered up.

Then with a last shattering of glass and a wail of metal, the car hit the boulders of the stream.

She hung there upside down in the sudden silence, not knowing whether she was alive or dead, whole or injured. There was no pain. She could not move. Sounds now came from above, voices and then faces. They meant nothing to her. She saw his face among the rest. He could do nothing now. Arms reached out to her but she could not feel them . . .

Perhaps that was death after all. To be aware for ever but to be locked in perspex like a paperweight. The thought horrified her but there was nothing she could do. She could not cry. Weep no more, sad fountains.

Someone was shouting.

'Get her out. It could go up any moment.'

'She was going too fast.'

'What's that got to do with it?'

It had all been too fast . . . what was the phrase? . . . the fast lane . . . She wasn't even on the hard shoulder.

'I'm not on the hard shoulder,' she thought. 'And if I were I wouldn't cry on it.'

She wished they wouldn't swing her so. Or if they must, would they do it the right way up, with not too much jerkiness, the way her father did.

There, she was crying now. But why were her tears red?

Fifty-nine

She woke up in hospital with a strange kind of helmet on.

'Why have I got this helmet on?' she asked. 'For my neck?'

A woman in a white coat came by and looked at her with interest.

'Ah,' she said, 'finished, have you?'

'Finished?'

'Finished your adventure.'

'My adventure?'

'Yes, you remember. Your adventure.'

'What adventure?'

A man approached who seemed vaguely familiar.

'Feeling good, Heather?'

'Good?'

'You've played it again, you know.'

'Again?'

'You wanted to. You love this game.'

'Love?'

'This game.'

'Do I know you?' she asked.

'I shouldn't think so.'

'I'm sure I do,' she said. 'In the adventure, but I'm tired now.'

'What would you like next?'

'A good rest.'

'The six or ten hour version?'

'What?'

'We'll give you the ten. And then you'd probably like *A Gentle Romance*. Hm?'

'All right,' she said. 'But no earthquakes.'

They put the disc into the machine and she was out again.

'Something in the drive's giving it the shakes,' said the white-coated man to a colleague.

He was a distinctive-looking fellow with jet-black hair that fluffed out at the back, giving him the air of a forensic blackbird.

'Or it could be a faulty chip,' he continued. 'Anyway, nothing to lose any sleep over.'

Acknowledgements

My thanks are due to Sonja Shields and Caroline Kennedy-Morrison who have inspired, helped, suggested, vetted, and not minded about being rung up for details of legal practice or forensic evidence at some grossly inconvenient hour, as I went along.

If I have committed solecisms, it is not their fault – merely mine for blundering ahead without sufficient consultation. However, I can assure you that there were many instances in earlier drafts where their beady eyes have helped me avoid making an even bigger legal ass of myself.

I should also like to thank Trinity College, Oxford, for allowing me to use their illustrious foundation in certain scenes. It seemed ludicrous to change the name when a description of the chapel so exactly pinpoints the place.

The people mentioned, on the other hand, are entirely fictitious and bear no intentional resemblance to Fellows past or present.

Lastly I must acknowledge my debt to Chrissie Michael, who made such a tidy-looking wood out of my trees, and to Terry Jervis, who has filled my head with delight and foreboding about the latest developments in the hardware and software of Virtual Reality.